Nick Tomlinson has been an English teacher, academic mentor, actor and singing waiter. He lives in Birmingham with his girlfriend, Jayne. *Saint Valentine* is his first novel.

To Lesky,

Happy Valentine's Day, and thanks for bumping my readership up to double figures.

All best,
Roman

SAINT VALENTINE

Nick Tomlinson

BLACK SWAN

SAINT VALENTINE
A BLACK SWAN BOOK: 0 552 77204 6

Originally published in Great Britain by Bantam Press,
a division of Transworld Publishers

PRINTING HISTORY
Bantam Press edition published 2004
Black Swan edition published 2005

1 3 5 7 9 10 8 6 4 2

Set in 11/14pt Melior by
Falcon Oast Graphic Art Ltd.

Black Swan Books are published by Transworld Publishers,
61–63 Uxbridge Road, London W5 5SA,
a division of The Random House Group Ltd,
in Australia by Random House Australia (Pty) Ltd,
20 Alfred Street, Milsons Point, Sydney, NSW 2061, Australia,
in New Zealand by Random House New Zealand Ltd,
18 Poland Road, Glenfield, Auckland 10, New Zealand
and in South Africa by Random House (Pty) Ltd,
Endulini, 5a Jubilee Road, Parktown 2193, South Africa.

Printed and bound in Great Britain by
Cox & Wyman Ltd, Reading, Berkshire.

Papers used by Transworld Publishers are natural, recyclable
products made from wood grown in sustainable forests. The
manufacturing processes conform to the environmental
regulations of the country of origin.

This book is dedicated, with much love,
to Jayne and my wonderful family.

drama

Tuesday morning, like every school-day morning, found Brendan and me under our tree. We were crouching in a clearing beneath the droopy branches, next to a miniature metropolis of toadstools. Someone had hung pink and yellow streamers over some of the branches. Veiled by the tree's straggly fringe, we spied on passers-by, mostly school-goers traipsing towards Denesgrove Secondary.

It was February 8th 1983, twenty years ago.

There was something about looking at girls while concealed that made us feel that we were seeing more than we were supposed to see, although we weren't. The girls were ambulating, not undressing.

'It's Sally Overton,' Brendan whispered. 'She's got breasts, and she knows how to use them.'

'Definitely,' I said. As far as I could tell, though, she wasn't using them at that moment.

'You can almost see them bounce,' he said. The wind was blowing Sally's shirt against her chest, then changing direction and pulling the shirt sideways, then changing again and making the shirt inflate.

Sally and her friends walked past. 'Imagine if they'd seen us here,' I said. 'Sarah Hancock keeps a brick in her bag so she can hit people with it.'

'They might have raped us,' Brendan speculated. There was a game in our school called Rape, played by some of the older girls. It wasn't really a game at all, if truth be told. It involved a group of very self-assured girls cornering a boy and forcibly debagging him. Being raped was allegedly an honour. Brendan and I were not the sort of people girls considered raping, even out of charity, which was fine by me, as it sounded like an ordeal. Brendan, though, felt spurned. 'If I got raped, I'd definitely make sure they didn't get my trousers down until I'd got a good feel of all of their fannies.'

'What if they were holding your arms?'

'I'd bite them on the baps.'

'How much fun would that be?'

'Not much. I'd prod them with my toes.'

Brendan thought that thirteen was not too young to start having sexual entanglements or being debagged. Personally I felt under-age. Sex struck me as the province of adults, like voting, driving or house ownership, which was not to say that I was not interested in it, only that I didn't expect to have first-hand experience of it until I was about twenty.

Sexual maturity seemed an awful burden if you weren't the kind of person that girls liked, and I felt I should view my own sexual maturity with scepticism until some girl came along who did like me, which was not something I could see happening soon. This left me with a surfeit of hormonal energy, which I diverted by becoming a romantic.

Brendan clapped his hands together gently. 'Third years. Maybe their skirts will blow up!' I looked at him. 'I mean in the wind,' he clarified. 'You know what we should do? Bring a camera here just in case.'

The row of trees to which our tree belonged flanked a cycle path that went under a couple of bridges and led up to the zebra crossing of a main road. On the other side of this road, another cycle path ran alongside a lake and then disappeared into a housing estate, beyond which was our school, Denesgrove Secondary. The trees along the cycle path were grotesque and entangled with bushes. The tree next to ours had fallen down. When we crouched in our hiding place, the fallen tree lay between us and the cycle path, with our tree's dangly branches tickling the fallen tree's flank. We hid behind this supine trunk, with our tree, which had two trunks and looked like a tuning fork, to our rear.

Now, during the winter, the lack of leaves meant that anybody who looked in our direction would see our faces bobbing above a recumbent tree trunk, hidden only partially by tangled branches and those apparently non-biodegradable yellow and pink streamers. But who looks at trees while walking to school?

We sat watching girls go by. Actually, we sat waiting for two particular girls to go by.

Today they were a little later than usual. For some reason they were jogging, but had to stop often because Gillian kept dropping her bag.

Gillian, whom Brendan loved, was a buxom beauty in the making. She had curly golden hair, not vague gold but bullion gold, the colour of opulence. Her eyes were blue and feline. She had a small nose dashed with freckles and when she frowned it wrinkled like a concertina. Her voice was deeper than you'd expect it to be. Brendan, who usually provided a cattle-market commentary on the girls who walked by, fell silent as she jogged flat-footed towards us. We both fell silent.

The girl running alongside Gillian was named Adele. For a short time I could feel the creaky vast rotation of the earth; the whole of the universe seemed the size of a pinprick, from which Adele flowed like life-blood. She flowed towards me, and my heart broke as it always did when I saw her, and Gillian dropped her bag again.

Adele and Gillian stopped jogging and started walking. As they passed us Gillian began swinging her hips from side to side in an exaggerated manner, and making her bag do huge loop-the-loops on the end of its long leather strap. She was talking loudly and laughing. Adele walked very straight, like a geisha, only without the subservience. She had nobody to be subservient to. She was as beautiful as it was possible for a girl to be; more beautiful, in fact, because she was also strange-looking. This gave her admirers the feeling that they were in love with something unique, admitting no rival, whereas Gillian's beauty was, all said, generic. I suspected that Adele was genuinely strange as a person, but I couldn't be absolutely sure, as I shared only one of her classes at school, and had never spoken to her.

Adele had pale grey eyes that always looked tired, dark vertical hair, and a mouth that turned downwards at the corners. She looked as though she never slept. When she smiled she looked knowing rather than happy. She was ethereally beautiful and not given to talking, showing emotion, or blinking.

After they had walked past, we stared at them for a while and then tried to summon enough courage to leave our tree. Our plan was to creep out from our grotto one day and follow Adele and Gillian to school, walking close enough so that they could overhear the pithy conversation that we would have scripted in advance. This plan may not sound adventurous; but the idea of being near to Adele and Gillian outside school, with nobody else in the immediate vicinity, seemed excitingly close to courtship. It never occurred to us that if we were to slip out from our hiding place and appear magically behind them, they would wonder where we'd sprung from.

Today we didn't have the nerve to materialize behind them, because we were planning on doing something tremendously daring later that day, and we needed to conserve our bravery. So we crouched behind the trunk for a further minute, then burst gracelessly from the shrubbery and took to the cycle path. Brendan snagged himself on something as we rustled through the branches, and let out a ladylike scream that caused Gillian, in the distance, to turn around. I grabbed Brendan's hand to stop him falling over. Gillian was too far away to recognize us. I hoped she was, anyway. I lifted my school bag in front of my face just in case.

Brendan didn't notice that Gillian had glanced at us, and I didn't tell him. It would have killed him to suspect that his true love had observed us, even from afar, stumbling from a row of trees, covered in streamers and twigs, momentarily holding hands.

I'd loved other girls before Adele, but only from afar. Even in infant school I found girls mesmerizing, and could not understand why other boys my age thought them repugnant. Secret admiration requires no great courage and is risk-free as long as it goes unnoticed, so I had become quite choosy and discerning – it is as easy for a boy to admire a pretty girl as it is to admire one who spits and has lice, so why settle for second best? This kind of discrimination does not serve a plain boy well, though, when he turns teenage and senses Nature prompting him to do something other than daydream. The world of actual romantic activity seldom welcomes skinny people with unreasonably high standards; it is, all said, a gladiatorial arena and not a pick 'n' mix.

Denesgrove Secondary was built in 1961, and was set quite far back from the main road. You could see why. Its designers had in mind a collection of buildings that screamed functionality, and the end result resembled some gigantic grey crates with windows. There was a long covered walkway leading to the Arts block, and it was easy to imagine that a lone aesthete on the design committee had lobbied for the walkway to stretch all the way to the main road, so that easily depressed pupils and teachers could enter the school without having to actually see it.

The red iron school gates were flanked by shops: a supermarket, a butcher's shop, a Victoria Wine, a newsagent, a pub and, mysteriously, a shop selling scuba-diving equipment. The tight ranks of shops part-concealed the sight of our concrete learning establishment from any outsiders driving past who might be considering moving to the area. Having passed through the gates, *en route* to the main school blocks, you encountered on your right-hand side a kind of suburbia of long, badly arranged buildings that looked like numerous cheap kitchen extensions joined together to form snaky parallel rows. It was as though someone had commemorated a World War I battlefield by erecting Portakabin museums where the trenches had been. These buildings, late sixties additions to the complex, comprised Lower School and the Craft block, and it was here that us second years spent most of our time, in the shadow of Upper School.

It was no architectural banquet, our school, but attempts had been made over the years to add creative touches. For example, back in the seventies a team of cutting-edge designers had hit upon the idea of removing most of the floor from the sixth-form area. The sixth-form area was situated on the first floor of the Humanities block, so you'd have thought that it needed a floor, but you would have been wrong. What it needed was a gaping hole that presented a permanent safety threat. A fence was erected around the hole, and so now sixth-formers, although deprived of much seating or standing room, could peer over this rail and enjoy the sight of children eating sandwiches in the school's second dining-room below. Very few people dared sit under the hole; sixth-formers tended to vent their frustration at having no floor by dropping things on anybody sitting at the tables beneath, and who could blame them?

The creators of the sixth-form hole clearly believed that floors were not so much practical as outmoded and creativity-stifling. After the hole, no further improvements were made to the school. No doubt the school governors rebelled against the idea of further renovation, having guessed that roofs or toilet doors would be the next things to go.

The dining hall beneath the sixth-form gap was a quiet, dingy place where no hot food was served, unlike the bright and bustling main dining-hall next door, which also had the benefits of fixed seating. The second dining-hall was reserved for those pupils who brought sandwiches to school because their parents disapproved of them enjoying hot dinners and socializing. There were no more than twelve such unfortunates in our school, and I was one of them. In our dining-hall you had to clear away your own table. The tables were round, with collapsible legs, so after you'd finished eating and dodging heavy falling objects, you would roll your table to the edge of the hall and stand there in a queue of people, harassed by a dinner monitor, and endeavour to stack your table against the wall without it rolling away or falling on anybody.

I detested being one of the sandwich children, but for a whole year I endured it because of loyalty towards my mother. Mum had sometimes felt that her only real contribution to the upbringing of her two boys was the making of highly nutritional baps – we had overheard her saying as much to my dad. Living with three exasperatingly untalkative males, she may have seen the baps as a line of communication, made on Sundays in batches and stored in the freezer, each bap a cling-filmed message bespeaking her concern for us. They said, *I love you, my dear sons*, and *You should ingest more vitamins*, though my brother and I didn't hear the baps speaking to us at the time. We'd pluck them from the freezer every morning and they would thaw in our school bags. Craig saved his for the walk home after school, and used his own money to buy hot meals, but I was the dutiful sort and so I ate mine in the sandwich hall under the sixth-form hole of death, even though, in our school, sandwich-eaters were looked upon as socially retarded loners and treated with the kind of suspicion usually afforded to dangerous cult members. I preferred to eat alone, but then so did everyone else in the sandwich hall, so we took a table each and ate in silence, disregarding any opportunities for fostering solidarity, then filed out without looking at each other, rolling our tables like oversized shields.

Shortly after my thirteenth birthday, however, Mum and Dad split up, and Mum moved out of our house and took up residence in a nearby flat. One consequence of this was that the freezer became bereft of baps, so now Dad gave Craig and me dinner money, and I could sit with Brendan and Martin in the main dining-hall eating iced buns, chips, and salt. I desperately regretted that my parents' split had occasioned such an improvement in my quality of life, but after a year of choking down my lonely homemade lunches, every greasy hot plateful tasted like a picnic luncheon served on Mount Olympus.

February 8th was the day on which Brendan and I intended to enter the world of romance. We were going to do it after lunch, during Drama, and had laid our plans, and in the meantime we felt a terror akin to that of entrenched soldiers clutching their bayonets before the big push, waiting for the whistle.

This is how it feels when you are young, and nothing that you want to happen to you has happened yet. Life seems like something you might have to risk death or maiming to lay hold of; it feels like something into which you have been conscripted. All of the luminous joys that existence promises are hoarded, it seems, in faraway bunkers guarded by the Germans, and you live in constant fear of the order to go over the top and tramp through the mud and bullet-rain to storm the enemy hiding places. Till then you crouch in hiding, risking detection and harsh weather and trench foot, which is what Brendan and I did every morning under our tree.

Today the whistle had sounded.

Drama was the only lesson that Brendan and I shared with both Adele and Gillian. This was because Drama classes were extra large, and contained pupils from several home groups.

Denesgrove had two Drama teachers, Mr Bennett and Miss Liptrot. Mr Bennett once joked that his first name was Gordon, but the joke was wasted on us; we all believed him. Most Drama lessons were spent getting into groups of two to four and improvising theme-based sketches, which Mr Bennett then critiqued without pity, while Miss Liptrot held her tongue for fear of crushing our spirit. It was like Bad Cop, Mute Cop. Once every term, though, the class did something different: we were forced to divide into groups of five or six, and spend four weeks creating major theatrical productions called Group Pieces.

Group Pieces involved writing, producing, directing and performing a play from scratch, and supporting it with all our own stage management. We approached Group Pieces seriously, unlike the theme-based sketches we did in lessons throughout the rest of the year. The theme-based sketches were opportunities to try to be comic. Even if the theme was 'Premature Death' you still felt you had to try to make it funny. A serious sketch just bored people, and your audience's boredom hung in the air like farts. Group Pieces, conversely, were always pretentious and arty, with thousands of guesswork-inspired lighting changes and no dialogue. It's easy to be funny for one minute, but hard to be funny for fifteen. And it's hard to achieve profundity in the space of one minute, but dead easy when you have quarter of an hour to build up to it.

(I hate to equate beauty with talent, but somehow Adele's Group Pieces always seemed the most mature and polished. It is a sad fact that the cleverest, most creative and most athletically able students in our school were also the most aesthetically blessed. Once, however, a really ugly group led by a spectral boy named Paul Thorpe managed to produce a staggeringly competent and dangerous Group Piece, in which the action took place on top of a Tower of Babel which kept growing as they added more chairs and tables, but this ended poorly when Paul Thorpe fell off the top level and then someone else fell feet-first on to his testicles, prompting a ghastly falsetto shriek from Paul, crazy laughter from the audience, and a worried look from the usually unflappable Mr Bennett, who really shouldn't have let such a risky piece go ahead in the first place.)

Naturally, Brendan and I had daydreams about getting into the same Group Piece group as Adele and Gillian. Sharing a group would mean being with them in every Drama lesson for a whole month. We saw ourselves laughing with Adele and Gillian, practising stage-kissing, arranging lengthy after-school rehearsals, going to each other's houses to try on costumes, and climbing lighting rigs together like excited monkeys. We saw them growing attached to us. Until recently, though, we had not thought of a way to make any of this happen.

In the first year we'd been allowed to choose our own partners for Group Pieces, which meant that some groups were filled with popular people and some groups were wholly talent-free. So, since the second year, Mr Bennett had started taking matters into his own hands. He would make us stand in a line and then walk down the line numbering us from one to seven, starting again at one after every seventh pupil. Then he'd make all the Ones get into groups, and then all the Twos do the same, and so on.

Brendan and I had failed to notice how we could exploit this arrangement, but luckily we had a mutual friend named Martin who was blessed with cunning. Martin pointed out to us that if, upon being told to stand in a line, he and Brendan and I made sure that there were exactly six people standing between each of us, and if none of us stood too near the end of the line, *the three of us would all end up in the same group.*

Brendan and I later discussed this plan in Martin's absence. It occurred to us that Adele and Gillian, both being quite clever, would probably also find a way to get in the same group as each other, so we decided to hijack Martin's idea and use it to get ourselves into the girls' group. Martin could fend for himself. As a result of our coup, Brendan and I would then enjoy a whole month of regular access to Adele and Gillian, and would also get to co-star with them in an exciting piece of theatre, and we would win their love.

This was the plan we were going to attempt that day.

Misfortune struck early in the lesson. As the pupils assembled in the studio, Gillian handed Miss Liptrot a note, then took the same note to Mr Bennett, then left and didn't come back. Brendan was heartbroken. I noticed that Adele was chatting with uncharacteristic esprit to a handsome sporty boy called Dean Millard.

After Gillian's departure, the next disaster was that Miss Liptrot, after giving her usual short speech about Group Pieces, told us to get into groups of five. On our own. No line, no numbers. A couple of listless-looking girls, Tanya Seyton (we referred to her as Satan, which was funny because she was a Christian) and Helen Cogo-Fawcett, wandered resignedly up to us as we stood looking shipwrecked, and affixed themselves to our group without saying anything. Adele was mobbed by Dean and his cohorts.

The noise was incredible. People were fighting all over the place, and someone was sent to the deputy head for hitting Paul Thorpe with a stray curtain ring. Our pathetic group stood at the foot of the wooden amphitheatre-style seating levels looking rejected even though we were the only cohesive social unit in the studio. Mr Bennett stormed through the middle of the class like Moses parting a puddle, and began wrenching children back and forth by their arms, forcing them into groups.

Suddenly there was a bellowing noise and everyone looked at Mr Bennett. Brendan stopped whimpering. Martin quickly started counting people.

'Everybody line up!'

To my surprise I was clapping my hands. I said to Brendan, very quickly and very quietly, 'Mr Bennett will probably let Gillian join whatever group she wants next lesson, and she'll choose Adele's, so let's get in Adele's group.' Brendan nodded earnestly. Everyone started lining up and Brendan, Martin and I hovered like pickpockets, counting people.

All of a sudden the line seemed to coagulate and Martin darted forward, landing between two girls. He looked at us and pointed down the line. Brendan ignored him and, counting from Adele's position,

22

rushed forward and stood next to Gavin Easement, who was Satan's cousin. He threw me a jubilant glance. I was having trouble counting. Then I found my place and headed to the line and waded into Helen Cogo-Fawcett, who seemed to weigh nothing and who fell over instantly. I garbled an apology and looked along the row of people and at that moment Mr Bennett appeared and grabbed me and wrenched me out of the line.

I didn't hear what he was shouting at me. I was gasping. Mr Bennett motioned for Helen Cogo-Fawcett to get off the floor and rejoin the rippling row of pupils, then cleared an inauspicious-looking space somewhere to Helen's right and shoved me in. By the time I was in place, Miss Liptrot was upon me.

She said, 'Four.'

I looked to my right and caught Martin's eye. He held up four fingers. Then I saw Brendan looking at me, standing several places away from Martin. Martin began shouting at Brendan. Brendan saw my four fingers. He held up his index finger.

'Ones, come and stand here,' shouted Miss Liptrot, pointing at a space on the studio floor.

Brendan walked timidly forward. Then Adele went towards him, clearly displeased. I felt dead and beaten; I felt blown-up. Standing next to Adele, Brendan mouthed something to me which looked like 'Olly noss-noss', and which I later found out was 'All is not lost!' But of course it was.

* * *

Later, at home, I felt so unhappy over the Drama fiasco that I developed a fever. Not wanting to be on my own, I tried moping in the lounge, but my dad shouted at me for staring at the carpet, so I resolved to be positive and think of ways to capitalize on the one strategic advantage that I now possessed, namely, that I was the friend of somebody who was in Adele's Drama group.

Unable to think of any really good ways to exploit my position, I went to my bedroom and started to read a book, one of the *Sweet Dreams* novels for teenagers that I had stolen off Brendan's sister, hoping it might provide inspiration.

When you are a boy who is quiet, polite and romantic, it's dangerously easy to equate yourself with the central male characters in *Sweet Dreams* teen romances. Many of these characters are also quiet, polite and romantic. What's more, the books' heroines all act as though the rarest (and therefore most appealing) thing on earth is a boy who is quiet, polite and romantic. So I believed that I, unlike other boys my age, at least partially resembled a *Sweet Dreams* hero, and felt that Adele would find me highly appealing if only she knew just how quiet, polite and romantic I was, even though my own quietness, politeness and romanticism were born from timidity, whereas *Sweet Dreams* heroes were generally good-looking loners.

I was not a good-looking loner. At thirteen I was lanky and startled-looking, and I mumbled, but I reckoned that love would give me volume when the need arose. I felt that I had nearly mastered the basic script of young romance. There were, I recognized, only so many romantic story-lines, only so many romantic things you could do before you exceeded your boundaries and became avant-garde. I knew what to say and also what to leave unsaid, although I did not learn until many years later that the really important thing, of course, is to know how to say it. Back then I assumed that *Sweet Dreams* heroes spoke how I spoke: without commitment, often into their hands, while staring at the floor.

Even at thirteen, though, I did recognize that it was not enough simply to know the basic script of romance. To enact the script with the object of your love – to practise even the most entry-level, rudimentary romantic gestures – you require one thing above all else to bind you to her, which happened to be the one thing I did not enjoy, the one thing that had been snatched out of my grasp and, incidentally, dumped in the lap of my hormonal friend; the one thing I felt I had to create between myself and Adele if I was to avoid having toothache of the soul for the rest of my youth – namely, proximity.

What I did not know at the time – as it was not covered in any of the stolen *Sweet Dreams*, *Sweet*

Valley High or Mills & Boon books I had secretly been reading – was that, in some cases, one need not be in close contact with one's beloved in order to forge a romantic connection. Under certain conditions, a lover finds a way to steal into the thoughts of his beloved without having to spend much time in her presence. It's as though the lover stumbles upon an entrance to the particular heart-shaped maze in which his beloved is roaming, the walls made of rosy hedgerow, and there dawns upon him, slowly and deliciously, the certainty that although a great deal of foliage separates him from his darling, they will at some point bump into each other in the middle.

It happens only rarely, but it does happen.

after bisto

That evening a new era in my family's history was heralded by a trumpet blast. The trumpet blast was provided by my older brother, Craig, as we sat around the kitchen table eating sweaty square hamburgers called Steaklets, crinkle-cut chips, and Dad's trademark underdone vegetables (broccoli florets, which made me think of Martians' shaving brushes), and gulping milk, which is all anyone ever drank in our house after Mum left, because Dad was an unimaginative shopper. The mountain of adamantine broccoli might have accounted for Craig's flatulence. He let one rip halfway through dinner – a compact bugle noise – and the clanging of forks stopped and Dad and I stared at him. It was the first fart our dining-table had ever witnessed, and I was mortified on Craig's behalf. He muttered something, an apology or plea for forgiveness, I presumed.

'What did you say?' Dad demanded.

Craig grinned stupidly. 'I said, "Ah, Bisto!"'

As in the slogan for the famous gravy brand. Craig was comparing his foul wind to the aroma of gravy, right there at the family dinner-table. I looked at Dad, horrified.

Dad shook his head, laughed, and carried on eating.

And that was it: we were now officially an all-male household. Craig waved his hand around to broadcast his pong, and my mother's absence rang through the house like a silent scream.

Craig and I did not look like brothers. Craig had Dad's tiny ears and nose, and also his kind eyes and straight brown hair and chubby cheeks, and his broad shoulders and shapely forearms, and numerous other appealing features that I felt I could have put to better use than Craig, who was a layabout. I felt I could really have made something of myself if I'd had decent shoulders and a kindly face. Craig and Dad were solidly built and so their small ears and miniature mouths looked incongruous and therefore interesting. I had my maternal grandfather's curly black mop and my mother's inability to smile convincingly. Smiling gave me the look of someone trying to hold still while a tarantula crawled through his hair. If God had wanted me to feel out of place in our motherless house, he'd succeeded by making me look so very different. But the thought that Dad and Craig were going to start sharing a mirthful appreciation of farting made me long suddenly for Mum's return.

Lately there had been a number of dramas on television that had addressed the topic of the trauma that marital breakdown can cause families. In these programmes, children of separated parents were nearly always wailing brats who slammed doors and lay sobbing in their bedrooms, or else they were jaw-clenching stoics who would spend the best part of an episode claiming they were just fine before eventually breaking into fits of weeping and plate-smashing. It struck me as shameful and uncalled-for, all this hysteria. The war films that Dad liked to watch were full of young soldiers whose limbs had been blown clean off, and men dying in the arms of nurses they might have married had they not been shot in the lung, and none of them seemed to complain except in a brave jokey way. They groaned, delivered speeches, attempted humour and left it at that – and they were facing *death*. In the face of such relentless heroism it seemed inappropriate to go insane with grief because your mother had decided to move to a nearby flat to get some breathing space, possibly only temporarily. It wasn't until I became an adult that I started to understand why I missed Mum so little in the months immediately after she left: I'd made no great effort to get to know her in the first place.

Our living conditions did not change dramatically with her departure. Despite Mum's absence, the fridge did not yet reek of sour milk and furred meat. The lounge had not become a scrapyard of discarded Wimpy hamburger boxes and copies of *Fiesta* and dirty vests. The bathroom didn't have soiled underpants draped over the toilet brush and a bearded sink encrusted with shaving foam and toothpaste and mouthwash and snot. We were a fairly clean bunch. Mum had trained us to observe the cardinal rule of running a household – use it, wash it, put it away – and we continued in this domestic groove. We still ate dinner at the dining-table, although from time to time we ate in the lounge when there was something good on television. It was during dinner-times that Mum's absence was most keenly felt, as it was Mum who'd always tried to get mealtime conversations off the ground (although once she'd got a discussion up in the air she would stand back and observe it like a kite, occasionally tweaking the string whenever we ran out of things to say or began talking nonsense). Otherwise, until the farting started, there wasn't much evidence to suggest that the Flack family machine was missing a cog.

There were tiny telltale signs betraying the lack of a woman's touch around the house, however, and I started to notice them almost immediately after Craig's Bisto comment. Dad had been in the army, so he was accustomed to being tidy, although his tidiness had something of a sorcerer's apprentice quality to it: left to his own whims, he could make the house chaotically orderly. It did not matter to him where shoes were kept as long as they were in a neat row, and so Craig and I were getting used to finding our footwear wedged under the front of the sofa, or lined up against the living-room wall. After the fart incident I looked at the cups standing like a firing squad on top of the fridge and I thought: *those cups weren't kept there when Mum lived here.* And although, scanning the kitchen, I saw that Mum's taste in décor remained very much in evidence – witness the spider plant on the table, the white tiles above the work surface, some of which were printed with colourful old-fashioned adverts for Bovril, Mart's Purified Orange Juice and Skaardal Crème de Kirsch – Dad's sense of functionalism was insidiously transforming the place (had we always, I wondered, kept our wooden spoons in a dented Smash Instant Mashed Potato tin?).

'Stop staring,' Dad told me. 'Eat.'

Craig looked at my plate and said, 'Is that Steaklet going begging?'

I saw an opportunity to say something sharp and hilarious, some quip that would make these men laugh and accept me as one of their own, but I couldn't for the life of me think what that quip might be. Wit, like shoulders and facial stubble, was another of Dad's traits I was unlikely to develop any time soon.

*   *   *

Since Mum had moved out, Dad had started seeing his old friends again, usually people from the forces, and they would sit in the living-room drinking bottled beer and discussing how to deal with estranged wives. I would sit hiding at the top of the stairs, in the dark bit where the stairs turned a corner and climbed a bit further before giving up and becoming a landing, and eavesdrop.

Recently I'd heard Dad telling his friend Terry that Mum was claiming that she and Dad were just having a trial separation, which Dad thought was nonsense. Mum had left us three months ago. She was working in a centre for the treatment of drug addicts and was also doing a part-time Philosophy degree at Reading University. She had become fond of travelling the country attending conferences, which struck Dad and Craig and me as impressive: once upon a time she'd been too shy to leave the house. What's more, she now wrote a column in a feminist magazine produced by the university. The column was called *Fifty Alternatives to Killing Your Lover*, and it contained subversive advice on relationships. The title suggested that Mum had lovers, ones that she wanted to keep alive. Dad banned Craig and me from reading the column, though of course we read it anyway, and understood precisely none of it.

So my parents had an unorthodox relationship,

and seemed to be in no hurry to be one thing rather than another, married or divorced. *Sweet Dreams* books sometimes mentioned 'soulmates'. As far as Craig and I could tell, our parents were stalemates. Our family therefore occupied an unidentified place betwixt the nuclear and the broken, a place that could be nicknamed limbo.

Craig, who was doing A-level Sociology, was concerned about the effects that our home life was having on him and me. He knew of at least three serial killers with backgrounds similar to ours. Sometimes I could see the appeal of being a murderer, roaming around alleys with a bowie knife. Craig said I would make a pathetic murderer, which I knew was true (what *was* a bowie knife?) but I felt insulted anyway. He said that he'd never seen me stab anything, but he'd once seen me throw a cricket ball, and somehow this told him all he needed to know about my murderous potential.

Mum was coming over to stay with us for three days this February, one of the days being Valentine's Day, which also happened to be my parents' eighteenth wedding anniversary. Even at thirteen I knew that if you are a separated couple with teenage children, it is irresponsible to reconstitute your nuclear family for your anniversary and then dismantle it again. So why were our parents doing it? If it was an attempt at reconciliation then it was not the first. Over the last three months, Dad had done a really poor job of trying to win Mum back. Sometimes she would come over and then she and Dad would stay up all night in negotiation, his voice getting louder and hers disappearing, then Mum would leave. But this hadn't happened for over a month now; none of us had seen her for about four weeks.

The official story? Dad told us kids that Mum missed us and wanted to spend some time in the house with us, and that he and Mum had a lot of talking to do, and that they'd decided that as long as they were still married, anniversaries should carry weight. But the whole thing struck me as abnormal, this yo-yoing; it was not the kind of thing parents did. Secretly Craig and I wondered if Mum's visit meant that she and Dad would be getting back together, though we didn't dare ask either of our parents whether this was a possibility. Neither of them appeared to have considered how Mum's stay might affect two confused teenagers, one of whom was close to becoming a serial killer. I felt that some-one should at least have mentioned it.

After school that day, Brendan's mum had asked me to stay for dinner, but I'd wanted to get home. I couldn't help feeling that Brendan was acting smug about being in Adele's Drama group. He wasn't; he just wasn't telling me what I wanted to hear, which was that Adele detested being in his group, and wanted to be transferred to a different group, specifically mine. Instead, Brendan indicated that Adele had managed to surmount her initial horror at being grouped with (a) Brendan, (b) a girl-bully called Karen who, last year, had pushed me over for no reason and had then stood over me laughing, and (c) two un-theatrically-gifted remedials.

He also said that Adele

(1) was basically polite in a prim way, and rather serious
(2) seldom spoke, but came up with really good ideas when she did
(3) tended to nod slowly and stare at you when you talked, and sometimes made a 'mm' noise
(4) laughed at one of Brendan's jokes (allegedly)

This last piece of information made me want to trap Brendan's hair in a car window and drive the car in circles until his head ripped off. But it wasn't just my jealousy of Brendan's access to Adele that made me feel distant from him. Lately our friendship had seemed, albeit barely noticeably, strained.

Brendan and I used to belong to a group of four friends. But at the end of our first year at Denesgrove we drove one of them away: our weird friend Warren, who, perhaps owing to hypersensitivity, got fed up with us ribbing him all the time and started hanging around with Gavin Easement, the cousin of Satan. Then, recently, we started to drift away from

Martin, who happened to be the only goodish-looking member of our small gang. It had begun when Martin told us he suspected that his dad kept pornography inside a locked trunk in what he called 'the junk room' of his house. We broke into the trunk and it did contain porn, but not the type we'd expected. The magazines had titles like *Hang Loose!* and *Pump Action*, and contained pictures of oiled men. Martin was aghast. He put his head in his hands and began moaning 'Dad, Dad!' Brendan and I sat wishing we knew how to teleport ourselves into a less embarrassing situation. Neither of us had the slightest clue how to go about comforting someone. Since that day, Martin's company had made Brendan and me feel uneasy, and guilty for not having been more supportive. Brendan felt especially bad about the way he had tried that afternoon to cheer Martin up by suggesting light-heartedly that we all wash our hands after handling his dad's magazines.

Theoretically, our alienation of Warren and our gradual snubbing of Martin should have brought Brendan and me closer together. But our mockery of Warren and our shared habit of living vicariously through Martin had, it turned out, become key components of our friendship, without which we felt a little stranded.

This was strange, considering that Brendan and I had managed to be best friends throughout primary school without Warren or Martin's assistance. Brendan and I had been among the very wimpiest pupils at St Michael's C. of E. primary school. Brendan was perhaps wimpier than me, but he was minuscule and therefore discreet. His diminutive stature made him cute and novel and he was quite popular with girls, some of whom loved him, and said so. I, on the other hand, was a tall wimp, a tall wimp made taller by a tall mess of hair, and so I was a target. At one point there had been a chant concerning myself and the leader of the boys' gang, Steven Fernley, which, if recited in Steven's presence, would deter him from beating you up:

> Neil Flack went to the moon
> Brought back a rusty spoon
> Steven Fernley went to the moon
> Brought back a GOLDEN spoon.

God knows how the song originated, as neither of us undertook such a lunar mission, let alone managed to bring back cutlery. But the chant demonstrated this: my peers considered me not only a waste of space, but a waste of outer space to boot.

Things had, of course, changed since Brendan and I had graduated to Denesgrove, which seemed to have an excess of both translucent nerds and overlarge bullies. Within this new ecosystem Brendan and I no longer sat at the bottom of the food chain.

True, we had once been beaten up on the cycle path during the first year, and smeared with dog mess by our attackers. But, generally speaking, we weren't eligible for unqualified wimp status, not like, say, Paul Thorpe. We were simply nondescript, over-lookable: not intelligent enough to be called boffins, not scruffy enough to be branded gypsies, and not pale and effeminate enough to be considered milquetoasts.

After dinner I sat hiding at the top of the stairs, peering down into the living-room and watching *Miss World* on the television. Dad and Craig were slouched in armchairs. I was of course free to join them, but I decided to keep my distance.

Then the phone rang in the kitchen and Dad got it and shouted to me. I leaned over, stretched out my arms, and patted the landing floor in a manner suggestive of footsteps, then rose to my real feet and came down the stairs.

Brendan was on the phone. He asked if he could cycle over to tell me a fantastic idea he'd had, an idea concerning the Drama groupings. On tele-vision, Miss Sierra Leone described herself as 'very fortunate to be so lucky', and Craig laughed so hard he started hacking. I felt suddenly sick. 'I'll come over to yours,' I told Brendan, because since dinner the house had acquired a kind of lonely feeling I wasn't used to and I didn't know quite how to respond.

Brendan lived between our spying tree and our school, in an old, massive property in which, until recently, three generations of his family had co-existed. His grandparents, who had owned the house, had both died the previous autumn, and Brendan was caught between grief at their passing and excitement over the possibility that his house might now be haunted. Half of the house was decorated according to Brendan's mother's wishes, the other half according to his father's. This made the place a sort of decorative oxymoron, with both of the furnishing styles cancelling each other out. Brendan's mother's taste veered towards simplicity and elegance, whereas his father had no taste at all. This was evidenced by the study, which had once been the bedroom of Brendan's eldest sister, who now lived with her married lover.

Brendan's dad had overhauled the study to give it a Far Eastern feel, but instead of exuding Zen tranquillity it now resembled the headquarters of a Japanese religious cult with militant leanings. It was decorated with endless potted marguerites, ivory Lao Tzus and priapic ebony idols, a full set of mock Edo-period armour mounted on what, on close inspection, turned out to be a broken Top Shop mannequin, a glass cabinet containing traditional

Ryukyu farming implements and the odd item from a highly suspect ninja weaponry catalogue, as well as two huge framed Utamaro prints and one Hokusai. It was, all said, a hideous room. It was also mine and Brendan's favourite hide-out, and the place where we liked to hatch our plans; it made us feel like a duo of conspiring ninja.

When I got to Brendan's house we ensconced ourselves in the Oriental study and Brendan took a bedraggled list out of his pocket. 'This is our agenda for the evening,' he told me.

Brendan enjoyed being formal. In this case, though, it was pointless, as his agenda only contained one item.

'Okay,' I replied. We were sitting on the carpet. I put a cushion under my bum and started playing with a couple of Okinawan rice flails.

Brendan cleared his throat. 'Right, do you want to hear my plan?'

I nodded.

'No – actually, it's too fantastic! Too fantastic for me to say.'

'Go on.'

'No, it's too fantastic. Give me a minute.' He pretended to languish under the pressure of contemplating his plan.

'You look so gay when you flop around like that,' I said.

Brendan draped himself on the floor and

started laughing while staring up at the ceiling.

'Get up,' I said.

'I was gay, I was naked. Were you there?' he sang, parodying a hymn we sang in school assemblies, then he choked on some spit while laughing and had to sit up. He cleared his throat. 'I'm ready now,' he said, shaking the creases out of his agenda.

'Is it about Drama?' I asked.

'It's badly good.' He put the irrelevant agenda-list to one side. 'Not this weekend but the weekend after, we're all going to come here.'

'Who is?'

'Me – because I live here. You. Adele. Gillian – if she gets put in our group (please, God!) – and the rest of my Drama group, although if we can think of a way to get out of inviting them, that would be better.'

'You mean to work on your Group Piece?' I asked.

'Yes. But there's more. That's not the main bit.'

I felt let down. 'Wait, you gimp. I'm not in your group, am I?'

Apparently this didn't matter. Brendan's parents were going out on Saturday and most of Sunday, and his sister was staying to babysit, but would not be in the house on Saturday afternoon. Brendan's plan was to propose to his group that they compose some kind of musical introduction for their Group Piece, and then suggest that they have a music session that weekend, at his house. I could come

41

round with my guitar and contribute my slim talents.

The problem with the idea was that Brendan was a pervert and could not be trusted to share a living-room with any girls whatsoever. Also, I couldn't see Adele or Gillian agreeing to come over to his house on so flimsy a pretext, no matter how hard he begged. And then there was the inescapable fact that neither of us was musically talented, and as party hosts we were underdeveloped.

But when Brendan asked me if I thought his idea was great I said yes, it was, because that is what I always said when he asked me that question. Having no ideas of my own, it seemed rude to criticize anyone else's, no matter how untenable.

Brendan was happy. 'I am a living genius,' he said.

The fake-ivory Boddidharmas watched us from the shelves.

doodles

February 9th.

I had been thinking about sending Adele a Valentine's card for some time, but by mid-January I had decided against it.

Valentine's cards struck me as risky. By age thirteen I was quite familiar not only with Sherlock Holmes but with Chesterton's Father Brown and Poe's Dupin, not to mention Scooby Doo, and these dogged sleuths proved that every crime leaves a trace, and every trace potentially leads to the perp. The act of inflicting a Valentine's card on somebody who wouldn't want one from me seemed precisely the kind of crime that I would get caught for. I imagined that my handwriting would give me away, or I would absent-mindedly sign the card, or I would get caught trying to deliver it. Also, the sending of Valentine's cards struck me as slightly distasteful. The closer one crept to achieving anonymity, the closer the finished product brought to mind a poison pen letter.

On Wednesday 9th February, though, I changed my mind.

Our English teacher was a plain-clothes, free-range Anglo-Catholic monk, though his beard made him look Orthodox, a little like Rasputin. He was also our school counsellor, which I can't imagine was a pleasant job. I never figured out how a monk could also be an English teacher, but I didn't lose sleep pondering over it.

Everybody in school, including the staff, called him Father Wigman, although his actual title was Brother Wigman. He kept reminding us of this, but we kept ignoring him; you don't call your teacher 'brother'. I don't even call my brother 'brother'. He said we should just call him 'Mr Wigman', but this seemed irreverent. Or, rather, it had probably seemed irreverent to whoever first started the trend of calling him Father.

Father Wigman was soft-spoken and eccentric, and his taste in attire suggested that he eschewed conventional clothes-shopping methods in favour of flailing through charity shops with glue on his hands. He was clearly committed to communicating to us the joys of literature, which I realize with hindsight was his chief failing as a teacher, as it made him seem desperate.

He chose his own syllabus. Because Valentine's Day was approaching, we were currently struggling through a course of love poetry. Every week Father Wigman gave us a photocopied poem and tried to get us to discuss it, then gave us a list of open-ended questions for homework. His chief objective while teaching us about love poetry was to convince us that:

(a) Poetry is cool and fun!
(b) Love poetry is NOT just for girls.

So far we had studied 'Daddy' by Sylvia Plath, which Father Wigman had completely failed to convince us was a love poem at all, and Marvell's 'To His Coy Mistress', which he'd probably hoped we'd find risqué and titillating. On Wednesday he gave us bits of paper sporting 'somewhere I have never travelled . . .' by e. e. cummings. He also supplied some other examples of e. e. cummings's work, including a poem about a Christmas tree and a heavily modernist poem that looked like it had been typeset by a cat. The tree poem was to show us that cummings was brilliant at blending social commentary with heart-melting sentiment. The cat poem was to demonstrate that Poetry is Fun! by showing that poets get to make up their own rules. In fact the second, typographically reckless poem looked very much like the poetry typically produced by our English class.

I think Father Wigman hoped we would take one

look at these poems and whisper excitedly to each other, 'I never knew poets enjoyed such wild freedom of expression' and 'To think that I wanted to be a police officer when I left school! No – today all that has changed.' In a way, the poems, and Father Wigman's accompanying 'poetry is freedom' lecture, did achieve something like their desired effect. We certainly became freer with our own writing, and throughout the rest of the year Father Wigman was bombarded with highly expressionistic poesy, and was not able to tell us off for writing dog crap without sounding like a hypocrite and a Nazi. (We'd learned about Nazis during the lesson on Sylvia Plath's 'Daddy'. I can't help thinking that Father Wigman had kind of shot himself in the foot.)

If you were naughty during Father Wigman's lessons he would punish the person sitting next to you. I used to sit with Brendan, but Brendan was a giggler and an idler so Father Wigman moved him away from me, sending him to be naughty next to somebody else while I was left to languish on my own. As a result I grew slightly bitter towards Father Wigman, and would spend his lessons doodling.

On Wednesday I spent the lesson drawing what I thought were Picasso-style naked women, but were in fact just naked women in cartoon form. Every time I looked over at Brendan he appeared nervous. Gillian was in our English class, although Adele wasn't (she also had Father Wigman for English, but belonged to a more advanced group) and Gillian's presence caused Brendan to fret. Tomorrow we would have our next Drama lesson, and would find out whose Group Piece group Gillian was going to be in. Also, Brendan was going to ask Adele if she wanted to come over to his house one weekend and listen to him shake a tambourine while I played my guitar. I had started to hope she'd say no. At any rate, he knew that he had to be on his best behaviour in front of Gillian, to lay the groundwork for her possible entry into (a) his Drama group and (b) his house in a couple of weekends' time. So: no disruptive behaviour. No crazed giggling. No throwing things. No farting. All that could wait till Geography.

English was one of my very worst subjects. I simply didn't know how to get my point across, either in speech or in writing. In this I resembled my dad, although Dad, unlike me, was superb at arguing, and became sharp-witted when annoyed. Mum, on the other hand, had a way with words, though she had rarely exercised it when living at home. She wasn't just articulate; she was pleasing to listen to. Her sentences were well-made and felt nice in your ears. They soothed and surprised and charmed you, owing to her knack of bouncing words together like wind-chimes. Whereas Craig had inherited Dad's traits – like manliness and lack of decorum – I inherited most of my traits from Mum: slight misanthropy, stodgy politeness, tendency to bottle feelings. But not her use of language.

If I was the poetic type, I decided during Father Wigman's English lesson, this is what I'd do: I would send Adele a Valentine's card with a home-made poem inside it.

After I'd used up most of my A4 rough paper drawing pictures of naked women, I set to work pondering Brendan's latest plan, which reminded me of the Oriental study in Brendan's house, and soon I was idly doodling little pictures of Chinese men in kung fu poses. Then I got bored and started reading one of the bits of paper Father Wigman had handed out.

I read the poem that began 'little tree, little tiny christmas tree' and for some reason it struck me as unbearably moving. I thought it was the most beautiful thing I had ever read, and all of a sudden I made a wild decision: although I was a very poor English student, I would become a great poet. I wrote the word 'Adele' on one of my doodle sheets: the title of my first poem.

At that moment, two unexpected things happened. First, I realized I had just overruled my previous judgement on sending a Valentine's card. In fact, I'd made up my mind to send Adele a card containing the most heart-rending message she'd ever seen, and a self-penned poem at least as lovely as the one about the Christmas tree. Second, I realized that Father Wigman was talking to me and that everybody else in the class was either giggling or being extremely quiet.

'Neil?' Father Wigman sounded reluctant to disturb me.

'Eh?' I said involuntarily. My desk, I suddenly realized, was a mess of paper. 'Sorry, sir,' I said.

'Can you read the poem?'

'Poem?' I had no idea what was going on.

'Poem,' repeated Father Wigman. Somebody tutted. I shuffled my bits of paper. My pens rolled out of my pencil case and clattered to the floor.

'Okay,' I said, bending down and scooping up the pens.

'Right!' said Father Wigman jovially. 'Now we're in business.'

I began to read the poem about the little tiny tree. Everybody began laughing and Father Wigman shook his head and walked down the aisle towards me. I realized I was reading from the wrong bit of paper. I flushed, and then, as Father Wigman approached, I remembered with horror that my desk was covered with pictures of leering naked women with outlandish bosoms, and the world flipped on its head.

Yes, it would have been easy enough to cover the offensive bits of paper with inoffensive items like my pencil case or my arm, but no, I didn't think of that, because I was panicking. Instead I did the worst possible thing. Feverishly gathering up as many bits of paper as possible, I screwed them into a large ball.

Father Wigman stopped and his eyes narrowed. I actually considered putting all of the paper in my mouth.

'What do you have there, Neil?'

'Nothing!'

Father Wigman strode over to me, looking uncommonly horrible. The rest of the class was squirming with car-crash-witness fascination. Father Wigman held out his hand. 'Give that to me.'

'I can't!' I yelped.

'*Give*,' he ordered. He was being scarier than anyone had imagined he could be. Leaning over my desk, it seemed he was about to start wrestling with me. I tried to weigh alternatives. What would be worse for my academic career: being caught with doodles of naked women or wrestling with a monk? Wrestling might impress my classmates, and possibly impress Gillian, who was after all a friend of Adele – but I was too scared to fight a teacher. Getting caught with crap pictures of naked women, on the other hand, would be social suicide. Leaning away from Father Wigman, I raised the bundle of paper to my mouth, feeling indescribably stupid. Father Wigman stabbed his finger at me.

'Don't you dare eat that!' he cried.

I opened my mouth. Some sort of whining noise

was coming out of my windpipe. I shoved the paper into my gob, and as I did so Father Wigman's bony hand shot towards me rather like a cobra, and ended up near my epiglottis. The next second he was holding a damp ball of papers and I was dribbling.

The classroom was, for a short period, Father Wigman's stage, and his pupils a mesmerized audience. He seemed pleased with his new celebrity status. He peeled open the sheets with great deliberation. I focused on one of the shiny buttons on his mauve blazer and, like every one of my peers, held my breath.

Father Wigman rotated the pile of paper round to study it from another angle. I noticed via peripheral vision that people were craning their necks to see what was on the sheets.

'Not a particularly accurate rendering,' he commented.

Then he examined another sheet. He looked at me with a blend of surprise and disgust. Then, screwing up the sheets, he walked back to the front of the classroom, sat behind his desk and dropped the papers into his metal waste bin.

I breathed once. I was thankful that the ordeal was not going to be prolonged. But then Father Wigman said, 'Neil, come to the front of the class.'

Quivering, I climbed noisily from my seat and crept over to Father Wigman's desk. He handed me a copy of 'somewhere i have never travelled . . .'

'To replace the copy you ate,' he said.

'Give him some ketchup!' somebody called, and Father Wigman smiled slightly. I took the poem back to my desk.

'Now. Would you like to read the poem aloud, Neil?' Father Wigman asked with pointed gentleness. I read it with a sort of tremolo.

'Thank you, Neil,' said Father Wigman afterwards. 'And be sure to stay behind after the lesson.'

For some reason I looked over at Gillian. She frowned and looked away.

By the close of the lesson I was a mess. The fact that Father Wigman was noted for his leniency was not a comfort. I was aware that I had a strange effect on teachers, and that the softest-seeming of them often contained a subcutaneous spikiness that I had a knack of bringing out.

Everybody left the English classroom. Father Wigman was sitting on his desk, his legs crossed, looking at a piece of paper, and appeared to have forgotten about me. I was aware that this was a ploy. He wanted me to make a dash for it so he could grab me. I hovered, fidgeting, while Father Wigman sat there reading his bit of paper. Under such circumstances, it is usually foolish to precipitate your own telling-off by drawing attention to yourself, but I got the impression that Father Wigman was engaging me in a battle of wills to see who would crack first, and that it would be best for me if I let him win it.

'Sir?'

Father Wigman looked up and smiled breezily. He said, 'Ah, Neil!' which sounded contrived, then sprang up from his desk as though about to shake my hand. He walked less than two feet to another desk and sat down on it. He gestured for me to find a desk of my own to perch on, but this struck me as overly informal, as though he intended for us to whip out guitars and start improvising folk songs, so I deliberately misunderstood him and shuffled a few paces to my right.

Father Wigman frowned. Then he looked at the floor and said, 'Neil.'

'Sir?'

He sighed. 'I think I'm right in saying you don't think a churchman could understand something like lust.'

I was appalled. A stern telling off I might be able to handle, but not a lecture on sex, not from a monk.

'But,' he continued, now looking at me as though I was Mary Magdalene, 'the fact that we don't indulge in sexual pleasure doesn't mean that we don't understand it. On the contrary; carnal pleasures are only understood by people who can distance themselves from them, who can view them objectively and avoid being enslaved by them. People who become enslaved by lust, who indulge

53

in it to the point that it begins to rule their behaviour,' he gestured towards the waste bin, 'are the people who understand it least.' He leaned forward. 'Is this making sense to you, Neil?'

I nodded, looking at the grey in his beard. In fact I was thinking of something that Martin had once told Brendan and me. He told us that priests and monks, when they get to heaven, are given a free run of women to shag by way of a reward for lifelong celibacy. According to Martin, that's why people become priests. It's in the Bible.

Father Wigman patted his knees, which I took as a signal that he was going to shut up and let me go. But he was just getting started.

'Neil, I'm going to say something that will surprise you. *Sexuality is not evil.*' I forced surprise. 'Yes, lust is a vice, but it's only a vice because it is an incomplete form of love. It looks at the body and not at the soul – do you see what I'm saying? If you don't want to use the word "soul", you can use a different word. Lust deals with the body but forgets the *mind*. Lust isn't sinful because it looks at the body – it's sinful because it chops the mind off the body, and chopping off someone's mind, or chopping off someone's soul if you want to use religious terms, is pretty bad! You see?' He sighed theatrically. I was not completely certain that he wasn't about to launch into a moving ballad. 'Neil. What worries me here isn't that you're thinking of

54

this girl in a sexual way. Don't be embarrassed. What worries me is that by drawing these kind of pictures, you're not really seeing her as a whole person. Are you? Because that's where the problems start – with not treating her as a human being. Think of it this way: how would you feel if she found out you were drawing these pictures of her?' I opened and closed my mouth. One of Father Wigman's hands levitated limply from his knee. 'You don't have to answer that. But you're intelligent, Neil. And you are sensitive. So go and *think* about it.'

He dismissed me, and I went away to think about it, leaving Father Wigman on his perch.

About a quarter of my English class were hanging around outside the room. I shrugged off questions about what was scrawled on the bits of paper Father Wigman had confiscated, and told interested parties that he hadn't punished me; he had just gone all religious.

Karen, the bully from Brendan's Drama group, looked at me like I was a fellow troublemaker, which made me feel sullied. 'That was the most fucking funny thing I've ever seen,' she said. A few people agreed with her and looked at me with something close to admiration. But as soon as my new-found fame seemed warm enough to throw on like a jumper, my audience had grown bored and I was dull again.

* * *

A couple of hours went by before I figured out the full import of what Father Wigman had said. I'd thought that it had been guesswork that had led him to assume, wrongly, that my Picasso nudes were pictures of a specific girl, and at the time of his lecture I had been too appalled to set him straight. But then I remembered something about one of the sheets Father Wigman had extracted from my mouth and thrown in the bin.

It was with a horrid, wanting-to-cry feeling that I ran sweatily back to the classroom during afternoon break, burst into the vacant room, raced to the bin and found it empty, and realized that someone, possibly a cleaner but more likely a curious member of my English class, had got to the bin ahead of me. Someone who, as a result, was now in possession of a drawing that I had tried to consume earlier, a piece of paper on which was doodled a grotesque, anatomically incorrect picture of a goggle-eyed naked female, a criminally stupid sketch that everybody in my English class knew I was responsible for.

A picture beside which I had written a single word: Adele.

I had sent my Valentine.

the keetleys at home

The evening of Wednesday the 9th. Everything was snowy and beautiful. The people I passed on my way to Brendan's all walked along huddled and self-enclosed for warmth. Cars sheared through the slush. Streetlights sprinkled orange luminescence from the ends of their crooked necks.

Brendan had been livid when I'd told him about the doodles and how they had vanished from the bin. Obviously this misadventure placed our plan to get Adele and Gillian to come over at the weekend in serious jeopardy. But he promised that he would come up with a solution, and said that I should come over after dinner, when he'd had time to consider our options.

By the time I got to his house, he had become quite positive, even excitable. In romantic endeavours, I have since learned, sudden crises can have a therapeutic effect. When the fundamental obstacle to winning a girl is the fact that she is not remotely attracted to you, less monolithic obstacles

– even obstacles like the unspecified whereabouts of incriminating amateur pornography – can be welcome diversions, provided they are potentially removable.

It was funny watching Brendan at home with his family. Mealtimes caused the Keetleys to become gyroscopic. Everybody zipped around the house accomplishing things, except Brendan, who would stand slap bang in the middle of the action looking bewildered, like a short-sighted traffic cop. People would trip over him and he would move somewhere else or try to be helpful, offering to dry plates or set the table; but wherever he was, he was always in the way. At home, in the heart of his family, Brendan's personality tended to be swamped by the personalities around him. He became a different person: a quiet fidgety thing with a slight stutter and his own dog named Savage, who wasn't.

It took Brendan's family an epoch to prepare the simplest meal. Once I saw them getting ready to serve up dinner only to realize as they took the lids off the pots that Mr Keetley, Mrs Keetley and Brendan's sister Harry had been working independently on different recipes (while simultaneously vacuuming the living-room and setting the video to record *Coronation Street* so they could watch it later with a cup of hot chocolate before going to bed). The final product was something like faggots in black bean sauce with plantain, and everybody grew angry with each other, but then they ate it anyway and it was so bizarre that they all began laughing. I sat in the living-room, having eaten at home before calling for Brendan, and listened to their noise with Savage dozing harmlessly on my lap.

Harry was not Brendan's sister's real name. Her real name was Ariadne. She had shortened her name to Harry herself, as a tomboyish elongation of Ari, and insisted that everybody else respect her decision. The deal between her parents was that her dad was allowed to name their male offspring, and her mum was allowed to name any girls she bore. Mrs Keetley had the crazy idea that romantic and exotic names make for romantic and exotic lives, although Brendan and Ariadne's older sister, Gwendolyn, had debunked this theory by becoming a splicer in a photo-processing plant, and having an affair with a married plumber named Barry.

The name Ariadne might have worked if coupled with her mum's maiden name, Leigh. But 'Ariadne Keetley' sounded muddled, a fact recognized not least of all by Ariadne Keetley herself. Harry rebelled against her former name by insisting on having her hair sheared short and not wearing skirts. As she was small and sparrowy, a little like my mum, this made her look like something from a Victorian poorhouse, which wasn't the effect she was after: Harry wanted to be tough, macho and boyish. She thought that by throwing away her ear-rings she had divested herself of her gender. But Harry was essentially a romantic and a daydreamer whose attempts at suppressing her soft centre were doomed from the outset. She spent her childhood and teens flouncing around in jeans and oversized T-shirts and talking constantly about her feelings, perhaps the most incongruous and emotionally delicate tomboy in the world.

Mr and Mrs Keetley treated me with unvoiced hospitality, which is to say that they rarely spoke to me but regularly brought me drinks of Coke. Harry treated all house-guests with suspicion. She must have known that someone borrowed her *Sweet Dreams* books, and, having no doubt searched the house for them, had probably reached the con-clusion that an outsider was filching them, perhaps with Brendan's help. But she couldn't openly accuse anybody, as her *Sweet Dreams* books were supposed to be a secret. Tomboys were not allowed to read romantic fiction, and there was no way she would admit that she kept a hidden stash of what amounted to pornography of the sentiments.

I told Brendan that I needed his sister's books to give me clues on how to win Adele's heart. I was always on the lookout for clues, and felt certain that somebody somewhere knew of a quasi-magical tech-nique that would enable me to get Adele to love me. I hoped this person had written a book, and that one day Harry would buy it and put it with the rest of her stealables. The closest thing to a seduction manual that Harry owned was *The Fine Art of Flirting* by Joyce Jillson, a book I had borrowed five months earlier and not yet given back.

My taste for romantic literature was tolerated by Brendan without comment, just as I overlooked his habit of trying to make himself look elegant by putting Vaseline on his eyelashes, a stupid trick he had learned from a women's magazine he once read in a dentist's waiting-room. Such things didn't worry me. Our unspoken consensus was that the role of boy, as traditionally defined, was way too restrictive, not to mention ill-fitting, especially as Brendan and I couldn't play sports. The occasional trespass was therefore acceptable as long as we each counterbalanced it by establishing our hetero-sexuality by frequently accusing the other of being gay.

While Brendan's family raced around making dinner and tidying the house, Brendan and I sat in his living-room hoovering the dog, who had con-tinued to moult throughout the winter. The living-room furniture was visible only through a thin membrane of settled dog hair. Brendan said that he'd thought of three plans to deal with the disappearance of my big-breasted-Adele picture, and that he would tell me them after he'd eaten. Then he went into the kitchen to have dinner, which was my cue to take two overdue *Sweet Dreams* books, one Mills & Boon and one *Sweet Valley High* out of my school bag and sneak upstairs to Harry's bedroom.

Harry's room was a showcase for posters of bands like Metallica, Slayer and Megadeth. I knew for a fact that her collection of records and tapes contained nothing by any of these artists, and veered more towards pop, which is perhaps why she kept it hidden under her bed.

Her bedroom floor, which served as a wardrobe, was covered with shapeless items of clothing, mostly in black or white. Some pastel and floral garments were kept in her pine cabinet, along with underwear that I found vaguely exciting despite the fact that it was nondescript. Her pine cabinet contained four drawers of clothing, guarded by two creaky-hinged doors. At the base of the unit were two more drawers, the uppermost of which had a semi-ornate brass handle. The bottom drawer, which was missing its handle and therefore looked precisely like the kind of drawer meant for hiding things in, was the drawer Ariadne used for hiding things in.

I sat down on a bundle of clothes in front of Ariadne's cabinet and prised open the bottom drawer. The books inside were arranged in small towers that supported several old school folders, some stray bits of cloth and a few magazines. Whenever riffling through Ariadne's stuff, I always made a note of the order in which things were piled, so I could leave everything looking un-tampered-with. First of all I searched for any new books. Janet Quinn-Harkin was my favourite *Sweet Dreams* author. She was formulaic and imaginative at the same time, and always wrote in the first person, which made me feel as though she was sharing love secrets with me personally.

There were no new books at present. I slipped the books I'd borrowed back into the drawer, and then I noticed something worth investigating.

It was a card. I took it out of the drawer and another card fell out of it. I held them both up. The outer card had a black and white photo on the front, showing two young children, a boy and a girl. The card that had fallen out of the first card had on the front a photograph of two figurines made from pipe-cleaners, with strawberries for heads, kissing. The strawberries had little eyes stuck on them and the tails looked like green hair. I thought it was very funny. I opened both cards. Both contained the opening salutation 'Dear Craig'. Nothing else.

The Craig in question was my brother. Brendan had informed me a long time ago that Harry had a thing for him. Craig and Harry had been an item in primary school, although that was perhaps too long ago to count for anything. Craig rarely had proper girlfriends, but he got quite a lot of female attention, as he was cheeky and funny, and knew how to conceal his flaws. He didn't come across as particularly romantic, and I seriously doubted whether he'd send Harry a card, though Brendan and I were of the opinion that one day he and Harry would get married.

There were some crumpled bits of paper in the drawer, and a crumpled sheet that had been smoothed out. I looked at these bits of paper. They contained Ariadne's experimental attempts at writing Craig's name in a manner that was at once anonymous and legible. The un-crumpled sheet was covered with snippets of poetry.

> Roses are red
> Violets are blue
> You're beefy enough
> To put in a stew.

Ariadne had put dismissive lines through the poems. In one corner of the sheet she had written: 'p. 46: FATKYL'. Fatkyl? Fat kill? Was this some sort of weight-loss drug? I put the bits of paper back into the drawer and continued riffling. I spied a recent copy of *Just Seventeen* and was about to read it when I noticed a paper bag.

Inside was a magazine with a bookmark in it. I recognized the magazine. Turning to the marked page, I found, to my great surprise, FATKYL.

Or: *Fifty Alternatives To Killing Your Lover*, a column written by Wendy Rostkowska, a.k.a. Wendy Flack, my own mother.

I was shocked and strangely delighted. After finding the cards addressed to my brother, discovering the article made it seem as though a Flack family reunion were taking place in Ariadne's cabinet. How on earth had Harry got hold of this? Perhaps Craig had given it to her. It occurred to me that Harry might have stolen it from my house while visiting Craig; this thought eased my conscience.

I'd only read FATKYL two or three times, and had not understood it. I had only been interested in reading it to learn about my mum. But now it began to dawn on me that most FATKYL readers did not read Ms Rostkowska out of a long-standing desire to get acquainted with my mother. They read it because Mum had useful and interesting things to say about topics like love and feminism. Useful and interesting things that I had somehow managed to overlook while reading the column in the past, or at least not properly digest, being pre-teenage and of restricted intelligence.

I re-plucked the de-crumpled bit of paper out of Ariadne's drawer and checked the page reference and flipped to page 46 in the magazine. Ariadne had underscored some of the lines in red biro:

. . . she eschews seduction and instead creates a fully-functional, air-conditioned simulacrum affair in her imagination, a make-believe relationship, complete with country cottage and set of saucepans, for her beloved to step into whenever he feels ready (or is coerced). It is a trick that shares its spirit with the art of sending Valentine's cards. <u>The skill of writing a Valentine's message lies not in impressing the recipient with one's eligibility or availability, as though one were sending a c.v. to a prospective employer. The skill lies in suggesting that something between sender and receiver *already* exists – a romantic edifice, pure potentiality, a (rather un-platonic) Platonic Form, elaborate and lovingly built to fill out a secret space in an anonymous lover's imagination.</u> The Expert Lover says to the beloved: 'This love already exists; you are already part of it' – because the romantic genius, the lover most beloved of romantic natural selection, is that lover who *determines for him or herself* when a love affair is in germination, and needs nothing to help him or her begin it. Not even the co-operation of the beloved. <u>The Valentine's card, then, is not a piece of seduction. It is not an invitation to *begin* something. It is an indication of what has already, secretly, begun</u>.

I held my breath while reading it. These were the kind of wordy obscure paragraphs that I'd skated over when I'd first read one of Mum's articles, some months after she'd left home. Now I felt as though I had found a treasure map. I understood none of what my mother had to say about Valentine's cards, but was tremendously excited to learn that she had anything to say about them at all. Then I remembered that my own enthusiasm for sending Adele a card had been dampened by the business with Father Wigman and the missing rude picture. And *then* I remembered that Brendan said he'd thought of three possible ways to clear me of blame regarding the picture, which he was going to tell me after his dinner. I was just about to remember something else when I heard a floorboard creak and the door to Ariadne's bedroom opened.

'What in the name of shit are you doing?'

It was Brendan. The fright of the door opening and the immediate anticlimax of seeing Brendan caused me to jump, then slump. 'I could have been my sister,' he hissed.

'Could you?'

'We've finished dinner. God, I am so full. You're so lucky I was me. Come on! Get off the floor and come into the study. Look at you sitting there on my sister's trousers. You big knob.'

'She's got my mum's magazine!'

'So you're both thieves.'

'No, I mean she's got a copy of my mum's magazine.' I waved the magazine at him.

'Get off her floor, or she'll have a copy of your balls. Come and hear my cunning plans.'

We went into the Oriental study, now looking slightly less Oriental because Brendan's dad had just installed two matching bronze Lakshmis and a smaller Shiva, who was dancing on serpents. We sprawled on the floor. Brendan had not written an agenda, and spared me any preamble. His cunning plans, designed for use if and only if it became apparent that Adele had seen, or was about to see, the rude picture with her name on it, were as follows:

(a) Spread rumours claiming that I had been commissioned by a beautiful aristocrat named Adele Smedley Smythe to paint her portrait in a modern (i.e. rubbish) style, and that the pictures confiscated in English were preliminary sketches of said woman.

(b) Somehow get Adele to believe that somebody else had drawn the rude pictures and then passed them to me, and as I tried to get rid of them Father Wigman caught me with them.

(c) Tell Adele the truth.

Brendan liked the first plan. I liked the second. The third was untenable. Contingency plans involving bald honesty are admirable, not to mention moral and perhaps even ultimately prudent, but bald honesty has no place in the life of a thirteen-year-old, especially when the contingency in question involves love or sexuality, which it always does.

'The second one,' I said.

'I suppose it would be easiest. Do you think it's damn good?'

'It's brilliant,' I judged. 'We definitely need to plan it, though. Wouldn't it be brilliant if the pictures had just got thrown away by the caretaker?'

Brendan screwed up his face. 'Don't count on it, Sonny Jim.' His face relaxed. 'I think that someone swiped them. I can feel it in my bowels.' He wafted some air towards me. 'Smell for yourself.'

I wasn't too convinced of the oracular capabilities of Brendan's bowels, but I did share their opinion. The situation stank. If we were to get ourselves in a position to invite the girls we loved over next weekend, we'd need to exercise some real cunning.

self defence

Thursday the 10th was a day of miracles.

Brendan and I were late for school, because we dawdled by our tree making plans, spying, and doing kung fu kicks at the tree's brittle branches. But once we arrived at our seat of learning, I started learning straight away, the first thing I learned being this: whether or not everyone now knew about the rude picture on which I'd blasphemously scribbled the name of the year's prettiest girl, I was, apparently, not deemed famous (or infamous). There was no jeering, no pointing of fingers. I drew no attention, which is to say that everything was, thankfully, business as usual. At one point, while being propelled by the throng of jostling pupils along the arterial corridor that led to our school's assembly hall, I found myself standing near Gillian, and although she *saw* me, she seemed not to *notice* me. This was a good sign. I could tell the difference between being snubbed and simply not attracting interest; all thirteen-year-olds can tell the difference.

This was the first miracle: I was not famous at school.

The next miracle happened in Drama, and was one that Brendan and I had predicted would happen, but neither of us actually dared expect: Gillian was permitted to join whichever Group Piece group she wanted to join, and she chose to join Brendan's (i.e. Adele's).

This meant that unless something went horribly wrong, it was all systems go for Brendan's weekend plan.

My own, less-miraculously-formed Group Piece group consisted of:

- Martin
- Paul Thorpe
- Satan
- Some girl called Anna Potemkin, whose name had once inspired Mr Bennett to give us a brief but informative lecture about Sergei Eisenstein, which in turn led to Anna being nicknamed 'Battleship'
- Leone Tilliard, who was about eight foot tall
- Me, Neil Flack

Here is how we operated as a dramatic body:

- Martin = the brains

- Paul Thorpe = the mouth (alas, not the testicles)
- Satan = the hair (her hair was huge)
- Battleship Potemkin = the ears (she never spoke but listened well)
- Leone Tilliard = the gigantic legs
- Me = the eyes (I was always staring over at Brendan's group)

By now you should have a fairly grotesque mental picture of a wildly hairy head attached to a neck which somehow sprouts legs. We were, collectively, this singularly useless theatrical animal.

Martin was eager to do a great Group Piece, and he wanted to star in it, which was perfectly reasonable, as he was the only one with real talent. (Paul Thorpe had talent, but his Tower of Babel ordeal had left him with stagefright.) It seemed natural that Martin should hope to grab what dubious glory might emerge from our group's efforts. It was like grabbing the oars if you were the only person in the lifeboat with arms. Martin also had good ideas, and some leadership skills.

As for me, I didn't want much. I wanted to get allotted some funny lines, or some cool lines, and I didn't want to do anything that might disgust Adele.

Drama lessons gave me ample opportunity to watch her. When she was called upon to do a small-group improvisation, watching her was a terrible bliss, terrible because I'd never managed to do any improvising with her myself, and blissful because of being able to just *look*, shamelessly.

I didn't like seeing Adele with Brendan, but in a way it slightly alleviated one particular agony, the agony of being unable to figure her out. I rarely encountered Adele outside Drama lessons, and when I did encounter her, the riptide effect of unexpectedly seeing her was often complicated by the fact that I could not understand what it was she was actually doing. Like the time when I saw her with two other girls, exiting the Humanities block, following the flock of pupils heading for their next lessons. The two other girls were talking, apparently to Adele, and then Adele slowed down a bit so that she lagged behind the others, and then she turned quickly and walked off in the opposite direction, and the other two didn't notice for about ten seconds, and then they stopped and looked around for her. It was like an inversion of pantomime: she wasn't behind them. Although I could guess the meaning of some of her beautiful strange gestures, there was perhaps an infinity of things I would never know, things lost, and I had the awful honour of being the only creature alive for whom these infinite losses *felt* like infinite losses.

At least, now that Brendan was in her company, I had someone to whom I could pose the question: what was that beautiful girl, my love, my life, doing at that peculiar moment? And: *why*?

At the beginning of the lesson, Mr Bennett made us run around the room playing a game whose rules I didn't understand because I hadn't really been paying attention. Something about having to race around then stop running and stand still whenever Mr Bennett shouted 'Stop!' That much I'd gathered. But you weren't allowed to just stand still in any old posture; you had to strike some dramatic pose, or something. I was the third person to go out: the second person evidently hadn't gathered that you were supposed to stop running, and the first one to go out hadn't even understood the bit about running around in the first place. Our school was not one in which MENSA scouted for new young members.

Brendan managed to stay in the game for a while, loping after Gillian with a shifty look on his face. The fourth person to go out was a remedial from Brendan's group, who, to my horror, came over and sat near me, because I happened to be sitting next to his bag. Then Karen – the bully from Brendan's Group Piece group who had once pushed me over and then laughed – went out, and to my even greater horror she came and sat between me and the remedial. An athletic-looking beast, too tall to be compared to a shot-putter, too muscular to appear incontestably female if viewed in silhouette (though her dyed-red hair was quite long), Karen always had a smug look, perhaps fixed in place by the large amount of brown foundation she wore. Sweaty from running, her face appeared to have the texture of wet clay.

She sat down and looked at me and grinned horribly and said, 'Don't worry, we're looking after your boyfriend.'

'Hey?' I said, aghast.

The remedial looked at us, hoping to join in the conversation. 'You think your friend Brendan fancies Adele,' said Karen. 'I've got you sussed. It's hilarious.'

'*Hey?*'

'Your boyfriend Brendan. You think he ran off and got himself into our group because he fancies Adele, I can tell. You keep looking over and giving her evils.'

I really didn't know what to say or think. It was terrifying to think that someone had spotted me looking at Adele, but at least the real reason for my staring was not apparent, at least not to Karen. Her understanding of the situation was so off-base that I didn't know if I should argue with her or just humour her.

'He doesn't fancy Adele,' I protested.

'So why are you giving Adele evils?'

'I'm not,' I said, sensing danger. I didn't know whether or not to worry about the possibility that *Adele* was under the impression that I was giving her evil looks.

'I don't like her much either.' Karen turned to the remedial. 'She's a bossy bitch and she's as thin as a twig.'

I hated Karen more than anyone on earth.

By now Gillian was out. She walked off, laughing, all sweaty, her golden hair in her eyes, and went over to her school bag with its long strap. Adele was laughing at her, a beautiful laugh, though I couldn't actually hear it; the sound of it was drowned out by voices. It *looked* beautiful. I looked round for Brendan but I couldn't see him. Karen watched me looking. Then I spied him, hiding behind one of the giant curtains that flanked the studio, waiting for the game to end.

The third miracle was huge and terrifying. It was this: during Drama, Brendan somehow persuaded his group (including, unfortunately, Karen) to come to the studio next week (exact day t.b.a.) to pose for a cast photo for their Group Piece programme. Miss Liptrot always told us to put stuff like photographs in our programmes, but nobody had ever listened to her before.

Brendan wanted me to take the photo.

That Thursday, the walk home was sleety and windy, but mostly windy. Trees convulsed. Umbrellas did hula-dances of inversions and reversions. The hoods of plastic macs flew off their wearers' heads. Grass bowed this way and that, as though worshipping different gods in turn.

My house was a modern, semi-detached building located on what was, at the time, the largest private housing development in Europe. In 1983 there were still fields between the estates, in which you could stroll, throw frisbees and witness the miracle of untended plant life. But they were being eaten by the march of progress. By 1990 almost everything resembling Nature within the development's gaping perimeter would be buried under housing or shops, or else reincarnated as rectangular gardens.

But development brought its own kind of charm. When I was thirteen, the built-up areas had been bulldozed but not flattened, and the estates were full of peaks and valleys. Some long roads were so gloriously steep that it took four people to push an abandoned broken moped up them, and freewheeling from the top almost killed all four of you. Upon entering the housing development, formerly uncomplicated main roads began to hiccup with roundabouts, and the tributaries that wriggled off the A-roads into the suburban estates were subjected immediately to great topographical variation. Streets undulated giddily. They curved like bass clefs and wound themselves tightly into cul-de-sacs. Psychedelic road planning had led to swirling, Paisley patterns of streets, making the estates mazelike. The concreted areas did not fit together seamlessly, but allowed for slim outbreaks of tree-lined grass that are known in suburbia as Dog Walks. Roads otherwise unconnected to each other were joined by narrow overgrown umbilical paths, saving you the bother of spending the whole day walking to a house whose doormat inscription you could read from your bedroom window. Sometimes the streets encircled small patches of green upon which rudimentary play-parks stood in beds of wood-chippings. They were like hidden gems. Some secret locations you could only get to if you had inside knowledge.

It was a great place to live, and a nice place to go home to, bursting with people who, like the natural environment, were restrained but not quite incarcerated by suburban custom and construction.

Nearby were shops, and on my way home from school that Friday, I went home via these shops, which stood within a protective perimeter consisting of a Lloyds Bank, a Halifax Building Society, an estate agent, a library, a leisure centre (still being built), a doctors' surgery with evangelical Christian affiliation and an evangelical church (perhaps with NHS affiliation). The shops themselves included a huge Asda supermarket, a Forbuoys newsagent and a video rental place called Video Box, from which I was, in later teenage life, to get fired for silliness.

In the Asda forecourt, next to the rows of trolleys, some boys were sliding around in the slush, playing a variation of hockey with a basketball and some pieces of plastic piping. I scanned the players to make sure that none of them were people who would recognize me, then headed for Forbuoys newsagent, which was glowing invitingly with warmth.

Inside, people were slipping on the slush they'd brought in on their shoes. I headed for the cards section, which stood next to the racks of budget-price games for the Commodore 64, and pretended for a while to examine the birthday cards while casting sidelong glances at the Valentines. Then I pounced on the latter, and began flicking through them at fantastic speed. Some were passable, most were dreadful. The very worst were the crude ones. Almost as bad were the ones depicting flowers or beribboned bears, with horrible troubadour poetry inside. None resembled anything you'd give to somebody of whom you were unambiguously fond, so I began to look at the birthday cards again, searching for ones without messages inside; something that could be mistaken for romantic.

Eventually I found one that looked strangely familiar. I held it up and stared at it from various distances before I twigged. It was the same as one of the cards Ariadne had bought for my brother: the one with two strawberries. I laughed out loud at it, composed myself, fetched a can of Quattro from the drinks fridge and went to the counter to pay.

While sloping home with the card in my school bag I tried to conjure up poetry. Ideally I wanted to think of something involving strawberries, but fruit-related words all sounded sleazy. Juicy, ripe, luscious: I felt uncomfortable applying any of these words to Adele. At one point I rhymed 'ballad' with 'fruit salad'.

Nearly home. I walked through the gap in a hedge that led from the main road to a five-house cul-de-sac. The mouth of the cul-de-sac opened on to a road which collided with mine at an angle, resulting in the creation of a new road, which then looped back to the main road. My house was the one on the corner, where the three roads met. Officially it was on Odell Close, but the garden, at the rear of which was a garage, lay along Selsey Way.

Our house looked different to the others on Odell Close in that it had a sausage-shaped curtainless window halfway up the stairs. My mum had placed an ornament on the tiny sill – one of those stick men, meant to ward away the evil eye, whose arms made a sort of rainbow or umbrella over his head. It was black and made of knobbly metal, and Dad said it made our house look like a pagan temple (he didn't remove it, though).

For some reason, the Volvo was outside the garage, which meant that Dad was at home rather than at work, probably faking illness. He did this whenever he needed to 'recharge his batteries'. His place of work was a big fleet-hire company, where he was a team leader in operations support. His job, which consisted mainly of doing unspeakably dull things with car registration documents, was not one that Craig or I could brag about at school, and we soon got bored with being among the few people who knew what MOT stands for.

Inside the house, Craig and Dad were lounging around with the television off, talking, which made me wary. I said hello and they grunted at me. I took my bag, with the Valentine stashed in it, upstairs. After changing my clothes I went to the kitchen to make a cup of tea, then joined Dad and Craig in the living-room, which was now getting quite dark; nobody had bothered to put the light on.

Craig had draped himself bonelessly across the armchair, his legs over one of the arms. His school tie was loosened and he'd wrenched his shirt-tails from his trousers. He was talking with what seemed to be forced nonchalance about some guy at school who'd been beaten up. I tried to listen, but the topic was too depressing and I was too happy. Ever since Drama I'd been full to the brim with underdog hopefulness regarding Adele and life in general. Buying the Valentine's card was such an uncharacteristic move for me that it caused an unfamiliar nice emotion to emerge. It was a sort of gritty gladness, the gladness that comes with being in real situations and doing real things rather than just daydreaming about them.

'When I was a boy,' my dad was saying, 'we'd all stand around shouting, "Hit him in the face!" But nobody ever hit anyone in the face, we just wrestled. We had a natural code of honour.'

'This kid's face was being bounced off the pavement.' Craig turned to me. 'Did you see it?'

'When?' I asked.

'At lunch break.'

'We were at Brendan's,' I explained.

Dad sort of lit up. 'Sneaking out of school?'

'It was work-related,' I explained.

He looked disappointed. I think that since Mum had left he'd expected some latent boyish mischief to bloom in me. 'What would you have done if it was *your* head?' he asked Craig.

Craig frowned. He has Dad's cheekbones but doe-like brown eyes that are all his own, and which make him look like a sap. But in the semi-darkness he looked more like Dad. 'If what was my head? Getting bounced off the floor?'

Dad made a chuckling sound. 'No son of mine would let himself get beaten up!' He'd obviously forgotten my primary school years.

'I think we've been through this already, Dad,' Craig said, trying to smile.

'Come on,' said Dad, standing up. 'On your feet. Let's see what you'd do.'

'Dad, this is embarrassing.' He didn't move from his chair. 'Neil, call social services.'

Dad laughed, but he didn't sit down. He was a stubborn brute, and he wanted to show Craig some of the tricks he'd learned during his two years in the army. This was a fairly regular occurrence. Usually Craig enjoyed Dad's tutorials, in which Dad would show Craig how to defend himself against school nuisances by crushing their tracheas and gouging out their eyes. But Craig seemed reluctant tonight. I could see why; Dad seemed uncharacteristically edgy, a bit unhinged.

I lapsed into a daydream where I was defending Adele against numerous attackers by snapping their necks with nimble movements. Then Dad scared me by grabbing my wrist and pulling me to my feet. With his free hand he pressed the light switch.

'Right,' Dad barked. 'Say Neil is some thug coming at me.' This was the first time I'd ever been involved in one of Dad's fighting lessons. During the months before Mum left, he'd made numerous attempts to have long conversations with me, conversations that never got beyond feeling like one's first meeting with a foreign exchange student; in retrospect I can see that Dad was trying to bond with me because he knew I would no longer have Mum around to be taciturn with. Now, apparently, three months after Mum's escape, I was ready for some *proper* father–son bonding, involving actual

84

physical violence. Perhaps he would make up for lost time by bonding with me so thoroughly that I died. I had no idea what to do.

'Come on!' Dad shouted. I realized he was shouting at me.

'What do you want me to do?' I asked.

'Just make like you're going to swing a punch at me.'

'You want me to punch you?' I asked, appalled.

He was still holding my wrist. He swung it in an arc. 'Just go through the motions! This could benefit you some day as well, you know.'

'Okay,' I said, stepping up to the challenge of being bonded with. I made a weak punching movement towards Dad's head. Craig howled.

'For Pete's sakes, Neil! Your opponent would be home having his tea by the time your punch got there. And don't dangle your other wrist like a jessie.'

'I'm not!' I shouted, defensive.

'Just pretend to punch me,' Dad ordered. 'But not like a disabled girl.'

By now I really did want to hit him, but I showed mercy and popped my fist out so it stopped short of his nose. But by the time it arrived, his nose was gone. He had ducked low and was going for my legs.

'Outside arm to the knee. Inside hand, hook foot.' He was leaning his elbow on my knee and holding my ankle with his other hand. 'Then push.' I fell on my bottom. 'See?' said Dad.

'Gotcha,' said Craig, nodding appreciatively. 'Nifty.'

'Ow,' I said.

'Now here's the coup de grace,' Dad said, anglicizing the term. 'Grab heel, grab toes. See? Control the foot.'

'Ow! Ow!'

'Sorry, Neil,' Dad said. He can't have meant it, though, because the next second he twisted my foot so I flipped like a frog on a griddle. 'Flip. Face down. Now, hook leg.' I felt a leg wrap around mine. 'Pull leg up.' My leg got yanked upwards. 'Keep your man's knee in the crook of your knee, then just drop down on to it, trapping the leg. Pop, broken leg!'

Pop! He knelt down and my knee made a number of snapping noises. I was too shocked to scream. Dad was suddenly deathly still.

Craig said, 'Fucking heck!'

There was a lengthy silence. Then Dad whispered, 'Hold very still.' I nodded. He said, 'Just hold there while I get disentangled.' I kept my leg still. Dad's pallor was scaring me. I expected my lower leg to fall away.

'Is it broken?' asked Craig, who was staring with grim fascination. 'Was it his ankle or knee?'

Dad freed himself and stared at me. 'Technique's . . . designed to snap both,' he muttered. 'Bloody hell, Neil, I am so sorry.' He knelt down and took my foot tenderly and lowered it to the floor. It didn't hurt; in fact I suspected the bone-cracking might have actually loosened the joint, like when you crick your neck. Then I realized that my whole knee was in fact numb. I sat with my legs stretched out.

'Can you move it?' asked Dad.

'Give me a minute,' I croaked. Dad and Craig watched politely as I sat there. It was quite nice being the centre of attention. Eventually I tried to move my knee. It moved.

'It's mobile!' said Dad, relieved. 'It's not broken.'

'Dad, do they teach you to put people back together again in the army?' asked Craig. 'Or just yank them apart?'

'Shit, I'm sorry,' said Dad, putting his hand on my head. 'What have I done?'

'I think you got your youngest son in a leg lock against his will, then, um, snapped his leg in half,' said Craig.

'No need to swear,' I told Dad.

A look of surprise flitted across his face. 'Yes, Wendy,' he said facetiously. Wendy was Mum's name. 'And you can shut up, too,' he snapped at Craig. He looked back at me remorsefully. 'Not that I was telling you to shut up.'

'Ow!' I cried, trying to stretch my leg out again. My leg didn't hurt that much – the knee itself was still insensate – but I wanted to interrupt the stupid conversation that was developing.

'I was telling your *mother* to shut up. Ha ha. If you see what I mean.'

'Neil, remember, Mum's coming over tomorrow night,' Craig said plainly. 'Dad's cooking dinner.'

Dad's weird behaviour suddenly became explicable.

'She still might back out,' Dad said. 'You never know.'

'I think she wants to check that Dad isn't, you know, beating us or anything,' Craig said, laughing. He pretended to be speaking to Mum. 'No, Mum, you must be mistaken. Our Neil was never blessed with *two* working legs.'

'This is your fault as much as mine!' Dad shouted.

'You may have noticed that Dad is a bit jittery,' said Craig.

I looked at Dad. His eyes were darting. He was scared and excited. My leg and I forgave him. It had been, all things considered, a good day.

craig

Back in 1976, in their last year of primary school, Craig and Ariadne were an item.

DECEMBER 1976

St Michael's C. of E. primary school. Ariadne was going through a phase of looking impish and pretty and not like a boy. Craig fell in love with her and made her a paper handbag, waterproofed with swirling thick wax-crayon patterning and held together with many tiny staples. He made me do the stapling. It was quite charming, and had a string handle.

FEBRUARY 1977

On February 11th something weird happened. Ariadne declared that she loved Craig, and by

Valentine's Day she and Craig were a couple. They gave each other cards. Craig still remembers one of the many little poems neatly written inside the card Ariadne gave him (most of them donated by her older sister, who was then still living at home):

> I wish I were a cabbage
> I'd split myself in two
> The leaves I'd give to anyone
> But the heart I'd give to you.

Although he appreciated the card, and kept it for many years, Craig told me that he thought this poem was the most grotesque he'd ever read. Neither did he relish the poem's allusions to promiscuity and dementia.

MARCH

Ariadne's best friend Serena decided that she too was in love with Craig. Unaccustomed to all this attention, Craig felt so flattered that, one day, when we were driving home from school, he asked Mum to stop to give Gillian a lift (we were about to drive past her). Ariadne found out about this infidelity and demanded to know who Craig loved more, her or Gillian. Craig tried to think of something deep to say, but burped involuntarily. Ariadne stormed off.

APRIL

Craig wanted to win Ariadne back. He wrote her a letter, but he never sent it. Dad found it on the kitchen work surface, where Craig had foolishly left it before going to school. Dad, who didn't know Craig had a girlfriend, thought the letter was the funniest thing he'd ever read, and blu-tacked it to the door of Craig's bedroom.

Craig returned home from school, saw the letter on his door and was mortified, almost as mortified as he would be four years later when Mum would find a copy of *Razzle* under his mattress and pin the pages up around his room. Dad spent the rest of the evening quoting from the letter in a Dave Lee Travis voice and laughing till he choked. Mum told Dad to leave Craig alone, but also told Craig off for misspelling the words *magic* and *Serena*.

Craig pretended the letter was just a joke, and started laughing along with Dad, saying that Ariadne was just some obsessed girl who fancied him, and that he wanted to wind her up. Dad and I believed him and soon all of us were laughing, except Mum, who was sitting silently in her wicker chair reading something by Virginia somebody.

Dad said to Craig, 'You know what you should write? You should write, "Dear unwanted admirer, I am not going to be tied down to any one woman, thank you very much." '

'Robert, don't be ridiculous,' said Mum in a small, dangerous voice.

'He knows I'm kidding,' Dad chuckled, but he winked at Craig, which sort of suggested he wasn't kidding at all. Craig looked confused.

Craig wrote Ariadne a letter, presumably saying he didn't want to be tied to one woman. Ariadne poured some poster paint over him in registration and they stopped speaking to each other. Mum made Dad wash Craig's paint-splattered clothes, as the letter was his idea.

MAY

Ariadne's dabble in femininity drew to a close, as did Craig's brief attempt at tenderness. By now I was friends with Brendan, who came round often. Ariadne and Craig somehow became friends too, platonic ones.

Craig and Ariadne met up sometimes to do homework and argue. Their arguments, on which
Brendan and I would eavesdrop while standing outside Craig's or Ariadne's room, tended to be quite
philosophical, and were presumably related to their
A-levels. (Craig was taking Sociology, Psychology
and Drama. Ariadne was taking English, Sociology
and Drama.) Usually the arguments involved
Ariadne explaining a concept and Craig criticizing
the concept in a way that suggested he didn't understand it, prompting Ariadne to reformulate her
explanation. This continued until Ariadne would
get fed up and they would put on a heavy metal
album to lighten the mood.

Ariadne, now Harry, still liked Craig, that much was
clear. As for whether Craig still liked Harry, that's anyone's guess. After Dad stuck the love letter on the
bedroom door, seven years earlier, Craig stopped
showing any interest in romance.

Thursday evening found me standing on my one
good leg outside Craig's door, listening to him and
Harry converse.

I'd been waiting for Brendan to phone so we
could dissect the afternoon's happenings, but he
hadn't. Usually this would indicate that he hadn't
finished his homework yet, but I knew for a fact that

Brendan only had to draw a picture of a wattle and daub house. I rang him and his mum answered. She sounded annoyed, and told me that Brendan couldn't come to the phone because he was in his room, which was not any sort of reason for not coming to the phone in my book. Reading between the lines, I concluded that he had been sent there and was not allowed to leave, which meant he had done something inadvisable.

When Harry came round later, wearing a mouldy-looking black leather jacket with ripped red lining, she shed some light on the matter. It turned out that Brendan had thrown one of his temper tantrums because his mum and dad had decided to go away this weekend rather than next weekend. This, of course, meant that our day of music-making with Adele and Gillian would have to be moved forward, giving Brendan only one day to arrange it. Also, Ariadne would be at home this weekend. Naturally, Brendan didn't explain to his parents why their new arrangements would inconvenience him, and his dad asked him if he'd been planning some sort of party. As he wasn't planning anything of the sort, Brendan was able to reply truthfully in the negative, but I knew that he had a habit of acting suspect when telling the truth, which is why his parents hadn't believed him. This led to a huge row concerning the issue of trust, and Brendan was banished to his room after he called his mum an unfair cow. He had not yet learned that arguing with your parents is the most fruitless activity in the world. The relevant authorities would probably have had something to say about his being incarcerated without being allowed one phone call, but he was unable to contact any relevant authorities, as he wasn't allowed out of his room to use the phone.

'Tell me the truth,' Harry asked me after I let her into our house. 'Were you two planning some sort of do?'

I said, 'Of course we weren't.'

'You're all jumpy,' said Harry, laughing. 'You're either lying, or an epileptic.'

'I was going to go round to yours and play guitar,' I told her. 'For Brendan's Drama Group Piece soundtrack.'

'Why can't you do that this weekend instead of next?' Harry asked. 'Does next weekend have religious significance?'

I wished that I could think up snappy comebacks, like Martin. Instead I tended to mumble whatever I thought the other person would like me to mumble. I tried to think of the kind of retort Martin would come up with.

'Yes,' I ventured. That was my snappy comeback.

Harry drew her head back, looking surprised. 'Next weekend *does* have religious significance?'

'Yes,' I repeated. Harry was about to give me

further chances to be snappy, but Craig leapt down the staircase three steps at a time and told me to hop off and rest my leg.

'What's wrong with the poor lamb's leg?' asked Harry, watching me drag it towards the stairs.

Craig was wearing horrible black jeans with rivets in them, and a black Jack Daniels T-shirt whose short sleeves he'd ripped or bitten off. 'Domestic violence,' he said. 'Our father practises old-style discipline.'

'Does he want to adopt my brother?' Harry asked me.

'Yes,' I said.

Up in my bedroom I tried to think of some romantic things to put in Adele's Valentine card. I heard Harry and Craig come upstairs and enter Craig's room. My attempts at strawberry poems were going nowhere.

> Strawberries are red
> Violets are blue
> You're tasty (yummy?) enough
> To put in a stew.

But I didn't like the idea of putting Adele in a stew. I tried to think of a less gastronomic image, but I couldn't think of anything at all, so I began to scour my English exercise books looking for some of the poetry sheets we'd been given. Then I got sidetracked by a batch of rude 'Mary had a little lamb' rhymes that Brendan, Martin and I had scribbled on scraps of paper one lesson. Mine were okay, Brendan's were awful and needlessly tasteless, and Martin's were outstanding.

ME: Mary had a little field
         It was very lush
         Her little lamb would eat the grass
         And nibble on her bush.

MARTIN: Mary had a little lamb
         Alas! it was ill-fated
         To keep its bleat both high and sweet
         She had the thing castrated.

BRENDAN: Mary had a little lamb
         It was very bad
         So she stuffed it down her knickers
         And now it's a panty pad.

Maybe, I thought, I should try to elicit some poetry tips from Martin, or sneakily get him to write a poem and then steal it. Or, I reasoned, I could just ask him to write a love poem for use in my Valentine. But if the poem made Adele declare love for me, wouldn't that mean she was technically in love with Martin? How ruthless should one be in striving to win somebody's heart?

*　*　*

I decided to eavesdrop on Harry and Craig, in case
someone said something poetic that I could steal. I
hopped along the landing as quietly as I was able,
and lingered at the end of the corridor, with the
bathroom on my left and Craig's room ahead of me.
If Craig or Harry happened to suddenly come out of
the bedroom, my plan was to pretend to be heading
for the bathroom.

Inside Craig's room, a heavy metal record was
playing. There were no lyrics to the track; it
was some sort of epic instrumental with baroque
guitar-twiddles. I started to get bored. Then the
instrumental ground to a close and I heard
the sound of a floorboard. Panicking, I fell into the
bathroom. It was a false alarm. But I decided that
while I was in the bathroom, I might as well wash
my face with the square Neutrogena skin-clearing
soap I seemed to spend all my pocket money on. Its
function was to dry out the skin, thus preventing
blemishes and build-up of sebum. If used as
frequently as I used it, it was also effective in preventing any dermatological vitality. I scrubbed my
face bright red.

Back outside in the corridor, I stood shining in the
darkness. A conversation could now be heard in
Craig's room; they were talking about writing letters
to Father Christmas.

'I didn't stop till I was twelve,' Craig was saying.

'That's really touching, Craig,' said Harry. She started making comical retching noises.

'I wrote him a letter saying, "Please don't give me anything this year. I've been too bad." Then I listed all the fucking grimmest stuff I'd done over the last year, and my dad found it and read it.'

'Stuff like what?'

'I don't know, just childish evil.'

'Did he punish you? Did he show you the hairy side of his hand?'

'Actually,' said Craig, 'I might have had extra presents that year.'

They moved on to an academic topic. Harry tried to explain something about the evolution of animals' sense organs. Craig said, 'I'm all ears,' and Harry found this unaccountably funny. Then she talked about toads for a while, and Craig made 'Mmm' noises. For a while he didn't sound like my brother at all.

Just when I was beginning to take an interest in the evolution of toads, Harry sighed and said, 'I'm suddenly all bored to shit.' Craig was evidently bored too. He said, '*Call of Ktulu?*' (This was the name of the lengthy instrumental.)

There was a sound of footsteps as someone went over to the record player, which was near the door. Once again I panicked, and spun on my bad leg.

The knee gave way and I gasped loudly. The

footsteps stopped. I stood like a petrified tree, leaning against the wall.

The door jerked open. Harry frowned into the narrow gap and spotted me there, glowing with guilt and soap. Behind Harry, the room was lit by Craig's orange lamp, giving it a seedy look that was at odds with the highbrow conversation.

Harry said, 'A-*ha*.'

'What?' asked Craig. I could hear him scrabbling around. I thought I heard something being hidden.

'A spy,' said Harry, glaring up at me. 'A one-legged spy.'

'One-legged?' asked Craig.

Harry looked over her shoulder at him. 'The KGB is literally cutting their staff.'

I fidgeted. 'I wasn't spying,' I lied.

'Oh?'

'I wanted to ask Craig something.'

Craig appeared behind Harry. 'What is it, boy?' He rubbed his eye and Harry put a hand on her bony hip. 'I wanted to ask you what we should do about Mum coming over.'

'Neil, can't we talk about this some other time?' Craig asked.

I said I thought I'd ask now because she'd be here tomorrow.

Harry turned to Craig. 'Are you going to be plotting some kind of *Parent Trap*-style shenanigans?'

Craig looked at Harry then back at me. 'I don't

understand what she just said,' I confessed to Craig.

My brother opened the door to his room, which glowed like the interior of a Hallowe'en pumpkin, and told me to come in.

Craig and I were sitting on the bed, while Harry lounged in a brown beanbag. The beanbag was like a lifeboat floating on a sea of bundled up clothes, magazines and piles of scribbled-on A4 paper. The beam of the orange lamp was on my face.

'Are you two planning to get your mum and dad back together?' asked Harry.

Craig told her to shut up and stop talking like a fool, and said that getting your parents back together wasn't the sort of thing people did outside films.

It occurred to me that I was in the world of grown-ups, albeit teenage grown-ups: people for whom some plans are not worth making because they do not tally with how life is outside films.

Brendan and I felt we got some of our *very best* plans from films.

I could feel the defeatism in the room. I could see it in Ariadne, too, clearly in love, distressing to watch. She sat looking at Craig too much, looking over at his foot as it dangled over the end of the bed, perhaps wondering whether to reach out and clutch it. The idea made me queasy.

'Anyway,' said Craig, 'We don't really know what Mum's up to nowadays.'

'You mean she might have met someone?' Harry asked Craig's foot. I must have looked horrified because she said, 'Sorry, Neil. I'm sure she hasn't.' She lowered her head and stared at me. Her eyes and the orange lamp bore deep. 'Neil?'

'Yes?'

She said in a deep voice, 'You may speak.'

Craig laughed.

'Oh, he's all sweet and serious!' Harry said. 'My brother looks like he might be sweet, but he's actually a complete fucking snot. Neil doesn't look sweet, but he is, bless his heart.'

'I'm not,' I said, feeling my face go hot.

Ariadne said to Craig, 'May I pet him?'

The conversation was getting stupid. I said, 'I just hope that they don't get into a fight.'

'Did your parents fight much?' Harry asked me. 'I never saw them fight.'

I looked at Craig, who shrugged. 'Dad was always the one who shouted,' I told Harry. 'Mum would just keep quiet.'

'Do you think your mum kept quiet to get your dad riled?'

'I don't get what you mean,' I said.

Craig said, 'She means that being quiet was Mum's way of annoying Dad.'

'I just don't think she liked being shouted at,' I said. I must have sounded peeved, because Craig said, 'Don't take it out on her.'

'Sorry,' I said.

But I didn't feel especially sorry. Harry's suggestion was stupid. If there's one thing I had learned from the time I'd spent at the top of the stairs, listening to the voices in the kitchen and occasionally the lounge, the sounds of my parents' marriage wheezing and gasping for breath, it was that neither party had any desire to rile or provoke or irritate the other. They talked about their relationship as though it were a third person.

'I don't think they should get back together,' I said. 'I think they'd just be unhappy again.'

Harry frowned at me, then at Craig. 'Poor chap needs cheering up,' she said. She reached behind the beanbag and when her hand reappeared it was holding a bottle of vodka.

Craig lay back on the bed with the back of his hand on his forehead. 'Jesus,' he said. He sat up. Harry was grinning. 'Neil, swear you won't tell Dad,' said Craig.

Harry sighed haughtily. 'Craig, your dad probably has a medal he's saving for you, to be awarded on the day you delight him by admitting you're a worthless lush.' She gave Craig a glass and I saw her fingers touch his and he whipped the glass brusquely from her hand. Ariadne pretended not to have noticed Craig rejecting her fingers. I felt sad.

Harry handed me a glass. I said, 'Sorry, I don't drink.'

Harry found this hilarious, and mimicked me, then passed me the bottle, which was almost full. 'Tonight you will drink deeply,' she said in a Christopher Lee voice.

'Harry, if he ralphs all over my room, we are all dead.'

'Then you will drink deeply, but you will add much orange juice,' she said in the same voice.

'The orange juice is downstairs,' said Craig. 'Neil, put that damned bottle down. And, by the way, I am not a lush. Just so you know. We were just having a tipple. Look. We've hardly had any.'

'What's a lush?' I thought it was something to do with vegetation.

'It's an alcoholic woman who forces young boys to get drunk. Put the bottle down.'

'You're not a woman,' I told Craig.

'Nothing escapes the boy genius,' said Harry. 'He's obviously too sober. Neil, go downstairs and filch some orange juice out of the fridge.'

'Actually, it's time to leave us, I think, Neil,' said Craig darkly.

Harry shot him a harsh look. 'Craig, for God's sake. Behold this brother of yours.' She gestured strongly towards me, as though I were tonight's star prize. 'He hasn't a clue about anything. He's never done anything in his life. All he does is mope around with Brendan making up stupid plans to woo two girls at school.' I let out a genuine gasp.

104

'Neil, in our house we spend half our lives clearing up the little love-plans you and Brendan leave lying around.' She was of course referring to Brendan's pointless agendas. 'Stop looking so embarrassed,' she said. 'Go and get some orange juice and join us for a bit of revelry. Girls love crazy guys.'

That settled it. I went downstairs to get some orange juice. In the living room, through which I had to pass, Dad was reading a magazine and looking depressed.

'Is that Mum's magazine?' I found myself asking.

'Just so we have something to talk about tomorrow,' Dad said, perhaps without meaning to. He didn't notice me sneaking the orange juice up to Craig's room.

At the top of the stairs I peered down into the living room and watched him study the pages of the university magazine Mum wrote for, looking for conversation topics, points of contact, clues.

I had the weird sensation that my hair was vibrating. Harry and Craig were quite tipsy, but I was reeling. My face was buzzing and I had an underwater feeling. We'd been discussing Mum's imminent visit and pouring vodka down our throats. Craig had angled his lamp so that the orange glow was absorbed by the carpet. We sat in the warm gloom, hoping Dad wouldn't come upstairs, though I guessed he'd fallen asleep on the sofa.

A long discussion about romance developed, in which Craig gave me what sounded like a rehearsed speech about playing it cool. He said that boys like me thought that girls wanted someone to follow them around and dribble over them. Apparently what they wanted was the exact opposite: someone who did not notice their existence. His argument was that beautiful people have an inbuilt imperialist streak – they get bored with those who simply worship them, and seek instead to conquer those who don't. Ariadne said she thought this idea was balls, and I agreed. Craig said he had proof. Once he'd had a thing for Suzie Winstanley, a posh horsy girl in our school, but then he realized that she had really enormous teeth, which put him off her, and as soon as he lost interest she began to pursue him madly. Apparently she was still after him. Craig said he might 'give her a go', which I thought was a shockingly insensitive thing to say in front of Harry. Harry looked murderous.

I told Harry that one day someone would sweep her off her feet and prove all of Craig's ideas wrong. Craig laughed so loudly that we had to shut him up in case Dad heard him. Harry said I was the most romantic boy she'd ever met.

'You wouldn't go out with him, though,' said Craig.

No, Dad did not find out about the drinking session: he had indeed fallen asleep on the sofa, with Mum's magazine splayed on his belly. When I woke up the next morning, although I had creeping flesh and a poisoned head, the strongest sensation I had (before I tried to straighten my injured leg and found that it wasn't working) was that of having passed the whole night with Craig's cynicism churning in my skull.

Thanks to my knee, which was frozen with pain, I got a day off school. On the one hand, this was just as well – I was bright green from the booze. But this meant that Brendan was going to have to handle our romantic affairs without my support.

Into the bathroom. To be sick. It didn't happen straight away. The face in the mirror was fascinatingly unhealthy. 'I am an alcoholic,' I told it. Was alcoholism appealing? I felt more interesting than usual. My stomach felt terrible but I made ugly faces into the mirror until I started laughing. I became hysterical. Mum was coming over later and would wonder why I was green. I brushed my teeth and let the froth spill out of my mouth and half-closed one eye.

'Hello, Mum,' I croaked horribly, letting big flobs of toothpaste foam dribble into the sink. I blew a menthol nose-bubble. 'Adele, why won't you go out with me?' I moaned. The toothpaste formed strings that stretched from my mouth right down the plughole. I laughed uncontrollably till I was sick, and when I was done I leaned against the toilet and started to think about all the things that would be happening today; and back in my room I thought of Brendan at school, and I wrapped my arms around my pounding head and prayed to Almighty God, God of underdogs, God of the impossible and the unlikely, that He would bless Brendan in his attempt today to get Adele and Gillian to come to his house this coming weekend; that in my absence He would keep my friend from irreversible blunders, if this was not too much to ask.

afternoon in

When Craig and I were younger, Dad would read to us at bedtime from books by people like Liddell Hart, Ludovic Kennedy and Sven Hassel, books with titles like *Sink the Bismarck* and *Blitzkrieg!* Craig, a man's man from the age of ten, responded to the stories by making, and filling the house with innumerable gigantic paper-and-sellotape battleships and tanks. He was constantly at war with invisible Axis forces. Often you'd walk into a room and find him spread out under the rug holding a plastic gun, or lying behind the sofa moaning, because of shrapnel. Dad, who'd joined the army when he was nineteen and stayed until his early twenties, and who acted as though he'd had to sacrifice his former hearty manliness so as not to offend my quiet, delicate-seeming mother, found in his relationship with Craig an outlet for his suppressed machismo. Craig became Dad's best friend, which somehow made me assume I was Mum's best friend, for the sake of symmetry.

Craig was Dad's recompense for having to give up his trooper's bawdiness and hard-drinking male friends. Not that Mum ever asked him to give these things up, as far as I know. But Dad always behaved as though he'd won Mum's heart, and her hand in marriage, by virtue of some noble sacrifice of his former self. He acted like this right up until Mum moved out.

Dad never knew how fascinated I was by the war stories he told. But then it wasn't the violence of the stories that fascinated me. It was the majestic beauty of the machines of war, as captured in the books' photographs. Snub-nosed fighter planes and Panzers with winter markings. Warships struck me as possessing distinct personalities, and I grew very attached to them: the *Tirpitz*, or the gigantic, doomed HMS *Hood*; proud durable sister ships like the *Scharnhorst* and the *Gneisnau*; the *Admiral Graf Spee*; the *King George V*; HMS *Rodney*. It never occurred to me that these machines killed people, only that they chased each other around in thrilling campaigns, large floating epic characters with majestic names (excepting HMS *Rodney*). The sinking of the *Bismarck* made me ache with sadness, even though my main sympathies were of course with the Allies. I was heartbroken when I saw on the news that the *Ark Royal* was going to be dismantled, even though by then Dad had long stopped reading his books to us.

Since Mum left, Dad hadn't displayed much fighting spirit, unless he was injuring his sons in hand-to-hand combat lessons. He spent a lot of time sitting around thinking. Not reading or watching television, just idling in a manner suggestive of reflection. In this sense he had started to resemble Mum, who was a big thinker. Mum also liked to stare at nothing. She read, but used to do it in the bedroom, where we couldn't interrupt her with low-brow chatter.

Mum now lived in a room in an apartment owned by an elderly woman named Jeannie, whose three black Labradors Mum had effectively taken responsibility for. Not that Jeannie was senile or otherwise incapable of caring for the dogs; Mum said she had just grown out of them. It is odd to think of a woman in her seventies growing out of something, the way children outgrow their shoes, but that's how Mum put it. Craig and I had met Jeannie many times, as she and Mum had been friends for a couple of years. It was Jeannie's now-late husband Owen, a former professor at Reading University, who first encouraged Mum to take up part-time studies in Philosophy as a mature student. He also critiqued the first article she wrote, which was published in a magazine for Christian women called *Home and Spirit*. I read it. It was about teaching spiritual values in schools, and was accompanied by a cartoon of a schoolgirl working from a massive textbook, the cover of which read:

GO FORTH AND MULTIPLY!
An Old Testament Guide to Times Tables

I didn't understand the article when I first read it, but I did understand that the person who wrote it was not the person who was my mother. The author of the article was someone bubbling with things to say, none of which she'd had a chance to say in a house populated by copies of the *TV Times*, Sven Hassel novels and three other people who had the combined intellectual depth of a handbag.

The fact that Mum's article was *argumentative* was another big shock. At home, arguing was one thing that Mum never did. Her inability to argue was probably the aspect of her that exasperated Dad the most. I think it stemmed from her manners. Mum was shackled by excessive politeness, so that even her close friends had to change conversational register when talking to her. I'd see them joke and gossip with Dad and Craig – both of whom managed to get on informal terms with people, including shopkeepers and police officers, in record speed – and then Mum would walk in, and her friends would adopt the same tone you'd use if you were interrupting a Quaker meeting to ask if anyone had some spare jump leads. Mum never got past this how-do-you-do phase with anyone, which I think made Dad consider her a bit socially inept. Dad obviously thought Mum's over-politeness was due to some sort of terrible fragility. This apparent fragility may well have been what he liked about her in the first place, not knowing that it would eventually make him so irritable that she'd leave our home to go and live with a youthful septuagenarian and some outgrown dogs.

Craig was more upset than I was when Mum left. Perhaps I didn't fully appreciate what was going on. I could get very sentimental at times, especially while reading *Sweet Dreams* books, whose honey-sweet plot developments sometimes forced me to stop reading and stare, overjoyed, into the air in front of me, as though willing the author to appear before my eyes to receive my congratulations, but anything worthy of genuine raw emotion made me switch off. Or maybe I thought it would be bad form to make a fuss. Craig made an almighty fuss. He made a point of reminding Mum and Dad of the times they'd sworn they'd never split up no-matter-what, which made Dad madly apologetic and then, when Craig pressed the point one time too many, made him angry. 'I didn't bloody *sign* anything!' Dad shouted at one point (referring to his and Mum's promise to us to stay together – presumably Dad did sign something when he actually got married).

Me, I felt nothing but numb, though I pretended to be devastated so I could have a day off school.

Two or three months before Mum left, she and Dad had been shouting a lot, or Dad had been shouting and Mum had been replying sparingly with well-picked words. On two occasions Craig and I, hiding in Craig's bedroom, too nervous to man our usual listening post near the upstairs landing, had looked out of the bedroom window to see Dad leaving the house with a packed bag, his shouting having reached its peak. He came back both times, but we got accustomed to the idea that if one of our parents was going to go, it'd be him. But then one day he announced that Mum was going to live with his parents, for reasons that he never fully explained. Our paternal grandparents lived nearby, and they liked Mum, at least enough to take her in despite the fact that she was abandoning their son. Dad broke the news to Craig and me that we'd be living with just him from now on, but he stressed that we would see Mum 'all the time' (we saw her quite a lot, actually, during the few weeks when she lived at the elderly Flacks' house).

Mum never sat us kids down to tell us why she was leaving, but we didn't expect her to. Dad was the one who filled us in on things. As it happened, Dad didn't explain either. Mum did apologize, though. Recently, nearly twenty years after the event, I was talking to Craig about Mum's apology and departure, and he said, 'I thought she was going to shake my hand.'

'Craig, she *did* shake your hand.'

'*Did* she?'

'And she gave you that signed photograph.' Craig has always been gullible.

Truth is, it struck me as a very positive development, my parents splitting up. It was certainly better than wondering constantly whether one parent was going to end up murdering the other with a garden trowel, which is something that had happened in one of the true crime books Craig read. Also, I felt a bit more grown up. I felt like I was experiencing real suffering, though without actually feeling any suffering, which suited me fine. In later teenage years, whenever I met people who weren't from broken homes, whose parents had stayed happily married, I'd look sympathetic and say, 'It must have been hard for you.'

'What do you mean?' they'd ask.

'You know, growing up in a minority. Different from all your friends. It must have been painful.'

I thought it was a droll, perceptive thing to say, but I recognize with hindsight that it wasn't anything of the sort.

On the morning of Friday the 11th, Dad came in and found me looking woozy and got me some tea. I told him that it had taken me about ten minutes to bend my leg, and then after I'd bent it I couldn't straighten it again. He telephoned work and then we went to the doctors' surgery at the Asda complex.

The surgery there was like a large Portakabin. We waited in the green waiting-room, me reading *Cosmopolitan* and Dad staring. Even though the day had hardly begun, I could tell he was already getting nervous about Mum coming over. Maybe he mistook my sick expression for a similar case of nerves, because he patted me on the shoulder and told me things would be okay.

Dr Ashley asked me what I'd done to my leg and I lied, saying I'd fallen over. I found myself sounding like a battered wife in a television drama who tells people, 'I just slipped.' Dad laughed and told Dr Ashley the truth, but somehow his words sounded really heartless, making Dad appear both abusive *and* nonchalant. We were not a great double-act. Dr Ashley looked horrified and wrote something on his pad. Dad cleared his throat nervously and stared at his knees.

I was tempted to mention to Dr Ashley that Dad was a very competent parent, and not at all tyrannical. This made me think of how much quieter and more pleasant and less complicated our household was without Mum at home, which made me feel guilty, but it was true: Dad didn't shout when his wife was not around. *And yet the very thought of her return made him break his son like a twig!* Dr Ashley made me lie down and picked up my lower leg and started rotating it. He felt around my knee and then dug his thumbs in. Annoyingly, my leg had stopped hurting the second I'd entered Dr Ashley's room, and so I had to try to remember where the pain had been, and moan at the appropriate times.

'Nothing's broken,' he said, and he mentioned a ligament behind my knee. He told me to avoid rotating the joint, and I tried to remember when I'd ever had occasion to do that. He gave me a beige knee support that looked too thin to be of any use. I was annoyed at not having to have an X-ray.

When we returned from the doctor's, Dad went to work and I stayed home and languished, hung-over. I think Dad was still guilty about my crippled leg, because before he went he said he would try to come home early. He may also have been troubled by visions of me stumbling around the house, knocking over valuables and crashing through windows.

As a matter of fact I ended up spending most of the morning looking at Polaroid family photos I found in a big clear plastic bag on the bottom bookshelf in the lounge, under the video shelf. There were further photos in two shoeboxes, and I looked at them as well. There was a good one of Craig as a young lad, looking distraught and holding a popped balloon by its string (a thorn bush had popped it). The rest of the shots of Craig pictured him looking up open-mouthed at the lens, or turning towards someone with an open mouth, laughing or gasping or shouting. Catching flies, Dad used to say. Most of the ones of me looked daft. I tended to look camp in photos, apparently unaware that I was being photographed, a beanpole who, if the photo collection was to be trusted, spent his life day-dreaming while leaning against things (trees, walls, a gun turret of the HMS *Belfast*) or else wafting lankily in search of things to lean against. I was always frowning at the floor.

There were also lots of pictures of Mum and Dad together, whose posturing looked weirdly formal. There was only one picture of the whole Flack household, all four of us, and I was embarrassed to see us all looking so joyless. We were like a Before photo in an advertisement for family therapy. Dad was the only one of us who didn't look miserable, but then he might have been, it was hard to tell. He was sneezing.

In the shoebox, along with the Polaroids, there were some older pictures I hadn't seen before. There was one of Mum's mum, Christina Rostkowska (who died when Mum was fifteen, a year after the photo was taken), looking suitably doomed. There was one of Mum as a girl looking black-haired and pretty, with big eyes and a trace of her later-trademark reluctance to smile. There were some of my maternal grandad, a sly genial dentist of Polish extraction. There were photos of Dad japing around as a teenager. He looked *exactly* like Craig. The photos gave me the weird impression of having a lost brother wandering out there somewhere, a prototype Craig. There were photos of Dad looking handsome in his army uniform, and I leafed through them and then felt moved to read some more of Dad's war books, namely Koch's *Medieval Warfare* and a book on warships, from steam-powered to nuclear, which kept me occupied until lunchtime.

Dad came back at about half one, by which time I had developed an unexpected appetite and was buttering bits of malt loaf in the kitchen. He came in with some Asda shopping bags full of food and asked me how I was feeling.

'Not too bad,' I said, in a brave voice, while deftly hiding my malt loaf in the bread bin, because I thought Dad might suspect I was faking my illness if he saw me eating. Then I remembered that I was home because of a bad leg, not because of illness, and was going to retrieve my snack, but by then Dad had opened the bread bin to put some breadsticks in there. He noticed the bits of buttered malt loaf and started chomping them without comment, even though one of the slices had a big bite in it.

'What are you going to cook tonight?' I asked as he unpacked the bags.

'What?' He seemed to have forgotten I was there. 'Ah, I was thinking perhaps spag bog.'

'Very romantic,' I said.

'You think so?' He sounded pleased with himself. Then he stopped unpacking bags and turned to me. 'Neil, this isn't *supposed* to be a romantic meal.' He gave me a piece of my malt loaf. 'It's the four of us being together as a family.'

'Okay,' I said. I limped over to the kettle.

'We should stop feeding you,' he said.

Dad saw me clutch my malt loaf. 'I meant you're getting really tall,' he explained. 'Like a basketball player. How'd you like to be a basketball player?'

'Basketball is too American,' I said, which made him laugh.

'Cricket,' said Dad.

I swung my foot. 'I'm not great at games.'

'You're more the academic type,' he ventured.

'Dad.'

He started arranging things on the kitchen work surface to the left of the hob: a jar of bolognese sauce, a packet of spaghetti, some carrots and some cheese.

'It's looking a bit basic,' I said. 'Mum always put in herbs.'

'God, did she?' He started looking through the cupboards. 'There are herbs in the sauce,' he said. 'I was going to put parmesan on top.'

'Parmesan has that smell, though.'

'I'm also putting in garlic, if that's all right with you. You haven't got a hot date tonight, have you? Ha ha.'

'*Dad.*'

I took a packet of garlic bread from an Asda bag and put it on the surface to the right of the hob, next to the cookery book on a stand, which Mum had left there, pointlessly open at a page that showed us how to make leg of lamb with rosemary and lemon.

'Girls like lanky boys, you know. Like David Bowie.'

'David Bowie?' From what I'd seen of him on television, he was about as far from my choice of ideal role model as could be imagined. 'Don't you usually make the sauce yourself?'

'I thought I'd buy it this time.'

'In case it goes wrong?'

'No, because – it doesn't matter. Sit down and rest your leg.'

'But why don't you just make the bolognese sauce and the garlic bread like usual? Yours is nicer than the canned sauce.'

'Neil, stop hounding me!'

I swung my leg.

'Neil, I'm not going to make some big song and dance about a dinner,' Dad said. 'This isn't a memory-lane bolognese. It's bog standard spag bog. I just want to rustle something up without any fuss.'

He put some teabags in cups as the kettle boiled,

then picked up the kettle too sharply, so that the boiling water jumped on to his hand. In a really impressive display of agility and responsibility, he managed to fling the kettle away from himself but somehow redirect it away from me and back to the kitchen surface, where its contents splashed over the last bit of malt loaf. Suddenly he seemed out of breath. He stared at his hand.

'Are you okay?' I asked quietly.

'Skin's still there,' he said. 'Let that be a lesson about safety in the kitchen to you.'

I ran the cold tap and told him to put his hand under it, which is what he'd do if I'd poured hot water over *my* hand, and to my surprise he obeyed. By then I'd forgotten what I'd wanted to ask him, which was: what is memory-lane bolognese? Then it struck me: he was nervous, like a boy going on a date. This was the first time I'd ever seen real live pre-date nerves, and the experience looked unpleasant. A thought shocked me: this was like going back in time and watching my parents get together. The thought of being a time traveller caused movement in my imagination – an underworked imagination at the best of times – and I felt the need to go to the living-room and sit down and think about this and similar scenarios, while Dad remained in the present, in the kitchen, trying to decide how much garlic to use.

* * *

Later, Brendan phoned. The girls had said no to the making-music idea.

I had to lean against the wall when Brendan told me. Disappointment gulped all my energy. It took Brendan thirty minutes to tell me every single detail of the fruitless conversations he'd had with every member of his Group Piece group, starting with the remedials and Karen the she-bully, whom he'd tried to win over first, in the hope that their compliance would give him leverage with Adele and Gillian. Apparently no one wanted to give up some of their weekend to be in our company.

But, he said, there was still hope. 'I told Gillian and Adele that we were in a band, and Adele said that she was in a band too. With some girls from another school.'

'A band?'

'Called Victorian Brickwork.'

'What?' I could not for the life of me think why anyone would call their band Victorian Brickwork.

'And Adele said she thought the music thing was a good idea. She plays a flute. So I thought maybe when we do our photo shoot, we could suggest that we all go to mine afterwards and make up a piece of music then. You remember we were going to do a photo shoot?'

I said yes. I thought: flute?

'So they're not coming at the weekend?' I asked needlessly.

He reiterated: no. But, he told me, Adele and Gillian said they'd definitely stay after school for a photo shoot next week. Adele had asked if we could do it after school on Tuesday, and suggested a venue: the Music room in the Arts block.

'Why did you tell them we're in a band?' I asked. 'What if they ask us to play a song?'

'We have to start a band, right now,' he said. 'You be the guitarist, I'll be the singer.'

'Can you sing?'

'I sing okay.'

'I've heard you sing,' I said. Brendan sang like a parrot might sing if it lived in Leonard Cohen's house. 'I'm not sure they'll believe that you are a proper singer. No offence.'

'And you think they're going to believe you're a proper guitarist?'

'I can play "Mull of Kintyre".'

'Our worries are over!'

We discussed our *ad hoc* band at length, and decided that it was going to be called Tramp, because Brendan flicked through a dictionary and that was the first word he landed on. (Actually, it was the third: the first was 'return' and the second was 'worthwhile'.)

'Wembley, please welcome: Tramp!' cried Brendan, his enthusiasm soaring. 'How does that sound?'

I thought it sounded crap. But now wasn't the

right time to quibble over our new band's name. Neither my brain nor Brendan's was working efficiently. We were too excited. True, our original plan had collapsed like a bad soufflé. But when you know in your heart that all of your plans are essentially idiotic, then one stupid plan, you can easily convince yourself, is as good as another, and if *any* of them work it is because of luck and divine grace rather than the plan's intrinsic merits.

So we agreed that Tramp would meet up for a band practice on Saturday, at Brendan's. Our set would include 'Mull of Kintyre' and any other songs involving less than four chords that we could find in the book *Start Playing Rock Guitar*.

Tramp! Brendan Keetley on vocals and Neil Flack on guitar and maybe backing vocals. And then (perhaps), next week – for one night only! – Tramp! with a guest appearance by Adele Collier, flautist with Victorian Brickwork!

After Brendan had rung off, I sat around with Dad, thinking: Victorian Brickwork – what a brilliantly peculiar name for a band! Unless it wasn't Adele who came up with that name, in which case, frankly, it stank. Craig came home and asked if Mum was here yet. Dad said no, and Craig told Dad he looked dapper, and Dad told Craig to shut up and stop grinning and set the table.

tiny christmas tree

The doorbell went and the three of us lurched. Craig and I looked at Dad, who stood up and reached for his throat as though to adjust a tie that wasn't there.

Craig pointed to the coffee table. 'Dad, you can't leave a copy of her magazine there. She'll wonder why the sudden interest in feminism.' The university magazine that Mum wrote for was lying half-concealed by a copy of the *Mirror*.

'Hide it!' hissed Dad, as though Craig had pointed out a bag of heroin. He headed for the door.

Craig hid the magazine. Outside the heavens had opened, and Dad rescued Mum from the storm by pulling her indoors. Craig and I got to our feet and found a place to stand.

Our mother had been rained on heavily, but she was a woman who wore rain well; being so small and pale, she didn't just look like she had been drenched in a downpour, she looked like she had *survived* something, like she had walked the plank on a pirate ship and somehow swum to shore, pursued by sharks. Her long black hair clung to her face, and her white skin shone with droplets. When she strode in she tried to pull her black scarf off too quickly and it almost strangled her. Craig said, 'Woah!' Mum grinned sheepishly and shook her head so that excess rain jumped out of her hair. She looked around the room at us: Craig standing by the coffee table; me with one leg, standing by the stairs; Dad holding out his hands to receive her enormous brown Pacamac.

'Hi, hi!' she said, unusually animated, waving at us as though we were far away.

We came forward. 'Give me that coat,' Dad said.

'With pleasure.' She let Dad relieve her of her mac, then held his hands and kissed him. Even in her tall boots she was much shorter than Dad, and her oversized black jumper diminished her further, but there was something about the way she moved that made her seem gangly, like me. Her austere face was softened by pretty eyes, with long black lashes that still retained raindrops. 'Sorry I'm barely-noticeably late.'

'You're half-drowned,' observed Dad, welcoming her into our home.

'I parked round the corner,' said Mum. 'On Bournbrook. Virtually a car-ride away in itself. Someone must be having a party nearby. The kerbs are chock-a-block.'

'I didn't think it was raining that hard,' said

Dad. 'I went out before and it was just a fine mist.'

'That's another fine mist you've gotten me into,' said Mum. She rubbed her hands together and said, 'What's for dinner?'

'Spag bog.'

'Robert, I wish you wouldn't call it that.'

'Right.'

'Makes it sound unappetizing.'

'Okay.'

Craig said, 'He doesn't want to get your hopes up, Mum, by making it sound posh. I've seen it, it's just slop.'

Mum went over to Craig and put her arms round him. 'Hello, you boys.' Craig towered over her.

I saw that one of Mum's arms was extended towards me, so I hobbled over and joined the scrum. Craig wasn't hugging Mum, he was just standing there looking surprised. He reached round to pat her on the back, but patted my hand instead. I withdrew my hand and put it in my pocket, not knowing what else to do with it.

'I must smell like a soggy beagle,' said Mum. 'I shouldn't wear wool in the rain.'

'Beagles have wool?' said Craig.

'Little sod,' said Mum, kissing Craig's head, which made him flinch with shock. 'Have you been wearing this sweatshirt since I last saw you?'

'Ha ha,' said Craig. 'It's the stubborn understains that hold it together.'

I heard Dad head for the kitchen. Mum released us. She held my hand as I stepped away from her, until she had to let go because I had reached arm's length, like a dog at the end of its lead.

Craig, now standing behind Mum, caught my eye, then nodded towards Mum and mimed swigging from a bottle. I thought: perhaps Mum has become an alcoholic. Two of Mum's friends, both husbandless, were alcoholics. I became upset.

'What's wrong with your leg?' Mum demanded of me as I tried to figure out how to tell if she was drunk. Craig, who was waiting for the right moment to sit down and relax, let out a sudden laugh. Dad came back into the living room holding a floral-print oven glove.

I remembered how unconvincingly I'd lied to Dr Ashley that morning. 'Well,' I said, 'Dad was showing us this fighting move where you have to break someone's leg. And I got hurt, by accident.'

'Very funny, Neil,' said Dad. 'He fell over,' he told Mum. Craig, who was still laughing, choked a little.

'Clumsy, *clumsy* boy,' said Craig. 'Always falling over.'

'What really happened?' Mum asked, sounding serious.

'We were just mucking about,' said Craig. He waved his hand. 'Nothing to worry about.'

'Fighting?' asked Mum. 'The three of you?'

'Don't be silly,' said Dad.

'Not *fighting*,' I said.

'Sort of training,' said Craig. 'Injuries do happen.'

Judging by the look on Mum's face, she was imagining us using the living room for no-holds-barred wrestling contests: Craig beating his bare chest and Dad with a tea-towel tied round his forehead, both taking it in turns to climb on to the arm of the sofa and belly-flop on to me as I lay unconscious on the rug.

She changed the subject and commented on Dad's choice of coasters for the coffee table: two Black Sheep Ale beermats. Then she remarked on the fact that there were two pairs of slippers on the windowsill.

It was only now that Mum was back in our house that I realized what a vast difference her absence made. I missed her, now that she was here. It was as though the air had cleared; the atmosphere lost its gloom of manliness. Here was a person who would never break my bones demonstrating ju-jitsu in the living room, a person who never slouched and never watched rugby on television. And it was only now that I recognized how different the *house* had become since Mum had last been round to see us. The relocated slippers and the beermats and the row of cups on the fridge, and the way the soapdish in the bathroom was full of about sixteen useless slivers, and the way the pans were left to dry in the kitchen (right-way-up, because none of us went

131

the extra mile and turned them over to let them drain) – these small details all added up to something quite big, I realized. How horrible for Mum, I thought sadly, coming back to a house that had changed. It was a wonder she didn't run screaming into the kitchen and start moving things around.

Dad must have been thinking along the same lines as me, because when he went over to the coat rack with the intention of hanging his oven glove on it, he stopped, looked at Mum, and changed his mind, then took it into the kitchen.

That was what Mum brought to our house: a sense of what was domestically appropriate.

During dinner we asked Mum what she'd been up to lately. She told us how she'd had a once-in-a-lifetime opportunity to stay in London for two weeks attending seminars conducted by well-known feminist thinkers, and had met a theologian called Mary something. She'd also helped out in a new women's refuge near Roehampton. For the last two weeks she'd been trying desperately to finish an essay evaluating the recent work of someone called Carol who was once a student of someone called Lawrence. Her tutor said that Mum might be able to get her essay published in a journal. Even I could see that Mum was trying to justify not having visited for a whole month. Personally I had no idea how often estranged parents were supposed to see their children; I'd never been the child of separated parents before, and did not know the protocol, so Mum was wasting her time trying to explain herself.

Next she told us a stream of anecdotes about people she'd spoken to on the phone at the clinic where she worked. We nodded continuously and when she finished her stories we made her tell us more. Soon she ran out of news, but we couldn't stop asking questions. We'd expected her to be much, much quieter than this, and we'd all mentally rehearsed things to say to keep the conversation going.

'I think you said you were going to do some editorial work with the college magazine,' said Dad. He, Craig and I were trying to copy the way Mum was twiddling her spaghetti round her fork.

'Oh, it was too much bother,' Mum sighed, waving her fork. 'When I get back to the flat after work or uni I just want to mope. But it's hard to relax with those dogs bounding around. Then there's Jeannie, with her endless appetite for discussing feminist ethics. Enough to send a woman grey.'

The way Dad was nodding sympathetically, you'd think his whole life was spent excusing himself from exhausting discussions with feminists. 'So you're not doing any editing?' he asked.

'Dad's on the ball tonight,' grinned Craig.

'No, I'm not editing. Actually – oh, I must be boring you all rigid.'

'No, no,' Dad insisted.

'I for one am on the edge of my seat,' said Craig. 'Any second now I'm going to get up and leave.'

Mum laughed at this. 'I don't see you for a month and you turn all cheeky!'

'Mum, I was always cheeky.'

'He was,' I confirmed.

'Why did I ever stand for it before?' Mum said.

Then she asked us what we'd been doing recently, and we gave her bland outlines of our lives. She seemed disappointed.

'These boys should get out more,' she informed Dad.

'They're teenage,' Dad muttered, apparently starting to get annoyed by Mum's unusual self-assurance. 'Getting them out of their rooms is hard enough.'

'Dad's attempts to interest us in fine art and the opera have been met with both mockery and ungratefulness,' said Craig.

'Oh, give that whale-size gob of yours a rest,' Dad commanded, a bit tetchily. 'Boy's got an answer for everything.'

Mum said she thought Craig was developing a fine wit. For some reason I thought of when Craig had compared his fart to the smell of gravy, and although I hadn't found it the least bit funny at the time, the idea of Craig doing the same thing now, with our Mum sitting here, struck me as irresistibly comic. A huge laugh flew out of my mouth. I wanted to turn it into a cough, but something went wrong and it came out as a sort of scream.

'Neil!' Mum cried. Dad looked concerned. Craig, for no reason at all, sprang to his feet. He sat down again.

'Just my leg,' I lied, rubbing my knee for emphasis. 'It twisted.'

As soon as I mentioned my leg I knew I had said the wrong thing. Mum pursed her lips. The sudden lack of conversation made the clinking of our forks seem abnormally loud. After an age, Mum said, 'Just to set my mind at ease, can you all assure me that you're not using Neil as some kind of stress relief toy?'

Craig laughed, but then he saw Mum's earnest expression and shut up. Dad was giving me a black look. Clearly I had ruined the meal by reminding Mum of the violence that had been going on in her absence. Why was I so thoughtless? Desperate to make amends, I said, 'It was my own fault.'

In retrospect, heaping blame upon myself for having been beaten up was not the best thing to say to a woman who'd just spent two weeks working in a women's refuge, persuading battered wives that they *weren't* to blame. Mum got heated. 'Don't you dare say it was your fault you got hurt!'

'Sorry!' I moaned. Dad and Craig were looking at me like I'd sold the story of my injury to the tabloids.

'And don't say sorry!' Mum ordered.

I stared at my plate. Unconsciously I'd twisted half of my spaghetti round my fork. It looked like a small Italian whirlpool. Dad sighed and said, 'Wendy, it was a one-off incident. Don't worry.' Then, after a pause, he added, 'We're muddling along just fine.'

Mum had brought a neat forkful of spaghetti to her lips but she lowered it. 'Meaning?'

Dad rolled his eyes. 'What do you mean, "meaning"? It meant what it sounded like it meant.'

'You know what I'm talking about.'

'And you know what *I'm* talking about,' said Dad. 'So give it a rest with this "meaning?" business.'

Mum said, 'I can't eat much more.'

Craig said, 'Meaning?' Mum and Dad glared at him. Poor fool, he was just trying to lighten the mood with some inapt humour, even I could see that. Craig said, 'Sorry, I just . . .'

Another big stretch of quiet. Then Mum said, 'How about I take the boys back to see the flat after dinner?'

Dad chewed slowly. 'See the flat?'

'Just briefly. Jeannie's going away for a bit, so we could see her off.'

'Ah, Mum, I can't,' Craig said. 'I'm supposed to be going over to Harry's after tea, just for a bit. We're working on a school project.'

'Oh,' said Mum. 'Oh, that's a shame.'

'I can come,' I said.

'Great,' said Mum.

'I thought you were coming over to do some homework with Brendan?' asked Craig, scowling at me. I tried to remember. 'I don't have any homework,' I said. 'I was off school today.'

'Maybe you could come over some other time,' Mum said to Craig. 'Jeannie is wondering how you both are.'

'Well, tell her I said howdy,' said Craig.

We finished the meal in silence, Craig and Dad and I exchanging glances over our forkfuls of badly-twirled pasta.

Things got ugly after dinner, while Dad and Mum stood in the kitchen washing up.

Craig and I were sitting in the living room at the time, arguing. Craig was telling me off for saying I'd go to Mum's flat.

'We were going to be leaving them alone tonight,' he snapped. 'They have stuff to sort out.'

'But I haven't arranged to go to Brendan's.'

'You should have,' said Craig. 'We were talking about it last night.'

'It was you who wanted to leave them alone, not me.'

'God, you can be selfish,' said Craig. 'Try to think about *them* for a change.'

'Anyway,' I said, 'I don't remember *any* plans we

made last night. You got me drunk, remember? I was sick all this morning.' Craig looked guilty for a second, and calmed down. I told him about Dr Ashley. Craig said, 'That man tried to get me and Dad to go to his church once. I only went to see him because of stomach-ache.'

'When they thought you had appendicitis?'

'Dirty bastard put his hand up my bum,' said Craig. 'And he calls himself a man of God.'

I asked, 'His whole hand?'

'Verily, I sat on his right hand,' said Craig.

'That's grim,' I said, getting up to hobble upstairs. 'Grim.'

'Wait, shush!' whispered Craig. He was listening to the voices coming from the kitchen. He crept over to the door and I followed. Mum and Dad were hissing at each other.

'What the hell are they going on about?' Craig whispered.

'Do they know we're in here?' I asked.

Dad was saying, 'Well, maybe you should leave it *two* months before your next visit. Give us more time to come apart at the seams.'

'Or to murder each other,' Mum snarled. I'd never heard her snarl.

'Oh, you'd love that, wouldn't you? The moment you leave we turn into Lord of the Rings.'

'Lord of the *Flies*, Robert. And no, I can assure you I wouldn't love it one bit. I don't love any of this.'

'Well, this was your choice.'

Craig and I listened in horror. We heard sounds of furious dishwashing. Unable to stand it any more, Craig cleared his throat loudly to indicate our proximity. Our parents went silent. I thought I heard Dad emit a quiet expletive.

Ten seconds later Mum came striding out of the kitchen, by which time Craig and I had retreated into the middle of the living-room and were standing there looking at our feet.

'Are you coming, Neil?' Mum asked sharply.

I glanced at Craig. He glowered. Mum was getting her coat. She turned around and fixed me with a look that prompted me to make up my mind. 'Okay,' I said.

Dad sloped into the living-room, looking dejected and heated.

'We'll be back later,' said Mum, not looking at anyone. 'Thanks for dinner.' She flung her scarf around herself and then went over to Craig and kissed him, holding him by the shoulders.

'See you in a bit,' I said meekly to Dad and Craig, following Mum out. It wasn't a promise, it was a wish.

Outside, the rain had lessened. Mum had been right about the parking situation: a conga-line of cars snaked along the pavement. Mum and I didn't talk as we trudged. When we got to her car, she saw that it had been hemmed in by other vehicles, and she stood and stared at it for a while. Then we got in and Mum said, 'Oh *dear*.' And she put her forehead on the steering-wheel.

'Mum?' I whispered. 'Are you okay?'

She exhaled and cleared her throat, and sat up. She put her hands on the wheel. 'Tight parking spaces,' she said. 'Bane of my life.'

'Mine too,' I said.

We sat in silence for what seemed like ten minutes. I was about to say something for the sake of saying something, like, 'Are we waiting for someone else to come and move their car?' when Mum started the engine and began checking around her blind spots. Then she stopped, the engine chugging.

'Are we going to fall through the floor?' I asked.

'What's that?'

'You always said the floor of your car was wearing thin.'

She laughed sadly. 'I think it'll last another five minutes or so.' She sighed and put her hands on her lap. 'This evening didn't exactly turn out how I'd planned.'

'No?'

'Not that I'd really planned anything. It's *wonderful* to see you and Craig. And your father. Believe it or not.'

'That's good,' I said.

140

'Neil, you and Craig don't feel abandoned, do you?'

This took me by surprise. I thought of what Dad had said to Mum in the kitchen, about how maybe she should stay away for two months before her next visit. Was he insinuating that she'd stayed away this last month to make us miss her? Maybe that's why she'd moved away in the first place! Maybe she'd hoped we'd fall apart. So what should I tell her? Should I tell her that we did feel abandoned, and that life without her was unbearable? But that wasn't true; it was only when she was around that I realized how big a gap she left. In the times in between, we muddled along, just like Dad had said.

I didn't know what to say, so I left her question unanswered. Mum seemed to read something conclusive into my silence; she turned to me and said 'Mmm.'

She reached for the handbrake, then changed her mind and put her hand back on the steering-wheel. She hung on to it as though it were a cliff-edge. 'I honestly thought that the three of you would be happier if there was a bit of distance between your dad and me,' she said. 'Please don't think it was something I wanted to do or felt good about. I couldn't see us all carrying on the way we were.'

'We don't feel abandoned,' I said. 'But it's not the same without you there.'

'Well, you seem to be doing very well.' She looked at her reflection in the rear-view mirror. 'Am I supposed to be having this conversation with you? Is this ethical?'

Was she talking to me or to her reflection? I said, 'Ethical?'

'My mum never spoke to me about *anything*! Even when Dad died we just carried on. Ours was a quiet house. And then when Mum died I became a very noisy person. Can you believe that?'

'You, noisy?'

'Before you and Craig came along I always thought that being a mother meant being the backbone of the family, but you three look after each other, don't you? All boys together. It's been a long time since I've known what my place was in this family. Oh, I shouldn't be saying all this to you! I'm sorry, Neil.'

I was getting distressed. I really wanted to tell her that I wasn't like Dad and Craig, that I was more like her, but that would have sounded like I was insulting Dad and Craig. I'd always assumed that Mum had known I was different, by virtue of the fact that I never made paper battleships or watched football on television. But how was Mum to have known I wasn't another Craig in the making? I hardly spoke. In fact, Mum had not been spoken to for over a decade, just shouted at occasionally by Dad. Was it any wonder she'd left? Why hadn't I bothered to talk to her instead of spending all my time in my room reading *Sweet Dreams* books?

Mum was staring at the steering-wheel. 'I'm sorry you heard that row inside,' she said. 'It was completely my fault. God, I messed up, didn't I?'

'Mum, don't be daft,' I said. I held her hand.

She looked at me with surprise. Then she looked closely at me. 'You've turned out a beautiful person, Neil.' She stroked my hair.

'Thanks,' I said, embarrassed. I didn't believe her. Just the week before, Brendan had seen the awful photo of me that Dad kept on top of some high shelves in the lounge, a photo in which I was sitting on a motor-trike wearing a hooded top, leering horribly at the camera with gigantic bags under my eyes and one eye half-closed like a prudish clam, my bottom lip dangling, and he said, 'Christ on a bike, you're an ugly mongrel,' and laughed so hysterically that I started laughing too. I laughed so hard at the poor guy in that photo that I started to feel sorry for him, which was a weird sensation as he was me. I knew for a fact I wasn't usually as ugly as that boy, but beautiful? That was stretching things. I hoped one day I might be vaguely handsome, though, preferably in the eyes of somebody other than my mother.

'We'd better go,' said Mum.

'Are you still staying with us?' I asked.

'I think so.'

*　*　*

Mum extricated the car from its sandwich, and we aquaplaned round the outskirts of town to a place called Hunter Court, where her flat was. There was a massive yellow barrier out front and she had to press buttons to make it elevate with a clang and let us through.

'You can see the dogs,' said Mum, pointing to a first-floor window. I looked and saw two dog faces. 'They always have a look to see who's just arrived. They hear the barrier go up.'

Jeannie's face appeared behind the dogs' faces. The three of them squinted out into the darkness, their heads floating and bobbing. It was the most disturbing thing I'd ever seen outside of horror films.

Jeannie met us at the door and told me how much I'd grown. I said she was looking very well, which was true. Every other elderly person I knew, like our antique Maths teacher Mrs Clamp, chewed their gums and had patchy skin that looked like a strong wind might blow it right off. Mum and I went into the flat and Jeannie went upstairs to finish getting ready: she was staying with her academic friends Hector and Kay tonight, then going with them to Wales in the morning to stay with more academic friends for a week.

And now with Jeannie upstairs the flat was silent, and I could well believe that my mum would not want to stay here on her own but would prefer her family's bosom, especially on hers and Dad's anniversary. She took my coat off me and hung it on the end of the banister.

I looked around. The flat was messy. The green curtains were too long and trailed across the carpet, and there were books everywhere, and copies of magazines with names like *Human Spirit* (25p) and *Humanist Review*. No less than three of those plastic fold-out constructions you leave your clothes on to dry stood in a small area behind one of the two identical floral-print sofas.

Mum gestured towards one sofa and I limped over and sat down on a book. I removed it and studied it for damage. It was titled *The Unselfishness of God and How I Discovered It*.

'It's not mine,' said Mum. 'It's Jeannie's. She's not religious, so I don't know why she's reading it. I think she was intrigued by the idea that someone else apart from her had discovered something.'

'Is she hard to live with?' I asked quietly.

'She's lovely, really, but stubborn. And argumentative. She has this kind of pugilistic intellectualism.'

I nodded thoughtfully. A dog sat at my feet. I stroked its ear and it tilted its head.

'The dogs are nice,' I said.

'You've only met Harry. Fleance is a horror and Toby is intellectually aloof.'

'They all look quite nice,' I said.

'I know what you're doing,' said Mum, grinning. 'You're trying not to hurt their feelings while they're in earshot. Ah. Once, when you were small, you were eating Hula Hoops and you dropped one on the floor by accident, and immediately threw another one down to keep it company.'

'That's stupid,' I said, though I still did that sort of thing even at age thirteen. I thought hard. 'The unselfishness of dogs and how I discovered it,' I said, trying to be sharp like Craig, and Mum laughed politely, a laugh filled with encouragement.

We drank tea. I picked up a copy of the magazine Mum wrote for and studied the picture of a carnival float on the front. On the float were some straggly-looking youths, students, holding a huge inflatable woman. The caption read ALMA MATER. I opened the magazine and started to read the contents page. The features ranged from the indecipherable (p. 45. The Cat in the *Chora*: Kristeva and deontological ethics) to the stupid (p. 21. Banshee! Why literary ghosts are a feminist issue). I frowned and nodded and flipped through the pages. 'It looks deep.'

'I'm afraid you might find it a bit dull.'

I said, 'I read one of your articles once.'

She looked shocked. 'Which one?'

'The one about Valentine's cards.'

She knew the one I meant. 'I don't suppose it was of much interest.'

146

'It was really interesting,' I said.

'Why did you read that one?' she asked.

'I don't know.'

'So are you going to send a Valentine's card to somebody?'

I realized that I wanted to confess to her about Adele. So I said, 'Yes.'

'To a girl at school?' Mum asked.

I described Adele as best I could, trying not to sound sappy. 'Is she pretty?' Mum asked.

'Totally,' I said, with feeling.

'Do you get on with her?'

I told Mum about the Drama groups, and about the photo shoot at Brendan's.

'You've managed to get her to notice you, then,' she said.

It struck me that I hadn't actually managed to do anything. Brendan had done all the work.

'What do you think I should put in the card?' I asked. 'Your article was a bit too complicated for me.'

'Anything that says something about your personality,' said Mum.

'What like?'

'What do you mean, what like? You take your personality and put it in a card. As a cultural artefact, the Valentine's card is really fascinating. You provide enough information about yourself to let the person who receives the card track you

147

down, if she tries hard enough.' She was getting really excited. 'If she tries to track you down and you want to escape being caught, you try to lead her away from you and cover your tracks. It's like being a fugitive.'

'A criminal?'

'A stealer of hearts.'

'I wanted to put a poem in it.'

'You write poetry? I didn't know that!' Mum put her head in her hands, which wasn't the response I'd hoped for. 'When? Since when?'

For some reason I didn't want to say, 'Since last week.' I said, 'Oh, for a while now.'

'What kind of poetry do you like?'

I said, 'Have you heard of e.e. cummings?'

'e.e. cummings!' Mum cried. 'Dear God!'

She stared at me, shaking her head. It was as if she was angry with me. Was e.e. cummings an enemy of feminists? I was about to denounce his work when Mum said she had a collection of his poems in her room, and raced off to get it.

It was a slim paperback and she wasn't overly keen on it, because it spelt his name E. E. Cummings (capital E, capital C), ignoring the poet's typographical rights. I didn't like the book either: it didn't have my favourite poem in it, the one about the tree. Mum had also fetched books by other poets, like Emily Dickinson, Charles Baudelaire, and Pablo Neruda, and a compilation of romantic verse by Americans. She tipped them all on to the coffee table.

With the books before us, we started talking seriously about poetry. All the time I was thinking: If I'd known that I could make Mum this happy by claiming to like poems, I'd have started reading Pablo Neruda in the cradle. Mum got some paper and encouraged me to leaf through the books and write down any lines I found that appealed to me, or that struck me as romantic. She jotted down some good ones. I felt awkward, writing poetry with my mother – not even writing poetry, just pasting together bits of other people's poems to make fake romantic verse. But at the same time I was really happy, and Mum was visibly transported, and the house was nice and warm, quiet save for the sound of pages turning and pencils scribbling. Mum said that if I strung together some sentences that said something about me, and something about Adele, then changed them a bit so that they related well to each other, I would have a poem to put in my card.

Jeannie came down and we had to stop being creative and help her with her bags and dogs. Then Hector arrived to take her and the Labradors away. When they drove off Mum and I waved at Jeannie and at the dogs' faces in the old white Mercedes's windows, and we stood there at the front door after they disappeared, both of us grinning like happy poets. Then Mum said we'd better be getting back, as Dad and Craig would be wondering if we were dead.

Mum let me borrow the poetry books, and when we got home I put my fledgling Valentine's poem inside the e.e. cummings book. It was late. I went upstairs, and Mum and Dad stayed up and talked, quietly, too quietly for Craig and me, secretly perched in the darkness of the top of the stairs, to hear.

verse

Saturday morning, 12th February.

The name had to go. 'Tramp' had seemed an okay provisional name as long as we'd assumed that nobody would ask us what our band was called. Then we considered the matter more carefully, whereupon we realized that if we somehow got Adele and Gillian to make music with us after school next Tuesday, they probably *would* ask us what our band was called, and if we said 'Tramp', they would laugh themselves sick.

I wanted to come up with something similar to Victorian Brickwork, as this would make Adele think that she and I were attuned to each other, at least with regard to obscure band names. I think my brother would have disapproved of my use of such a basic seduction tactic. Even when he was seventeen, he knew that the only psychological techniques that really work in romantic situations are ones in which you feign indifference. But some of us are not cold-hearted enough to act indifferent.

Personally, I wasn't a good enough actor to pretend to be indifferent towards Adele, given that she was someone for whom I would happily eat gravel.

'Victorian Stonemasonry,' said Brendan.

'The Jacobean Abbeys,' I said.

'Gentleman's Masonry. Hmm.'

'How about Jacobean Masonry?'

'Gentleman's Underpants.'

'Get the dictionary,' I said.

'I like that,' said Brendan. 'Please welcome Get the Dictionary.' He thought. 'We could call ourselves What If Thesaurus?'

'Don't be gay,' I said.

'Imagine if Gillian and Adele asked to be in our band! Wouldn't that be cool? You bet your sweet ass it would.' *You bet your sweet ass* was something Brendan had heard on an American television show a couple of weeks ago, and he still made himself laugh whenever he said it. He laughed softly now.

Eventually we had about fifty ideas, all taken from the dictionary at random. We had to give up the naming game after about half an hour because we'd lost all sense of what might be good and what might be rubbish. We were tired of words. Carton, Meld, Figurine, Slump (or The Slumps), Bowsprit, Glade, Gland (or The Glands), Backwash, Fungal, Effervescence, Nadir, Plinth. We each chose one, and decided that whoever was asked first would get to say their preferred band name. I chose Plinth, for no good reason. Brendan chose Gland. He wanted us to be called The Gland That Time Forgot. I said no.

Brendan had already made a little sign for me to stick on my amplifier. It had the word TRAMP on it. We threw it away and didn't bother to make a replacement.

We'd lugged my guitar and amp to Brendan's for our inaugural band practice. His house was many times larger than mine, and therefore easier to hide in. When we arrived, I realized that I'd forgotten to bring *Start Playing Rock Guitar*. Brendan got angry and I had to pacify him by saying that it was probably best if we worked on some original material, so that's what we did after the death of our band-naming efforts.

'All we need is something that we can play really loud if they ask us to play one of our songs,' I said. 'We can say we're a thrash metal band.'

'They're not going to ask us to play anything.'

'But you never know,' I said. 'If they ask us and we don't have anything to play, they'll know you were lying about us having a band. We need something short but brilliant.'

'Okay, you're right,' he said. 'Play "Mull of Kintyre", but then play the notes backwards, so it sounds like a different song.'

The chords I'd learned to strum were:

GGGGGGDDDDDDGGGGGGDDDDDDDGGDG

Not very inspiring played forwards, let alone backwards, but I humoured Brendan and within a minute we had our first song virtually written.

Next we had to come up with some lyrics and a vocal melody. We decided to base the lyrics loosely on 'Mull of Kintyre', for the sake of cutting corners. (We figured that they need not be good lyrics; in fact, they could be pretty much anything you liked, as Brendan could moan or scream them, rendering them unintelligible. All they needed to be was memorizable.)

We took the key word from our list of band names.

> Plinth of desire
> I miss running in from the sea
> Oh, you liar
> There's always a tree here
> The plinth of desire.

By now we were starting to enjoy ourselves, but time was running short – when Harry emerged from her room around noon she would surely find us and laugh us to scorn – so we reverted to solemnity. I plugged the amplifier in, turned the volume very low but the distortion very high, and played the chords savagely but quietly. It sounded like someone was using a chainsaw a long way away. Brendan sang our lyrics to a tune in his head, quietly so as not to wake Harry, or to attract the attention of his parents, who were upstairs getting ready to go out.

We performed our song quickly: five seconds. We bulked it up to one minute fifty seconds by adding two guitar solos, which sounded more like I was tuning-up, three repetitions of our verse, and three repetitions of the chorus, which was:

> Plinth of desire
> It's my Plinth
> Of desire.

What was a plinth? We'd found the word in the dictionary, but hadn't bothered to find out what it meant. We decided that the definition was immaterial. We had our song.

I got back home just after midday. While I was at Brendan's, Mum had gone shopping and Craig had remained in bed. Dad looked happy enough, sitting in the living room thinking and staring at the coffee table. He said Mum would be back later in the afternoon.

Upstairs, in my room, Mum had left something for me: a frayed book about saints. Protruding from it was a book token that served as a bookmark, marking the entry on Saint Valentine. I read it until I got to the bit where he was martyred, either by having his head cut off, or, according to another tradition, by being beaten to death. The saint's alternative deaths were making me feel less, not more, romantic. So I started to work through Mum's books of poetry.

For all Mum's failings, I now appreciated that she of all my family-members had this in her favour: she had depth. I possessed special proof of this depth. One of the books Mum had lent me was a notebook full of her own verse. There were little dates under each of the poems, which had been hand-written out in neat, tiny print. The poems spanned decades. The first was written in 1968, when Mum was seventeen:

Box

My friend most beautiful told me of the 3 people
she keeps in her head for latenight advice and
conversation. They come out, she said, when it's
warm – whether warm within me or simply
because of heavy clothing, a woolly jumper, warm
makes warm and I wonder who I'll talk to tonight,
him or him or her. Usually there's an issue on my
mind. Who are they? I asked. There's him, him
who's made of unfeasible striations, the pillars of
each limb towers of energy, buzzing – a huge
elongated robotic ghost who is wisdom and I can't
say we've ever talked. Other him, she said very

seriously, is a pixie of goodness, tender spoken and
plum-chubby with loves who always seems to
bland moralize in a weak watery way. But leaning
closer, but, she said in a tomb whisper – it is to her
I always seem to go, dark, the sexless phantom
devoid of suckle or hair under the goblin cloak,
who reads me the faults I would love to be, from a
scroll I would otherwise keep in a box in a box in
a box. Like Pandora, said I, and my sweet most
beautiful mind friend said no! with a happy laugh,
for Pandoras shudder to be curious, and I will
open the box one day which Pandora herself is in,
and let the poor girl out again.

The last was written eight months ago, while she
was still at home:

No longer, no once more, can I sublimate the seasons,
having unmasked the centricity of poem-words; the
    footfalls
no longer tread and mete but lie for me, and here in
    this
summer train the dandelion spores do not so much
    play out
my convictions, in and out the carriage, as skip across
    the
platform to another mind, no-mind.

157

No one is here for the journey but I – not even the
    train.
Respectful, flower and machine weld voiceless into a
thankfully deeper union. Would that I could melt
    through
the portal to where the flower is its own metaphor,
    where
    these unintentional spores, snowdrops on the
    no-wind,
would settle on my happy death. They rejoice without
rejoicing, free now from my tyranny.

But the mouldering which eats the summer flourishes,
    and in
the carriage makes a sickly season. These tiny angels
    are
not in my attendance, poet devoured by her own
    gaudy muse –

                             Yet here, still
here, is an elysium where the air is more than mere
dilution of breathings;
(where we and all are endless speech,
no-speech, no ears to hear).

See? Depth. The moment I began in earnest to compose my Valentine's poem for Adele, having binned
my first timid attempt, I became convinced that I
had depth too. It was a delicious conviction,
because I had the pleasure of not yet knowing

exactly how deep my depth was. I'd never plumbed it before. (Perhaps, I considered, all deep people are initially shy of this kind of plumbing.) My depth had potential, like the beginning of the summer holidays, or like a drizzly but lovely Saturday afternoon such as this.

I sat in bed with books of poetry on the duvet, putting small pencil marks next to lines of poetry I thought might be worth filching, but after a while I found that my depth demanded more of me than pencil marks. It demanded that I get some paper and write out my purloined lines. This was not something I could comfortably do lying in bed, as Craig or my dad might burst in, see my poetry, plumb my depth and call me a nancy boy. So I decided to find a place where I could be absolutely alone.

Where can a sensitive soul go to know the solitude from which great poetry is born? Where indeed, when one lives in a semi-detached house with two unromantic apes – a brother who is a foul womanizer, and a father who is a breaker of young legs? Where, when one lives not in town or country, but in suburbia, where there is much in the way of diversion but little in the way of inspiration? Where do suburban poets go when they feel like being surrounded by things worthy of poesy, or, for that matter, other poets?

I had to rule out the outside world, unfortunately, as

(a) Dean Millard, Martin, Brendan or any one of a dozen
people, the likes of which Pablo Neruda never had to
contend with, might discover me.

(b) It was raining outside. My poetry would get wet.

We had a garage, which would have made a nice
cave-like creative environment, but how could I
justify spending a couple of hours in the garage to
my dad? He'd think I was going there to hang
myself, and would probably come in to stop me, or
to show me some nifty and efficient ways of
strangling oneself that he'd learned in the army. So
I opted for the bathroom.

'I'm having a bath in a bit,' I told Dad as I made
some toast downstairs. 'Freshen up.'

'Wait a minute,' said Craig. 'I need the bog.' He
then said something about spag bog that doesn't
merit repeating, and I had my toast and went to my
room and wrapped the poetry books in a towel so I
could sneak them into the bathroom once Craig had
finished.

The toilet flushed and Craig emerged from my
cave of poetry, wafting his hand and grinning. I was
clutching my towelled books to my chest. He told
me in a low voice that he'd found out some information about Mum and Dad's conversation on
Friday evening, the one they'd had after Mum
drove me back from her flat. Dad told Craig that
Mum had apologized for being rude, and apparently

said that she wanted to see Craig and me more often.

'Great,' I said. 'Can I get in the bathroom now?'

'What's in the towel?' he asked.

'Underpants,' I told him. 'Socks. My brush.' I pretended to think. 'That's it. Can I have my bath now?'

'Neil, it's obvious you're hiding stuff in your towel.'

I realized that it would be stupid to continue lying. 'I've got some homework.' I opened the towel and showed him the books. 'We have to read poems for English.'

'Why didn't you just say?' he asked. I rolled the books in the towel again.

'It's embarrassing,' I said. 'You know. Poems and things.'

'You thought I'd think you were getting into poetry?' he asked, laughing loudly. 'You're no Lord Byron.'

I laughed too, even though I was cut to the quick. 'Not me!' I said.

He was right in at least one sense: Lord Byron never wrote poems in the bathroom. Or did he? Perhaps we will never know. I turned the bath taps on so that the water ran slowly, put the toilet seat down and sat on it. I was actually going to write Adele's poem on the toilet, when I realized what I was doing and what might happen as a result.

ADELE: Dearest, on this, the fiftieth anniversary of our marriage, I want to see where it all started. I want to sit where you sat when you wrote that masterpiece, the poem that won my heart.

Adele was unlikely to say this, but she might, you never know, and one has to prepare for such possibilities, so I got off the toilet and lay on the floor as the water ran into the bath. For a while I lay with my ear pressed to the side of the bathtub, listening to the water pound. Then I opened an anthology of American love poems, flicked to Gregory Corso and located the pencil marks I'd made earlier, and copied the marked lines into my notebook. After a minute of reading and scribbling, I put some bubble bath into the tub, and turned off the cold tap so that the bathwater would get roasting hot. By the time I'd finished my poem, the water would hopefully have cooled to a just-right temperature. A bath would be a nice reward for completing my work, I thought, and probably symbolic of something.

Saturday, 11.45 a.m. Comment spoken on upstairs landing:

'Hey, I think Neil's gone down the plughole! Heh heh.'

I reach into the bath and agitate the water with my hand, to suggest my presence in the water.

12.15. Comment spoken on upstairs landing:

162

'And the award for world's cleanest boy goes to . . . Neil Flack! Ha ha. Come on Neil, hurry up in there.'

More agitation of water, then agitation of mind, because I have got soap bubbles on Pablo Neruda.

12.55. 'Neil. Get out the bath.' (Dad.)

'Neil, after a while you stop getting cleaner and start to absorb the dirt again. So get out. I need the bog.' (Craig.)

I say: 'I'll be out in a second. I think I fell asleep.'

Craig: 'That's dangerous. Dad, if Neil ever drowns in the bath, promise we won't give him an open-casket funeral. He'll look like a white raisin.'

I shout, 'I can hear you out there, you know!'

Dad: 'Neil, will you be much longer?'

Craig: 'All I'm saying is, Dad, it's not how any of us would want to remember him.'

So my poem was rushed, but I got it done. The bathwater was cold by the time I'd finished, and I had only managed to get into it as far as my watch, which was not, I discovered, waterproof. It still worked, but it had heavy condensation under the casing.

I undressed, got into the bath for thirty seconds so that my story about having a bath wasn't a total lie, dried, then got dressed, and wondered if I was the first person in the history of the world to do that: to take a thirty-second bath. Maybe, maybe not. But to take a thirty-second bath, having entered the bathroom a normal schoolboy only to be leaving it a poet: that felt unique.

Even though I had already chosen what lines my poem was going to consist of, it had still taken me two hours to turn them into a finished product. I'd had to make the different lines, stolen from diverse sources, fit together by inserting *and*, *but*, *then*, *for*, and other words between them. I also chose to introduce sophisticated techniques like making plurals out of words that shouldn't be plurals, in the style of my mother, who did this all the time (she did it in the poem 'Box', printed above). And, of course, I felt the need to change the lines slightly, so that they were more properly my own. So, for example:

> I'm faint, and horrors! it's with love –
> (from Jacqueline Mitchell's 'Ages of God and
>   Romantic
> Novelists' in the *Anthology of American Love
>   Poetry*)

Combined with –

> Now I perceive the hearts of things:
> Your witchery, and taste for
> puppet strings
> (from Stanley Everdene, 'Mystagogue',
> in the same anthology)

Equals:

> **I am faint with loves**
> **And now I perceive the heart of**
> **Your tiny witcheries**

(Note: the insertion of the word 'tiny' was entirely my own innovation.)

Then I stretched the poem. It was originally twenty-two lines, but I took the last words of some lines and gave them lines all to themselves, which is something Mum did in some of her poems:

> The heart of your tiny
> **witcheries**

Also, I wanted to include something from cummings's 'little tree' poem, but it wasn't in the book Mum lent me, and I had eaten one of the copies I got at school, and lost the other. So I wrote a bit myself, which was this:

> Every moment with her is like the
> poem
> by e.e. cummings about the little tree

Which eventually turned into

Like the poem of e.e.
cummings
About the little tree
is every
Moment with she

because I plagiarized *another* American poet, who
wrote something similar-sounding, except the
American poet was writing about a he and not a she,
and wrote 'he' instead of 'him' so it would rhyme
with 'be'. I even stole the shape of that American
poet's stanza.

Did I care that most lines of my poem were stolen?
No. The process of choosing what to steal in order to
convey sentiments that were mine – to seek a
perfect match between other people's phrases and
the peculiarities of my own feelings: this was itself
a poetic process, and when I looked at the printed
poem in the card, it felt absolutely unquestionably
mine.

Later in the day, I took my Valentine card into
the bathroom and copied out my beautiful thirty-
six-line poem. I finished it just as I heard Dad come
up the stairs, so I flushed the toilet and, under the
cover of the flush, bit off some Sellotape and stuck
the back of the envelope down, having slipped the
card inside. I'd tried licking the envelope, but it
kept popping open. I would have taken this for
some sort of omen, had I been in less of a hurry.

I had the most incredible feeling of accomplishment.

our night out

On Saturday night Craig consented to join his parents and his younger brother, none of us great fashion accessories for a seventeen-year-old, on a trip to the ABC Cinema on Friar Street. It was the first time we had all been to the pictures together for maybe half a decade. Craig put his foot down regarding the choice of film, saying no to *E.T. The Extra Terrestrial*. He opined that science fiction films were politically suspect, xenomorphs usually being symbolic of foreigners. Mum, who didn't know that all of Craig's opinions were stolen from Harry, was so impressed that she suggested we instead see a long film about women bonding and growing old gracefully. Dad said he would rather be murdered, but he gave in after Craig glared at him, and on the whole we bore it bravely. Later that year, when I learned more about the contents of *E.T. The Extra Terrestrial*, I guessed that Craig's real motive for snubbing it was not wanting to cry in front of his parents and younger brother.

Craig and I didn't sit with Mum and Dad, as Craig thought we should leave them to sit on their own, as part of his plan to get them back together. Halfway through the film, giddy with boredom, my brother and I went out to the lobby for ice creams, and after eating our lime-flavoured Mivvis we tried to prolong our absence from the theatre by jumping repeatedly down the dark and dusty red staircase leading to Cinema 3, and doing forward rolls when we landed. Or rather: Craig demonstrated jumps and forward rolls, while I, with my bad leg, merely leapt down the steps, landed on one leg and fell on to the floor, then got Craig to help me up. This was before CCTV.

We sat outside Cinema 3, listening to *E.T.* Craig said, 'They look happy now, don't they?'

I said, 'Mum and Dad?'

'No – *them*,' he said sarcastically, pointing to a large cardboard display for *Terms of Endearment*.

I said, 'They don't look anything. They're just watching the film.'

'They're both completely miserable,' said Craig. 'I mean generally. Mum's lonely living away in that flat, you know. And Dad's lonely when she's not around.'

'Oh,' I said. I remembered what Mum had said last night, about how leaving us wasn't something she'd *wanted* to do, and I felt sick. But I said brightly, 'How can they be lonely? It's not like they live on their own.'

Craig said, 'This isn't a joke, Neil.'

'I never said it was!'

He regarded me with disgust. 'You have a brain like a fly's ballbag.'

Mum came into my room later, on her way to bed, to say goodnight. She was wearing Dad's navy blue towelling dressing-gown, and had to shuffle rather than walk to avoid tripping over it. I expected to hear Dad coming up the stairs as well; when Mum had lived at home, they'd come upstairs at the same time. But he didn't. 'Is Dad staying downstairs?' I asked.

Mum said, 'He's doing some paperwork.' She asked me if I enjoyed the film, and I said it wasn't my cup of tea.

'No, it was more like a cup of sick,' she said, and she laughed suddenly.

'How are you enjoying your stay?' I asked.

She said, 'I've had a lovely night. I could tell your Dad didn't think much of the film, but he was very polite and said it was interesting, and then we discussed it in depth and he admitted he thought it was nonsense.' She laughed again and put her hand in my hair and moved it around in an untrained gesture of affection. She was clearly excited that she'd managed to rope Dad into having a proper discussion with her about something. I tried to think of things to say, to prove I wasn't sullen and uncommunicative, but nothing seemed appropriate. We both stared around my room for something to comment on, but there wasn't much. A framed map of Europe with the names in German (Dad's); a Snoopy poster (mine – I didn't take it down until I was nearly fifteen); some stuffed toys on a shelf. A cup with sludge in the bottom from when I'd failed to stir my Horlicks properly.

'So, my favourite poet,' said Mum eventually. 'Have you finished your Valentine's card yet?'

I said no, in case she asked to see it. Suddenly brave, I asked if *she* was sending any Valentine's cards this year.

'Hundreds!' Mum said, and she laughed suddenly, a weird and uncomforting cackle.

February 13th: Sunday breakfast. Dad was up early, and had put boxes of cereal out on the table, and there were knives and forks and spoons out, and eggs boiling and making strange whistling noises. 'Listen!' Dad said to Craig and me. 'You can hear the birds trying to escape!'

Craig laughed, but I was horrified.

Mum came in and asked if she should make some soldiers, and Dad said something hilarious – what she did in her own spare time was her own business! – a comment we all thought inappropriate, except Dad, who got annoyed at our prudery. But it was Sunday, the Lord's Day, the day of rest, and it seemed as though we were a new family waiting to hatch, we weren't fighting, just chirping together in our egg, so Dad cheered up and hummed 'Oh When the Saints'. But then he put our eggs in the yellow-and-white striped eggcups and he asked Mum what she wanted – he'd bought some Scotch pancakes specially! – and Mum said, perhaps wearily, 'I'd have liked an egg or two, Robert, actually,' and Dad said, 'I thought eggs gave you the runs?' At which Mum clapped a hand to her forehead and said, 'There's a time and a place, Robert, for God's sake.'

And there was a silence, which I hastened to dispel by asking, 'What are runs?' – because I'd only heard the term in relation to rounders, a sport that seemed inappropriate to the matter at hand, unless people back in my parents' day had played rounders with eggs, which was conceivable, wasn't it?

'Squits,' Craig said to me in a stage-whisper, by way of explanation, and that was the last straw, nobody felt like eating their eggs.

'I'll just have some Rice Krispies,' said Mum.

'This is like breakfast at Brendan's house,' I said cheerfully. But it wasn't. At Brendan's house, stupid conversations like this counted as funny.

That afternoon in my room I thought: *Tomorrow I will be giving Adele Collier, the most beautiful girl in the school, a Valentine's card.* I decided I would put it in the register, or into her coat pocket, provided she hung her coat in the cloakroom. Then I thought: am I adequately prepared to be loved by Adele? I shampooed my hair six times and conditioned it four. By the time I'd finished, my hair had a squeak that was almost deafening.

My sleep that night was troubled. Was I tense about the fact that it was Valentine's Day tomorrow, or was it because my family seemed to be reconstituted and the house was an awkward place again? Both, of course. I was waking up every hour or so. My dreams and the reality of my dark bedroom were getting smudged together: I kept dreaming about dark bedrooms, only to wake up in one. Then I heard a noise like faraway singing and became electrified with fear, not sure whether I was trapped in one of those dreams which are like real life but with weird singing and everybody seeming shifty. I wriggled out of bed and went to the window and looked out to see the crescent moon hanging somewhere over Asda like an oddly-angled smile.

Then it occurred to me: Craig had sneaked downstairs, and was watching an adult programme, one with sexy music.

I got up and left my bedroom and crept along the landing, on which there were five places where you could place your feet without making the floorboards groan, as long as you moved fairly quickly and didn't raise your feet much. You had to glide and skate at the same time, which was hard with an aching knee, but I managed. I was generally a clumsy person, but in my own house, with whose architectural idiosyncrasies I was profoundly familiar, I was like a cat, like a phantom.

A phantom cat!

I was scaring myself again, thinking no longer of Craig watching porn, but of ghosts and burglars, and I crept fearfully to my listening-post at the turn of the stairs, but as I arrived and sat down, a feeling of recognition arose in me. I knew the song that was playing. It was 'Handyman' by James Taylor.

I looked through the banisters and peered into the living room – which was lit by just one lamp so that shadows glowed everywhere – and I saw my dad sitting on the sofa, leaning forward, his elbows on the coffee table, writing something, and singing along very quietly in his tuneless voice. It was funny to hear my dad sing about not being the kind [of handyman] to use a pencil or rule, he's handy with love, and he's no fool! – because Dad was in fact hopeless with a pencil or rule, despite his manliness. His first ever attempt at DIY in this house had fallen from the wall and disabled Penny, our dog, who had previously been quite active. But then Dad wasn't handy with love either. Was he a fool?

I watched. What was he writing? I thought, with a jolt of realization: *he's writing a Valentine's card for my mother*. Was it a card? His hunched torso obscured it from my view. Dad got up and took it with him to the stereo and rewound the tape, and after a few stops and starts 'Handyman' came on again. Returning to the sofa, he lay back and started dancing with his head. His head went left and right, and back and forth, to no particular rhythm. I felt suddenly sad, and also guilty for being there. Dad was twiddling something in his hand – definitely a card. He sat up and put it back on the coffee table. He wrote some more, then put the card in an envelope, singing about how the main thing he wants to say is that he's busy twenty-four hours a day, mending broken hearts.

I realized that I had to get back to my room before Dad got up to go to bed. The part of my brain that handled this particular procedure was beginning to stir and whirr, but Dad was quicker. He got up and peered around. I wondered if he'd heard me moving. He walked over to the stereo and switched James off.

I leaned forward to see more of the lounge, and then I saw something on one of the armchairs. A big bundle. Pushing with my good leg, I lifted my bum and started to levitate up the stairs. Dad had picked up the bundle and threw it on the sofa, keeping hold of a corner of it. It was a duvet, and a pillow was cocooned inside it. He made the sofa as bedlike as he could and then turned the lamp off and

everything vanished, was swallowed into the darkness's gleaming gullet.

I realized I had not continued moving up the
stairs and round the corner on to the main part of
the landing, which is what I thought I'd told myself
to do. Now I sat very still. Time passed. The darkness was buzzing. It looked textured, grainy. I heard
the silence surging with high-pitched frequencies.
Dad cleared his throat and passed wind and I felt a
loneliness that I would never have credited with
existence, not my loneliness but *his* loneliness, his
adult loneliness, and my mum's, and the world's –
my emotions were superheated by the night-time,
and it was a horrible feeling for a delicate boy to
feel, this sudden dawning of so much cosmic loneliness. Dad snored and turned. I cried a little, into
my hand.

After a while all this raw emotion seemed oddly
comforting. I thought some more about my dad
lying in the dark, just over there, and about his
Valentine to Mum, and about what he might have
written. What would Mum think if Dad gave her
some awful, amateurish poem? The idea of my own
father being rejected by my own mother on the basis
of substandard poetry made me wring my hands.

We'd driven Mum away once before, by not communicating with her. How awful would it be to
drive her away a second time, by not managing
to communicate intelligently or artistically enough?

It's one thing to alienate your mother through negligence, another thing entirely to alienate her through bad rhyming. I pictured it: Dad and I presenting Mum with our hopeless poems and Mum realizing once and for all that we did not have what it took to make her feel at home with us, and secretly making plans to flee the house at the next possible opportunity, through the bathroom window if necessary, never to return.

But later, in my bedroom, I took out the poem I was going to give to Adele at school in a few hours' time, and I could not bring myself to consider it anything less than a masterpiece.

Maybe Dad had written a masterpiece too. Maybe us male Flacks were born to surprise.

It was one twenty-six in the morning, so I would find out soon enough.

valentine's day

Monday, February 14th. Something unexpected happens: despite the events of the previous night I wake up on Valentine's Day feeling not miserable but poetic. Feeling like a poet. Feeling like a poet with one goddamn beautiful poem under his belt (or in his school bag) and one goddamn beautiful girl to give it to.

What does it mean, to feel like a poet?

For a start, it is very different from feeling like a *Sweet Dreams* hero. In fact I feel superior in every way to *Sweet Dreams* heroes. *Sweet Dreams* heroes are handsome and charming, but you wouldn't ask them to write, say, a thirty-six-line love poem with heavy modernist influences. You wouldn't ask them to do that unless you wanted to see them flounder like an ape in a sandstorm. You'd ask someone like me, a poet.

And now: a breakfast fit for poets. Bran Flakes. I am nearly faint with my own greatness. I feel the same way people feel when they are going out for

179

the night *knowing* that they look fabulous, that their clothes and hair and features are all so magnetic that they fear they might stick to fridges. Except, in my case, *I am* the alluring garment, and my inner poetry is wearing me. That's why people haven't seen it before. That's why *I* hadn't seen it before, until I assembled Adele's poem. Now everybody is going to see it.

I am a poet, unstoppable, and I am damn well going to enjoy this day at Denesgrove Secondary. Luckily, Brendan and I possess a number of wonderful features which, when combined, make for a unique enjoyment of the classroom environment. First, we have *absolutely no interest in getting educated*. Therefore we always need some way of keeping ourselves amused during lessons. Second, we are genuinely afraid of teachers, and are scared to death of getting told off. This makes school exciting. Out-and-out rebels, the kind who insult teachers and laugh at threats of detention or expulsion, have much less fun than Brendan and me, as the thrill of being caught is not, for them, particularly thrilling. Third, Brendan and I are massively creative when it comes to the pursuit of self-entertainment, and now that I am a poet, this creativity is undoubtedly going to reach new heights.

When you and your friend are afraid of teachers, especially harsh teachers who demand silence during lessons, everything you and your friend whisper to each other becomes fantastically hilarious. Today I feel I have deep reserves of hysteria. I have even more hysteria today than I had on that day when Brendan and I made each other laugh non-stop through a French lesson just by saying the word 'curry' to each other in a deep sexual voice. (In no other circumstance could this be construed as funny.)

Today we will play some of the many games that we created to serve as frameworks for our inventiveness and stupidity. We'll play a complex game called You Bet Your Sweet Ass, which Brendan invented just last week, and at which he is (as yet) unbeaten. You Bet Your Sweet Ass requires paper if you want to play it properly. Usually we start by playing it properly, and then when order starts to break down, we abandon the paper and just play verbally. To play the game you have to think of a well-known phrase, and then engage in a written conversation with your opponent. The aim is to write down your phrase as part of the conversation before the other person can guess what the phrase is. The only catch is that you have to make the phrase fit naturally into the conversation. Before you start you have to write your phrase on a secret piece of paper. The game got its name from the first time we played it, when Brendan won by writing down the phrase *you bet your sweet ass* before I had a chance either to guess it, or to put down my own phrase, which was *please sir, I want some more bush*. (When I said 'well-known phrases', I meant well-known to Brendan and me.)

Abridged transcript of first-ever game of You Bet Your Sweet Ass (notice how I play right into Brendan's hands):

BRENDAN: Do you want to play cards?

NEIL: No, I'm hungry.

BRENDAN: I bet you could eat a horse.

NEIL: Was that your phrase?

BRENDAN: No. Here, I've got you a small horse.

NEIL: I can't eat it, I'm a vegetarian.

BRENDAN: Here. I've put sugar all over it, now eat it.

NEIL: Can't I have some vegetables? Or grass?

BRENDAN: You'll have to pay for it.

NEIL: I don't have any money.

BRENDAN: So let's play cards for money. If you win, you can have some vegetables.

NEIL: I'd prefer grass. Or a hedge.

BRENDAN: Is the grass always greener on the other side? (That was a guess at my phrase.)

NEIL: No.

BRENDAN: Here are some cards, let's play. I bet fifty pence, what about you? Put some money in.

NEIL: I told you, I haven't got any money. Just give me something bushy to eat.

182

BRENDAN: Why don't **you bet your sweet ass**?
         (Brendan has won the game.)
NEIL: What?
BRENDAN: (Explaining how he has won the game) Small
         horse = ass.
NEIL: Why is it sweet?
BRENDAN: I put sugar on it – sweet ass.
NEIL: What?

We don't sit down as a family to have breakfast this morning; we're all hurrying, hurrying, except Mum, who doesn't have to be at work until ten, and who comes downstairs as I finish my Bran Flakes. She puts a hand on my shoulder and quizzes me about my Valentine, and when I tell her I've finished it I realize that she expects me to show it her. 'It's in the envelope,' I say.

'Oh,' she says, crestfallen. She brightens. 'Well, she'll love it, I know she will.'

I want to ask if Dad got her a card, but I don't.

I arrive at school three full minutes before the bell, having left my card at home, next to the bread bin.

By the time I get back home, Mum has left for work, and so I am unable to scrounge a lift back to school. I grab my card and run, cursing myself aloud. By the time I arrive at my first lesson to find Brendan sitting alone, looking forlorn, I am so sweaty I look like I swam here.

183

Mr Timmer is furious with me. I tell him I had to go back home because I forgot my bag, and everyone laughs at me, except of course Mr Timmer. I sit down next to Brendan, who is locating things like palm trees and shops on a photocopied map, and writing in his exercise books how far above sea level these things are.

'You forgot your bag?' he asks.

'That was just an excuse,' I tell him, hoping that the girls on the table behind can hear me.

'So why are you late?'

Suddenly I feel guilty about not having told him about the card earlier, although my reasons for not telling him had been perfectly sound. So I tell Brendan that I had to go home to pick up a card for Adele, and that I am thinking of putting it in the register at break, and he glares at me and says, 'You *arse.*'

'What?' I blurt, though I know perfectly well What, and immediately regret having told him. Sending a Valentine's card is major, the type of thing we plan in detail, *together* – it is supposed to be a combined effort. I have betrayed my friend and ally. I am no different than Judas, except I do not kiss men.

'I can't believe you went and did that,' he says.

'Get her a card? I just did it last night.' I am determined not to act guilty.

'Well, thanks for letting me know. What if I'd wanted to send one to Gillian?'

'Actually, my mum made me do it.'

'Your mum made you write Adele a Valentine's card?'

'Sort of, yes.'

He refuses to answer.

'Anyway, I didn't think you were interested in sending Gillian a card. You said that it was too risky. Remember, you said it was risky, because you might get some snot or something on it by accident.' I want to try to make him laugh. 'A long snot skid mark.' He turns away, which either means that he is grinning, or he is really angry. 'That's when I had the idea,' I continue. 'I wrote Adele a Valentine's message in snot.'

When Brendan turns towards the front of the class again his profile is stern.

We work in silence.

Near the end of the lesson, after we've finished our work and are drawing artist's impressions of the landscape on the photocopied maps, Brendan says, 'So. You're going to pull Adele without my help, are you?'

I say, 'Don't be dickish.'

'I'm not the one being dickish. You're the one running around making your own little plans.'

'It's just a card!'

He is silent for a few minutes. 'Putting it in the register is a balls idea.'

'Oh?' I try to sound deferential, as it seems he is beginning to forgive me.

'Someone'll catch you putting it there.'

'Yeah, you're right.' But I sound patronizing.

'Oh, *shut up*. Do what you want.' Some people turn to look at us, as Brendan is getting noisy. Mr Timmer peers up at us, then goes back to reading something on his desk. Brendan lowers his voice. 'I can't believe you just went ahead and *planned* to send Adele a Valentine's card on your own.'

Nothing is resolved.

After Geography, Brendan goes off with Abigail and Liz, two of our mutual friends, and I follow. Liz and Abigail are best friends, the female equivalent of Brendan and me, and are in the same social bracket as us, which is to say that they lack a clearly defined social bracket.

Abigail and Liz can tell that things are rocky between Brendan and me; Brendan rolls his eyes whenever I speak.

Feeling miserable, I decide to go to the cloakroom in the Technology block, which is where the second-year form-rooms are located. I know Adele's coat will be there, and I know what it looks like: a sort of Red Riding Hood coat, but without the hood. A red coat, basically. I can't remember if it has pockets, but I hope it does, because putting my card in her pocket is my Plan B. As Brendan has pointed out, Plan A (the register plan) is foolish.

I trudge away, and start to feel angry. Of course I was right not to tell Brendan about the card before. Poets are not pack animals, and they don't have to submit their plans to any committee. They are solitary and catlike, and if they announce that they have spent the previous day doing some poetic work, well, people must understand. Writing a poem for a beautiful girl isn't something you can plan with a pal, which is something Brendan is incapable of understanding.

BOB: Hey, e.e. Whatcha do last night?
e.e. cummings: Wrote a poem.
BOB: Without me?

Would this conversation happen? No. Or –

JIM: Why didn't you come out last night?
VAN GOGH: I was painting a picture.
JIM: Didn't you stop to think that I might have
            wanted to paint a picture too? Did you?

No no no. People make allowances for the solitude of artists, unless they're dumb.

Breaktime. In the Tech block cloakroom – a horse-shoe-shaped corridor with no lights – I find Martin lurking with a weasely friend of his, Kieran.

I know what they were doing. They're going

through people's coat pockets and stealing lunch money. Martin started thieving last year, during some family trauma (it might have been during the time of the gay porn incident). For a while he made Brendan, me and a boy called Paul Shand go on missions with him, lifting things from people's bags, or from teacher's desks, from stock cupboards. As long as the people from whom we were thieving were members of staff or people we disliked, it was exciting, and we became quite good at it, but eventually we got bored, and instead of looking for bigger challenges, we gravitated towards easier pickings. By then Martin had discovered that people left money in their coats. Stealing from cloakrooms was easier and thus less thrilling than stealing from people's school bags during break, as there was less chance of being caught, but as criminal activities go it had a certain charm. The cloakrooms were cool and dark and you'd have to search for ages before you found anything of value. But I had moral qualms about stealing from people I didn't know. Luckily we got bored with being burglars before we managed to hit any jackpots.

So why is Martin stealing again? Has he continued stealing since the first year, despite the fact that Brendan and I have kicked the habit and replaced it with girl worship? Maybe he's gay and needs something to do instead of fancying girls. Maybe that's why he is in here with Kieran! Or –

maybe he and Kieran fancy Adele and Gillian, and are putting cards in their coats!

No, they're stealing. They jump when I slip into the cloakroom. As soon as they realize who I am (not easy in the dark), Kieran brings his hands from behind his back and scrutinizes the stolen things in his palms.

Martin looks at me and says, 'Oh. You.'

'What are you doing?'

'Want some lunch money?' Martin asks.

Aha – I can see it now. Here's what is happening: Martin is getting in with a bad crowd, of which Kieran is a key member, and Martin is trying to impress him. Kieran has dozens of unsavoury brothers and uncles, and a sister who wears sovereign rings so she can leave circular bas-relief pictures on people she punches.

'What are you doing here?' asks Martin.

'Getting my coat?'

'It's over there.' Martin points round the corner of the cloakroom's U-bend. I know where my own coat is, of course. Martin just wants me to know that he knows too. 'Nothing worth stealing.'

'You looked?'

'Well?' says Martin. 'Aren't you going to get it?'

'Um . . .'

'Neil, it's completely obvious why you're in here.'

'Is it?' asks Kieran. He riffles through a pocket,

pulls out a long rope of tissue, makes a face and drops the tissue on the floor.

'It's Valentine's Day. You're putting a Valentine's card in someone's coat.'

'Whose?' asks Kieran.

'Adele Collier's,' says Martin.

'Don't be stupid,' I spit. 'I am not.'

How on earth does Martin know what I'm planning to do? Am I transparent? If Martin has guessed that I am giving Adele a Valentine, who else has? Will Martin tell anyone? My nerves begin to jangle.

I snatch my coat and head down the corridor to CDT, thinking hard about whether I should try to get Adele's card into the register, or whether I should go back to the cloakroom at the end of CDT, or whether I should forget the whole idea.

When I get to the CDT workshop, most of the class have already arrived to claim good benches.

Five lessons to go, and lunch break as well, and already I have alienated all my friends. If e.e. cummings walked into the workshop right now, I would saw his head off.

Craft, Design and Technology.

Brendan is sitting with people I don't like, no doubt on purpose, and although I linger near his bench looking hangdog in the hope that he will come over and sit with me, he doesn't look up at me. My stomach is aching. I sit at one of the front benches, with two girls, one of whom was voted the most popular girl in my tutor group in the first year (not much of an honour), but who is now over-weight and unnervingly religious. Her name is Anne. During the first year I went through a phase of having lewd fantasies about being in a bath with her.

The front bench is a dangerous place to sit. Mr Lund has a habit of straddling the corner of the bench while teaching the class. He actually rests his genitals on the corner. It is fascinatingly horrible. Also, he looks like the man from *The Joy of Sex* (allegedly).

Once, when I was lounging with Brendan on the front bench (this was in the first year), our legs sticking straight out and our feet jutting off the edge of the bench, Anne, then popular, came over and did the Mr Lund straddling-thing *on my foot*. As though my foot was a small pony. She was talking to me normally, as though she wasn't sitting on my foot. It seemed unspeakably rude, but she was being so nonchalant about this action that I wondered whether I was making too much of it. Did people do this sort of thing? Had I been mistaken all these years in my assumption that if I walked over and leaned my crotch on someone, they would mind or even notice? Brendan claimed not to have noticed Anne on my foot, but that's what he does when he's jealous, when something unexpectedly sexual happens to someone else and not him: he pretends it is not newsworthy.

Anne and I talk about our jigsaw puzzle designs.

'Hey, I like your picture, Neil. Is that a car? A sort of . . . truck?'

'Um, it's the *Admiral Graf Spee*.'

'Look, Alison!' She nudges the other girl. 'Who did you say it was, Neil?'

'It's a battleship.' She is beginning to make me feel uncomfortable.

'Great, great. Neil, you'll have to show me how to use the jigsaw machine.'

'Um–'

'I just *know* I'm going to chop my fingers off! Aggh! Ha ha.'

'I think Mr Lund is going to show us how to do it.' At this point, if I'd been sitting with Brendan, we would undoubtedly launch into an insightful discussion about whether Mr Lund will be resting his balls on the work-face of the jigsaw while demonstrating its use, perhaps lopping them off. I look over at him to see if he is enjoying life without me, but he looks depressed, which makes me feel even worse.

Now Anne is talking to the other girl. 'Alison, that's a good – what is it? A horse?'

'It's *The Scream*.'

'Look, Neil! It's a scream. Or do you mean–'

'The painting,' mumbles Alison. 'The painting *The Scream*. By Edvard Munch.'

'*That* Scream. Great.'

Woah, I am bored. And I think Anne fancies me. She is a weird mixture of spooky religiosity and overactive sexuality, and so, being inoffensive and quiet, I probably strike her as a win-win pro-position: both corruptible and/or potentially interested in attending, and singing and clapping in, her freakish tabernacle. So later, on the way to History, when I sneak nervously back to the cloak-room and find it vacant of people, and put my card in Adele's pocket, and then check my own coat to see if a) it has been riffled through, or b) Adele has left me a card of her own – and I find *a card in my pocket* with florid writing on the front:

To Neil

– my first thought is:

(1) Adele! Oh, my Adele!

And the second is:

(2) Bloody *Anne*.

Still, there is always a chance . . . I look around to see if anyone else is lurking in the cloakroom darkness. I don't want to open the card there and then (too risky), or anywhere else in school, in fact (much too risky), so I hastily put it in my bag and think about how nice it will be to open it later, at home, and find out it wasn't sent by Anne at all, but has telltale Adele-isms –

What *is* a telltale Adele-ism? Anything short of an actual signature would be ambiguous. Oh, but this is stupid, it'll be from Anne, I can feel it, it'll have some kind of awful message, punctuated exclusively with exclamation marks, millions of them!! So many that the message inside will read like a ghastly shriek!!!!! And it'll be one of the cards sold by her sinister church, and will say on the front

HAPPY ST VALENTINE'S DAY!
FROM THE
BRETHREN OF THE BLOOD-WASHED
SAINTS OF THE ONE TRUE GOD

with a picture of Saint Valentine himself on the front, *being martyred*. Oh God, I can sense it –

But what was I complaining about? Someone had given me a card on Valentine's Day – wasn't that enough? It's not like I was drowning in hordes of admirers. At least if somebody asked me whether I'd received any Valentine's cards – and Adele happened to be nearby, eavesdropping – I could say in a loud voice, *Yes*, even if the card was only from Anne, the straddler of feet.

I decide to open it at the first viable opportunity. Perhaps at lunch break.

History.

We watch a video called *The Cult of Hitler*. I sit on the long table at the back, with two people I don't know well separating me from Martin, who is at the other end of the table. The video is fascinating, but Martin keeps whispering comments all the way through, especially during the bits about the Hitler Youth and their summer camps and dreadful sing-songs.

Then a boy called Jeremy gasps. He is the first to notice that one of the grainy, head-dressed black-and-white League of German Women girls on the video looks exactly like Heather Lawlor, one of the girls in our group. Soon everyone is laughing. Then Martin starts calling her Fräulein Heather, and claiming she is 'as hard as Krupp steel'. And soon all the boys at the back of the class are quoting from the video but applying the words to Heather, who looks stricken. Then we see footage of planes and barrage balloons and the programme's narrator says the word 'flack' and that cow Karen shouts, 'Neil Flack!' But nobody laughs, which for some reason makes me feel worse than if everyone had laughed.

History videos always lead to some sort of

persecution: last time it was the one about Vespasian's Rome, after which some of the meaner members of the group started calling a big-nosed recluse named Peter Rolph Maximus Spasticus. I write a poem about my History group in my head. It is quite good, and I am sure I will be able to remember it, but it vanishes, goes up in smoke, some time around Kristallnacht, or the Berlin Olympics.

After History comes lunch, after which, I've decided, I will go to a toilet cubicle in the Drama and Music block and open my mystery Valentine. I considered retrieving my poetic Valentine from Adele's coat pocket and begging Brendan's forgiveness, but then I think about how Mum would feel if I told her I'd chickened out of sending the card.

Lunch is a plate of chips, a small pile of salt that serves as a dip, and a flan. Without Brendan to sit beside and talk to, I feel lost. Telling you who I had to sit next to is something I would only do if I were desperate to garner sympathy.

On the way to Drama, I open the mystery Valentine's card.

My God, my God.

It's that picture of the two strawberry people.

Whoever sent me a Valentine has picked exactly the card I've picked for Adele, which happens to be the same one that Harry has bought for –

Wait a second. Is this card from *Harry*? Oh, God help me, my one card! My one, only, Valentine's card, and it's not even from an admirer, it's a sympathy card from Harry! Even worse – it's a card she originally bought for my brother! It probably has his name scribbled out inside. Of course it's from Harry! Harry who sees me as her secret fellow-romantic ('Neil's the most *romantic* boy I've ever met') and who has pitied me enough to send me a card so that for a so, so, so-short spell I think that *someone* – even if it's just bloody Anne, Anne of the high church of the puritanical foot-riders – likes me, but then I have to discover that no, it's from my brother's friend, my possibly-no-longer-best friend's older sister, whose tawdry and ghastly books I used to steal before I convinced myself I was a poet –

Why don't I just look inside?

TO FLACK

YOU ARE SEXY AS HELL

I LIKE THE WAY YOU

LIE ON THE FLOOR

What?

It is not from Ariadne. It is from someone else, someone clearly deranged.

When do I *lie on the floor*? What awfulness is this? Who has ever seen me lie on the floor? Has Anne ever seen me lie on the floor?

Oh, but maybe she saw me lying on the floor when we all went on a week's trip to Wales in the first year. To some residential thing involving outdoor activities. Where we spent some time lounging in the lounge, yes, and yes, God! it's true, whenever I am forced to sit on the floor, I eventually end up reclining because I am too lazy to sit there, hunched over, my lower back hurting from the strain of having a physique reminiscent of spaghetti.

Has Anne been treasuring this thought of me lying on the floor in a converted Welsh mansion *for the last twelve months*?

No one has ever referred to me as sexy before. It seems almost sick.

Drama.

In shock.

We all sit down on the floor and Mr Bennett tells us where in the Drama block we are and are not allowed to go to practise our Group Pieces. Brendan is still refusing to look at me, which is making me alternately upset and angry. Mr Bennett dismisses us to go and find somewhere to work on our plays.

Satan, Battleship Potemkin and Paul Thorpe mill around, waiting for Martin to take charge. Leone is away, probably truanting. Martin and I ignore our group.

Martin, referring to Brendan, says to me, 'Girl trouble?'

'I'm going to speak to him.' I get clumsily to my feet.

'I wouldn't,' warns Martin.

'Why not? Has he spoken to you?'

'He's not too chuffed about your card.'

'What?'

'Forget about it.'

But how can I? After all Brendan's hard work to get us into Adele and Gillian's social orbit, I have repaid him by sneakily becoming a poet without telling him. Our Drama group heads for the costume room, with its racks of garish sweaty outfits, and the wooden benches on which people paint their papier-mâché masks, and we try to run through our fledgling play, and Martin repeatedly reminds me to concentrate, which I can't.

And then it is Maths, then hometime, and the solitary walk home, and now I arrive at the house with Dad's Volvo outside but not Mum's Beetle, because my parents have finished work early and Dad has let Mum drive him somewhere to celebrate their anniversary; and now I am at the front door, and now I am in the kitchen, and now on the stairs I stop and shudder to think of Adele reading my poem, a poem that has made my best friend hate me, and now I am entering the bedroom with the clothes on the floor, the floor upon which I might lie if I wanted to be sexy, which I don't, and the bed with the poetry books on the duvet.

Question. What kind of dickhead have I become? (Answer. A *poetic* dickhead. A dickhead, yes, but, for what it's worth, a *poetic* one.)

valentine's day ii:
retrospective in a kitchen

When I got home, Craig was in the living room watching television and drinking something alcoholic-looking from a brandy glass, possibly brandy. He told me that Mum and Dad were still out. Eventually Dad phoned to say that he and Mum would be home later, and said that Craig and I should make our own dinner. In the background I could hear loud voices and a song by Joan Armatrading.

I told Dad I was going to go round to Brendan's, and he gave me his customary advice: don't get murdered. Dad only let me go over to Brendan's in the evenings if I cycled, as it is apparently much harder to be murdered if you are on a bicycle than it is on foot. However, owing to my bad knee, I could only turn one pedal, which in practice proved less efficient than hopping. The sight of me cycling one-legged, however, was probably disturbing enough to deter most would-be killers.

Outside, an invisible blanket of cloud kept the night in. The air was filled with the kind of incredibly fine rain that doesn't seem to be actually falling, rain that's just a tickly swarming presence in the air, like wet gnats.

Life felt different.

The world had changed completely since last week, and had changed significantly since yesterday.

Life felt different now I was suddenly bereft of Brendan and everyone hated me, of course. I'd crossed some boundary, struck off on my own, was doing my own thing. My unpopularity with girls had acquired a ruggedly individualistic character. It did not feel like a positive development, not at all, which is why I was going to Brendan's: to sort things out, to get him back on board, to reaffirm our partnership.

But something else had changed, too: I was now a young poet who had just given someone a poem. On Saturday the poetry thing had made me feel happy and free, and while I didn't feel so happy now, the feeling of poet-hood was still there, though it had evolved somewhat.

The feeling is hard to explain. Its most concrete, and therefore most prosaic, symptom was that I'd somehow, suddenly, lost interest in *Sweet Dreams* books, after all this time. In fact, the idea of wanting to be a *Sweet Dreams* hero now seemed rather absurd.

Poetry had somehow made me a realist. I was aware for the first time that other boys would never secretly envy me my coolness, my lone-wolf air of danger, if I ever took to skulking around the school glaring moodily and reading *Catcher in the Rye* in the manner of a *Sweet Dreams* boy. They would call me a dick.

Sweet Dreams heroes have friends who come up to them at precisely the moment they are talking to the girl of their (sweet) dreams, and say, 'I heard how you saved that kid from a bear last week. Nice move.' And the hero has to play it down. 'It was nothing. That bear probably wasn't even going to eat the child. It was probably just shaking her out of playfulness.'

Not so with me. My friends came up to me and said things like, 'I was thinking how someone should invent a new word for fanny. How about "gwap"?'

Even *Sweet Dreams* heroes themselves would strike us as unconvincing if the authors of *Sweet Dreams* novels did not give them certain qualifications. They are good-looking, with deep rich voices that never unexpectedly leap an octave in a manner suggestive of yodelling. True, they are often misunderstood, but that is not because they mumble, or because they have to keep a hand positioned in front of their face while talking, to hide their objectionable skin. It is because they, unlike other boys, even other good-looking deep-voiced boys, were born on the wrong side of the tracks, and were encouraged from a marginally post-partum age to escape into great literature, poetry and the recognition of constellations. Their exotic lives, not the bad haircut their dad gave them after a long speech about the cost of haircuts and how difficult can it be to do it yourself? it's only bloody hair! stop whinging and sit down! – a haircut that would make even Quasimodo think that he'd turned a new corner in terms of ugliness – set them apart from other boys.

But now I had a new way of defining myself and the world, one that depended on my rich, limitless, solitary inner life, not on my ability to integrate at school, not on my complexion.

True, I hadn't understood a single one of the poems I'd read in Mum's book, poems that I'd taken to reading in bed before going to sleep. I'm not even sure I liked them. To me, the meaning of a poem, any poem, was just that it made someone a poet. The meaning of my own poem was that it made *me* a poet, and it was through this new role of poet that I had made romantic contact with Adele, via the giving of the card. She might have been reading the poem even as I rode to Brendan's. Re-reading it, for maybe the fifth or seventh or twelfth time. Maybe she and I were, at that moment, connected by the poem I'd sent. Adele and I, connected!

Until I could convince Brendan to like me again, the possibility of this connection was the only consolation I had.

At *Martin's*?

Why the bloody hell was Brendan at Martin's? He didn't even *like* Martin. They hadn't spoken properly for days, weeks. The pair of toerags!

By the time I arrived at Brendan's, I had remembered why I was visiting him, and was feeling bad about having spent half of the cycle journey fantasizing about Adele's reaction to my poem. Harry answered the door holding a plate of pasta. She had a piece of tagliatelle dangling from her lips, and as the door opened she was trying to flick it into her mouth. Evidently she had been trying for a couple of seconds, and had no doubt expected it to be safely out of sight by the time she opened the door.

'Oh, sod it,' she said. She grabbed the bit of pasta and put it in her mouth. 'Sorry about that. I should wear my nosebag.'

'What?'

'Nothing. You're after Brendan.'

'Yes.'

'He's over at Martin's.'

'Which Martin?'

'Martin who lives near you. He didn't call for you?'

'Well, no. Unless – no. *Martin's*?'

'You've had a fight?'

'No—'

Harry shrugged and said, 'He should be back soon. He hasn't had his dinner yet. Maybe he has anorexia. I hope so. Come in and wait.'

I didn't want to. I felt upset and wanted to go back home and write a poem about being abandoned by friends. 'I'd better go.'

'Neil, don't be stupid. It's a long way. Come in, and if he doesn't come back soon you can eat his dinner. Do you like peppers?'

'They're okay.'

'They're roasted. Ah, perfection. Here.' She offered me an oily, flaccid bit of red pepper.

She watched me hold it. 'You can eat it. It's not for saving. Open your mouth. That's it. Delicious, eh? Come on in and wait.'

Why was she being so nice to me? Again I thought of the possibility that *she* had sent me the Valentine with the strawberries, out of pity. She seemed a bit crazed, actually. Her voice was even faster than usual.

I went in. Harry said, 'Take your shoes off! God, they're filthy. Kids nowadays are so mucky.'

Mucky? Filthy? Could she mean *sexy*?

We were standing in the beautifully tiled hallway with its big oval mirror, mahogany telephone table and broken clock (a dusty grandfather with a limp pendulum), and the house gave off a spooky emptiness. I felt awkward about being alone in the hall with an older girl, virtually a woman. There was nothing I could possibly say that would be the slightest bit interesting. Unless – perhaps she would give me alcohol, so I could get drunk again and be conversational. But surely that would be a bad development. I'd seen what alcohol abuse does to a man. That man being Terry, Dad's ex-policeman friend, whose problems included dribbling.

'Harry, how long do you think he'll be?' I asked as I took my shoes off.

'Should be back soon. I think he left because he knew I was making the dinner.'

'Your parents are out?' I asked, horrified.

'Only till eight.'

'I might go and sit in Brendan's room.' I shuffled towards the immensely tall staircase that led to the first floor, where one could find the kitchen and living (sic) quarters of Brendan's deceased grand-parents. Brendan's room was the only room on the fourth floor, an attic room, balanced high up in the cold night sky, creepy as anything. There were gusts of wind outside. I didn't really want to have to pass through the domain of the dead grandparents on my own. They had been frightening enough when they were alive. What would they be like – *as phantoms*? I couldn't remember having ever walked through the Ghost Floor of the Keetleys' house alone, in the evening, with nobody but a girl in the house to hearken to any screams I might emit if spectral geriatrics came at me. No wonder Harry wanted me to come in and wait for Brendan. Sometimes she was so convincing in her imitation of a tough, fearless hard-nut that I forgot she was nothing of the sort.

While I was looking up at the staircase, a ghastly claw grabbed my coat sleeve. I lashed out involuntarily, realizing too late that the ghastly claw was Harry's hand and I had just accidentally whapped her across the face.

She was still holding my coat. With the other hand she clutched her nose. There was something in her hand, apart from her nose. Her dinner was on the floor; I looked down at the plate to see if it had smashed. I hadn't even heard it fall. I was about to apologize but she swore at me and pushed something into my face. It felt spongy and wet. It was a piece of bread that she'd been using to mop up pasta sauce. I wriggled to get away but slipped on the tiles and fell on the floor and Harry leaned down and picked up a handful of pasta and threw it at my head. I cried out as though she had hurled acid in my face, realizing as I did so that this response was not warranted. The harmless pasta ribbons clung to my cheek.

'Bloody hell, Neil.'

'You grabbed me.'

'Because you were staring at the stairs. *Staring*

at *stairs*! You spend your life in a bloody trance.'

Later, after we'd washed our hands and faces in the kitchen sink and sat down at the enormous pine table with some tea, we talked about life and watched Savage slide across the waxed kitchen floor looking for food or distractions. He slalomed around the table legs.

'This has been a shit day,' Harry said. 'I hope Craig's day was also shit.'

'Valentine's Day?'

'Exactly. Happy Valentine's Day! Mother of Shit. I really hate Valentine's Day. It's always either really shit or just toss. Depends on who your friends are. It's shit when you have the kind of friends who all get millions of cards and you don't. And you know that if you got a card, it would be from someone appalling. Someone who smells of sour milk. You know people who sit on buses and smell really strongly of old milk? People who have a rotting aroma. Well, they always sit in front of me, right under my nose. You know why? It's because they know I'm too mild-mannered to move away. And then there are Valentine's Days that are just toss. They're the ones where most of your friends are just scum who don't get any cards, but a few of them do, and you have to put up with their disgusting, vile smugness.'

'I don't know anyone who got a card,' I said helpfully.

'I know for a fact that your brother got one from Suzie Winstanley.'

'The horse?'

'From what I've heard, she gives free rides.' Harry made her eyebrows go up and down very quickly, something she does in accompaniment to innuendoes. It's very funny. Brendan attempted it sometimes, but couldn't do it quickly enough. 'She's more Blackpool Pleasure Beach donkey than thoroughbred. No – more inbred than thoroughbred. You should see the size of her gnashers.'

'Tombstone teeth,' I said, repeating a phrase I'd heard once.

'I just hope Craig isn't biting off more than Suzie can chew. Do you think he's going to ask her out?'

How would I know? 'How would I know?'

'He doesn't talk to you about that sort of thing, does he?'

I shook my head. Then I said, without really meaning to, 'Do you like Craig?'

I expected her to be coy or something, but she said, 'Yeah.' She looked sad. 'The bastard.'

I said, 'Did you send him a Valentine?'

'I chickened out.'

Did that mean that she'd sent me the card with the strawberries that she'd intended for Craig, out of pity or charity? I had no way of asking.

'Didn't he send you one?' I asked.

'I got zippedy shit.'

'Sorry,' I said.

Harry asked, 'Did you give that girl a card?'

'Yeah.'

'*Really?*'

I nodded, trying to look nonchalant. 'I put it in her pocket. Hopefully she got it.'

'That's fucking great! What did it have on it?'

What should I say? 'Fruit.'

'Fruit?'

'Just . . . fruit.'

'Like, fruit salad?'

'Um, human fruit.'

She frowned. 'Oh, *that* kind of fruit.' I think she was suspecting me of sending the same card as her. Either that or she thought I was insane. 'What was inside it?'

I said, 'I wrote a poem.'

For the first time since we'd been drunk in Craig's room, I saw her face rearrange in a way that communicated tenderness. 'Oh, Neil,' she said. 'You wrote her a *poem*.'

I was blushing, and grinning with embarrassment and pride, so I put my head down, tucking my chin into my collar.

'Neil?'

'Hmm?'

'Has your neck just broken?'

'No,' I said defensively.

'Was it a good poem? Oh, of course it was. Stupid question. Can you remember any of it?'

I could probably remember most of it if I tried, but there was no way I was going to recite it. If I recited it and she gave me a look of horror or pity, and I realized that the poem was in fact terrible, I would not be able to live. So I said, 'Not off the top of my head.'

'Still. It's a lovely thing to do. Not many boys your age write poems. Did you actually write it yourself, or was it copied?'

'I wrote it.'

'How sweet!' She let out a deep sigh. 'Why isn't your brother sweet? Have you met Suzie Winstanley? Do you know her at all?'

'I don't think I've ever seen her.'

'She's a whore. She would be awful for Craig. Probably break his shrivelled heart.' She leaned towards me and grabbed my arm. 'Swear on your life that you won't let him go out with her.'

I swore it.

Harry's parents returned just after eight. Brendan was still at Martin's, unless, of course, he had been murdered while cycling home (unlikely, if not impossible, according to my dad's theory of the invulnerability of cyclists).

When I got home, my parents were still out; Craig said Mum had phoned to tell him to make sure I got to bed at a reasonable time. He said she'd asked if we'd had a nice Valentine's Day, and he'd told her it had been okay.

Brendan phoned at just after nine o'clock, when he'd realized that our plan to woo Adele and Gillian tomorrow while taking photographs of them would be infinitely more difficult if we were not on speaking terms. Even though I had sent a Valentine without his help, and even though he had got into Adele and Gillian's Drama group without my help, we were still mutually dependent, whether it suited us or not, a fact attributable not to circumstances but to the fact that we were both wimps – something we would continue to be, presumably, until Adele and Gillian transformed us with their love, which was something we hoped would happen in the next twenty-four hours.

please welcome tramp

Tuesday 15th February: the day of my first real meeting with Adele Collier.

There may well be a cosmic law to the effect that people who find true love are precisely those who expect to do so. I expected to find true love, a fact that, given my self-esteem, mumbling and unsightly haircut, would have baffled evolutionary psychologists. But the explanation was simple, and involved a loophole in the workings of natural selection. Lacking the good looks and charm necessary for successful breeding, and finding solace by spending the last two years imagining myself as a *Sweet Dreams* hero, I had accidentally programmed myself to expect the same romantic opportunities that *Sweet Dreams* heroes enjoyed.

I didn't expect my first real meeting with Adele to be exceptional, though. Rather, I expected factors like my Valentine, and the machinations of a cosmic Cupid, to draw us together. I knew that I would have to take a photograph of her after school, but I didn't expect to have to try to impress or entice her, not yet. All I had to do was not strike her as cretinous or evil or obscene or unhygienic or mentally unsound or gay, and I wasn't any of those things, so why would I act like I was?

Such was my view. But all day I waited for the end-of-school bell with so much fear in my intestines that it felt like a snake was in there, coiling.

That afternoon I was behind her in the lunch queue, and when she was halfway through paying at the till she popped back to the food counter to grab something spongy with icing, just as I myself was trying to choose my own spongy dessert, and she looked as though her life had not changed *in the slightest*.

What had I expected to happen as a consequence of my Valentine? Honestly? I had expected the poem to explode in Adele's life like a hand grenade. More than that, I had expected the explosion to be felt throughout school, to leave scorch marks on tables. I'd expected whispering in corridors, and rumours about a nameless poet who had won Adele's heart. Then I expected to have to step forward, possibly because of public pressure, and admit that I was the mystery poet. Celebrity would follow. We would be a very high-profile couple, and very happy: Adele blissful to have found a truly romantic *poetic* guy; me equally ecstatic and also (incidentally) no longer considered a nancy by my peers.

I had not expected the card to have no concrete consequences. I had not expected Valentine's Day to disappear, to evaporate. But that was what appeared to have happened.

That morning, I'd told Mum that I was nervous about going into school in case everyone knew about my card. Mum said, 'Don't expect everything to happen all at once.'

I'd also asked Mum if she and Dad had enjoyed their Valentine's Day evening, which they'd spent in a restaurant and later in a pub. Mum said that after two glasses of wine she was banging her hand on the table and ranting about ordination of women priests while Dad stared at his hands. Apart from the obvious message about the dangers of alcohol, the moral of the story, as I understood it, was that none of this gets any easier as you get older.

That afternoon at home time we stood in the Arts block foyer: Brendan, Gillian, Karen, a remedial, Adele and me, all gathered for our photo-shoot.

We were not standing together. We were grouped according to social status and distributed across the foyer – Adele and Gillian near the main Music room door, Karen and the remedial by the broken piano

217

that stood under the notice-board, Brendan and me next to the boys' toilets – all waiting for the remaining remedial to arrive.

Brendan and I stared goggle-eyed at one another as we contemplated the prospect of taking colour photos of Adele and Gillian. I looked over at them. Adele was yawning widely and was so endearing I felt bad for not yawning too, and briefly considered trying.

'Nude, please, girls,' said Brendan, miming photography. He laughed nervously to himself. 'I'd best go over to Gillian. You come with me.'

'I'm so scared,' I said.

Adele went into the Music room. Music wafted out of the door. She emerged thirty seconds later and suddenly she was walking over to Brendan and me, her step weightless, her sad mouth pursed a little, her grey eyes mesmeric in their symmetry, her frame willowy and insubstantial but with definite shape, and I lost control of my movements, I had no idea how to stand, whether to do something with my hands, where to look. Basic rules of speech became trigonometry. She came right up to us, and I became aware of all the room's colours, and of my hair, and of my open mouth, and of her nose and of the fact that she seemed taller than me, though she wasn't.

'There's nowhere to do it,' she said to Brendan. 'The rooms are taken.'

'We could go to mine,' said Brendan. 'It's just nearby.'

She pondered. 'I'll check with Gill.'

'Anyway, I forgot the camera,' said Brendan.

Adele did not chide him. She walked over to where Gillian was standing with Karen and the remedial.

'This is a major victory,' Brendan whispered. 'We're going back to mine!' Then he turned to me with wide eyes. 'Should I go for a poo now, before we go? If I wait much longer I'll do it in my willows. Could you keep the ladies amused while I sneak off?'

Willows was our word for underpants (as in *Wind in the Willows*). I said, 'You're kidding.'

'Actually, there's no time. And anyway, they'd guess what I was doing in there.' The toilets were right next to us, there in the Arts block foyer, and Brendan no doubt had visions of us all waiting outside, timing him. 'He's doing a long 'un,' Gillian might say, and everybody would laugh.

'But I can't go at my house,' he said, panicking. 'What happens if it bobs back to the surface and won't flush, and then Gillian goes to the toilet and sees it swimming around?'

Adele and Gillian and the others came over.

'So is it far to yours?' Gillian asked.

I'd never spent so much time close to Adele, and my nerves could not cope. Brendan and I were shaking with fear, and for a moment it looked suspiciously as though Brendan's should-I-or-shouldn't-I-defecate problem had solved itself. I sniffed loudly and Brendan, somehow guessing my motive, suddenly snorted with ghastly laughter. Everyone stood back a bit.

I said to Gillian, 'It's, um, just near.'

Brendan remained bent over from his laughter outburst. His nose had run, and he was trying to wipe it surreptitiously. Gillian tutted.

The remedial asked, 'Can we get a drink at your house? I forgot my drink today.'

'We could have some booze!' said Brendan, straightening up, and everybody looked at him like he'd just leaned over and licked the remedial's face. The other remedial arrived and Karen, seeming worryingly animated, explained our new plan and we all started walking. I couldn't keep my eyes off Adele.

'Neil's coming to take the pictures,' Brendan said, primarily to me. We walked through the covered area outside the Arts block, out past middle and lower school, and on towards the school gates.

'He got badly done in English,' Karen told Adele. 'It was the funniest thing I've ever seen. He ate a piece of paper in front of Father Wigman.'

I looked at Karen, horrified.

Adele said gently, 'What?'

I was in love and was also petrified. My heart felt like a bird trapped in a box. I wanted Karen dead. Adele looked bored, and kept doing spontaneous, appealing things like stroking her own hair. She kept her eyes on the ground.

'You had to be there,' said Karen. 'It was hilarious.'

'It wasn't my fault,' I snapped at her. I waited for somebody to respond, but they all ignored me.

We arrived at Brendan's house. I wanted to see if Adele would wipe her feet, and she did, which I found delightful. She then went the extra mile and said, 'Shall I take my shoes off?' I glanced at Brendan, who looked as though Adele had just offered to strip for him.

'If you want,' he said.

She removed her small shoes, one slightly scuffed, the other not, and placed them neatly beside the door. Gillian and the remedials went into the lounge, shoes and all.

Karen said, 'I'll keep mine on. I've wiped them, though.'

'Keep them on, take them off, whatever you want,' said Brendan.

I said to Adele, 'If you want to put yours back on, you can.'

She laughed. 'I'll remember that. They might come in useful when I leave.'

I should have laughed politely, but instead I tried

to justify my stupid comment. 'You're not leaving yet, though, are you? That's why I thought that you might, you know—'

Brendan let Savage in from the garden to gallop around the living-room leaping at people and depositing hair. Adele tried to give him a stiff-handed pat on the head, but he ran off. I thought: bad dog! impolite dog! Brendan took Savage upstairs.

Meanwhile, the rest of us sat in the living room watching a soap opera on television and drinking Brendan's family's cola. Outside, rain was washing away slush. Inside, Adele, Gillian and the male remedial sat on the sofa. I thought: this is what Adele looks like when she's at home, watching television. She looked serious. The other remedial sat on an Italian leather beanbag, Karen sat on one of the chairs, and I sat on the other chair. None of us spoke.

There was something surreal about sitting in my best friend's house with this exquisite girl, with her waterfall hair and luminous seriousness, the constellations of freckles on her face, the dark rings under her grey eyes – here in the very room where Brendan and I once watched a video entitled *A Hole in One,* ostensibly about golf. I was dying for her to say something about having received a really beautiful Valentine. I began wondering what kind of things she might say to hint that she'd received a

Valentine, or, better still, to hint that she knew it was from me and she'd found it irresistible.

'Where the fuck has Brendan gone?' Karen demanded.

'To get the camera?' I said.

We heard a toilet flush, then Brendan bounded down the stairs with Savage bounding after him.

'What were you doing?' Adele asked.

'Did you get the camera?' I asked, boldly redirecting Adele's line of questioning.

'I'm letting the dog back into the garden,' Brendan said, wafting his hand. 'He stinks!'

'You let your dog use your toilet?' a remedial asked.

'Get the camera,' I ordered sharply, and everybody looked at me because my voice had sort of yodelled.

'You've upset the dog,' Adele told me. Me and the dog hung our heads.

Brendan looked at Adele and at me, then went through the archway to the dining area. He stood in front of the patio door and patted his thigh and called Savage over, but Savage was now playing with the boy remedial. The boy remedial got down on all fours and started panting at the dog.

Gillian observed the remedial with disgust. Brendan went over to the tall shelving unit and felt on the top shelf for the camera. He was too short to see what was on the shelf, so Gillian, who was almost as tall as me, went over to help him. Brendan looked petrified. I looked over at Adele. Now that she had told me off for upsetting the dog, I realized that I no longer feared talking to her: I had spoken to her and lived, and presumably there was no reason why I should not continue to speak to her and live. And having moved into this new territory, I felt yet a new kind of love. Or, rather, I loved a new Adele: an Adele with whom I was on speaking terms.

I looked at her, hoping that there was something we could *do* together, but she was watching the crouching remedial with scientific detachment.

I thought: should I cunningly mention something about strawberries kissing? Or about little tiny christmas trees, or e.e. cummings? I looked back at Brendan. Gillian was on tiptoes, searching the shelf, reaching up with one hand, and Brendan was standing right in front of her, hypnotized by her bosom. Afraid that Adele would see him being perverted and associate him with me, I jumped up and went over to help look for the camera, but as I wandered over, the crouching remedial started whooping.

'Look!' he cried. 'The dog wants a piggy back.'

Gillian, looking over, started laughing loudly and unattractively. Brendan gasped with horror.

'He's humping you,' spat Karen. 'You're being humped by a dog.'

Brendan raced over and tried to lift the dog off the now-distraught boy. For a second it looked like

Brendan was humping the dog who was in turn humping the remedial, who was thrashing around. A flash went off; Gillian had taken a photo. She laughed crazily, possibly imagining the photo on the cover of her Group Piece programme. Now the room was filled with manic laughter, so I joined in, but then I noticed Adele and stopped.

Adele was looking confused. I realized that she didn't know what was going on. Gillian went over to her and whispered something, and Adele looked at the floor as though ashamed of her naïveté.

And suddenly I felt another kind of love, one that I'd never thought I'd feel for Adele. I pitied her. Of course, I felt some sympathy for the remedial, who looked disgusted at himself for letting a dog have such high-profile sex with him, but the novelty of pitying Adele took up most of my energy. Innocence in any form always made me feel heartbroken; it seemed so doomed and fragile. Very few people get to thirteen years old without feeling somehow sullied, and Adele might have been one of them, and I wondered if I'd witnessed her first encounter with the sleaziness of life.

But then she surprised me by walking over to Savage, kneeling down and patting him on the head, the same stiff-handed pat as before. His tongue was hanging out and he looked deranged, but he seemed soothed by Adele's bouncing hand. It was as though Adele was forgiving him for humping the remedial in front of her. Or it was as though she was aware that the dog was being laughed at, and wanted to comfort him. Maybe she was expressing fellow feeling with the dog, recognizing that he was as poignantly ignorant of human etiquette as she had been of dog sexuality.

In the end, Savage got in the photo. He lay splayed in front of the group, looking at Adele's hand. A dog, I decided as I pushed the button, of impeccable taste.

I moved near to her as people were getting their coats on and I waited. What I was waiting for I didn't know. Karen was frowning at me and Gillian had sensed my presence, but still I lingered. I was waiting for the right time, without knowing what the time was supposed to be right *for*, which complicated matters. Then I gave up waiting, and moved further into Adele's orbit, and I said to her: 'Brendan says you want to do some music for your Group Piece.'

Adele looked at me as though I'd spoken in Latin. Her sharp eyebrows bowed to each other, and I could see her front teeth. Moving her hair away from her forehead, she said, 'I think they all want to go home.'

'Oh,' I said, the muscles in my face knotting, unravelling, knotting. 'It was a good idea, though.'

Karen threw a coat at someone.

'Bye,' Adele said to me. A posh, polished, well-formed word.

I thought: she can tell it was me who sent her the card. I don't know why I thought that; I had no evidence whatsoever. Something about the way she said that last word.

I said, 'Can't you stay a bit?'

Adele said, 'My flute's at school.'

I said, 'I've got my guitar here already.'

To my surprise Adele asked where, and, seizing the moment to introduce a conversation piece, I went over to the door to what Brendan's family called the Snug, in which stood the guitar in question, and I opened the door and Adele came over and I pointed to the guitar, a horrible shiny red spiky thing with two black humbucker pickups and a black tremolo bar.

Adele said, 'You could stab someone with that.' My mind swam with stupid replies.

Gillian walked up to us and told Adele that she was going, and asked was Adele coming? Adele, now crouching by my guitar, which was leaning menacingly against my amplifier like a street punk, said she'd be coming out in a second. Gillian, as surprised as me, said she was going to the shops, and told Adele to catch her up.

As Gillian left I saw Brendan attempting to get between her and the door, trying to field her as though she were a slow-moving cricket ball. Karen was lurking. And now Gillian had departed and Brendan was trying to make Savage lie down. Then finally the remedials had gone, though Karen, annoyingly, remained. She was looking at Brendan, and I suddenly thought: Karen loves Brendan.

Brendan crossed the living-room and came into the Snug and said to Adele, 'Our music studio.' Karen joined us, looking suspiciously happy. Brendan clapped his hands and rubbed them together. Savage, who thought he was going for a walk, pelted over and started jumping up at us. Karen said, 'Get this fucking pervert dog off me.' Brendan made Savage lie down.

Karen went over to my guitar. 'What is *this* supposed to be?'

'It's a flying-V guitar,' I said.

'You like heavy metal?' Adele asked me.

'It's okay,' I lied. I thought about the song Brendan and I had written.

Adele looked from Brendan to me and back to Brendan. 'What's your band called?'

Brendan and I looked at each other. Brendan said, 'Tramp?'

Karen burst out laughing. Brendan started laughing too, a strained, fake-sounding laugh. 'Not really,' he said. Then there was a throbbing silence that went on and on, a silence that could have eaten us all, during which Adele and Karen just stared

228

at us, waiting to hear what we were really called.

I couldn't think of the word plinth. 'We're called The Victorians,' I said.

'Really?' said Adele, agog. She told us what her band was called and I acted surprised and delighted.

Adele took charge. 'So, what kind of thing would we be trying to do here, with the music?' she asked in her lovely posh voice. 'Would we make up some music and then build the play around it? Or are we coming up with a mood for the play and then writing some music to fit it?'

Karen looked at me and rolled her eyes. She was still under the radically mistaken impression that I disliked Adele. I looked away. Karen said, 'We can't just make up some music and then do a play to it.' She looked at Brendan, then at my guitar. 'What if the music's shit?'

'It won't be,' Brendan lied.

'Do you have anything you've already written?' asked Adele. 'I want to hear what that guitar sounds like.'

Suddenly I saw 'Plinth of Desire' for what it was: the direst piece of music ever created. Brendan looked at me and seemed to read my thoughts. I shook my head.

'Sure. We have loads of stuff,' Brendan said.

'Brilliant,' Adele said enthusiastically. 'You two play some different things and we'll see if

229

there's anything that we might be able to perform to.'

I almost laughed out loud. I wanted to say something to Brendan like, 'Can you imagine actually playing that awful piece of crap to Adele?' But although we were sitting only feet away from each other, we were incapable of communicating, not having created an elaborate system of signals in advance.

Everyone sat waiting. I cleared my throat twice. Finally I said, 'Okay. Choose a key, major or minor.'

Karen said, 'Key? What?'

Adele laughed and said, 'Key? *Que?*' which meant nothing whatsoever to me, but I laughed loudly anyway. She looked at me with her narrow grey eyes and smiled sweetly, as shyly as a deer. I felt unimaginably proud of myself for having had the intelligence to pretend to understand whatever she'd just said.

Adele gave the matter some thought. 'I think *minor* sounds nice. We can change, though, can't we? We could start with something minor and build up' – here she gesticulated grandly – 'then break through to the other one, major, then sink back to minor, then finally have a happy ending.'

'Well I haven't a fucking *clue* what she's on about,' mumbled Karen. 'Have you?'

'Well,' said Brendan, equally baffled. 'You see, it's sort of . . .'

'That's really cool,' I enthused, ignoring Karen. 'So the play is kind of already written in the music. Or the moods are already written. That's brilliant.'

Karen laughed and said sarcastically, 'Yeah, Adele, that's *brilliant*.'

'So,' said Adele. 'Something in the minor key to start.'

I said, on a whim, 'Wait. What's your favourite fruit?'

Adele said, 'What? I suppose oranges.'

Oranges? Why not strawberries? Karen said, '*Fruit?*'

Adele looked puzzled. How was I going to find out what she thought of my Valentine card? I switched on my amp. Because the guitar was leaning against it the amp yelped with feedback. Everyone made an 'Agh!' noise apart from Adele, who laughed. She was happy and excited. I sat down on my amplifier and picked up my guitar. It was slippery. I realized that my palms were gushing water. Adele seemed joyful and eager to get to work but I wanted to linger in this lovely moment, this moment pregnant with promise, for as long as possible, and to delay the occasion of her discovery that I only knew how to play the following chords:

MAJOR CHORDS (happy):

E MAJOR, which I rarely found a use for.

A MAJOR, which I could also live without, and

231

which I could not play without a buzzing sound coming from under my left-hand third finger.

C MAJOR, indispensable, especially in songs in the key of:

G MAJOR, my favourite chord, a chord which sounds like a smile, and even looks like one, albeit a lopsided one. Found at the heart of hundreds of classic songs, two of which are 'Mull of Kintyre', and 'Take It Easy' by the Eagles. Unfortunately, however, it is not one of the . . .

MINOR CHORDS (gloomy):

E MINOR, a crucial chord, which adds bathos to songs like 'Take It Easy' by the Eagles, which also involves G and C (see above). Simple to play, requiring only two fingers.

A MINOR, essential for 'Take It Easy' by the Eagles, adding a lovely sad note in the chorus. Has many other uses outside 'Take It Easy', the discovery of all of which still lay before me, possibly quite far away.

Also, my chord changes were less than smooth. Sometimes you could be forgiven for mistaking one of my chord changes for the end of the song. To get round this problem I tended to strum all of the strings irrespective of whether they were necessary for the chord, and let some of the open strings continue to ring out, sustained by the sandpapery reverb of the amplifier, while my fingers crawled at geriatric pace into their next configuration, so that at least my chords were linked together by *some* kind of noise, no matter how unpleasant.

I strummed E minor. Brendan shouted, '*Plinth–*' and Adele and Karen and I looked at him, terrified. I stopped playing and said, 'Brendan!'

'Is this an actual *song*?' asked Adele. 'Brilliant!'

'Wait, I've got an idea,' I said, damping the strings with my palm. 'We should just do something off the top of our heads.'

'What kind of music do you like?' she asked, looking at me, then at Brendan.

I said, 'Um, poetic music.'

'Poetic?' Adele asked, frowning.

Brendan said, 'We like our own music.'

Adele laughed. I laughed too. Karen looked at Brendan and said, 'You're a dick.'

'What do *you* like?' I asked Adele.

'I like someone who's dead,' she said.

'How can you like someone who's dead?' asked Karen. 'That's sick.' She had the intelligence of soap.

'Beethoven,' said Brendan.

'Nope!' said Adele.

'More old or less old?' I asked, wanting to join the game.

'More dead or less dead?' asked Brendan, and Adele laughed.

'Less dead,' said Adele.

'Almost alive?' I said, but the window of opportunity for jokes on degrees of death had shut like a coffin lid. Adele chided me with a gentle, motherly look. I loved her desperately. 'Frank Sinatra,' I said.

'Close,' said Adele. 'But he's alive.'

'Dracula,' spat Karen. We ignored her.

'Vivaldi,' said Brendan. 'Is it someone who died recently?'

'It's the King,' said Adele. We looked at her blankly. 'That's a clue.'

'Oh, Bruce Springsteen,' said Brendan.

'Elvis!' said Adele. 'I love him.'

'*Really?*' I said, as though I were about to add, 'Me too!' Which after a moment's consideration I realized was a bad idea. However, I did know one of his songs. 'As in "Hound Dog"?'

'Yes!' said Adele. 'Brilliant song. Can you play it?' Her beautiful eyes were twinkling.

'Never tried,' I said.

'Try now.'

I was so caught up in the excitement of the conversation that I could not refuse. I suggested we all go back into the living-room, where we could sit in comfort. We relocated, and I sat in a chair with the amp in front of me and put my guitar on my lap and activated the amp, which emitted excited metallic noises, and I looked at Adele, who was on the sofa with Karen. She was smiling. Surely she knew –

knew from the noise of the beating of my heart!
– that it was me who sent the card. Dissemble no
more! I took a breath and tried to remember whether
the song was happy or gloomy. I strummed G.

'Turn it up,' said Adele. 'Right up.'

Brendan, sitting cross-legged in front of the
amplifier, turned the volume up until the amp
started to buzz steadily. I started to strum and
settled into a rhythm, playing a loud, crunchy G.
Adele looked at me, perhaps impressed, then looked
away and cooed the first line of 'Hound Dog'. It was
the happiest moment of my life.

The way Karen looked at her, you'd think Adele
had just removed her own head and hurled it out
the window. But Adele didn't care about Karen. She
was swaying a bit from left to right as she started to
hum the rest of the song. Then I realized she was
waiting for me to change chords, and I tried to think
which of my five remaining chords would sound
most appropriate. Brendan slapped his thigh to keep
rhythm, prompting Savage to get up from his resting
place near the velveteen footstool and come over to
sniff us, which made Adele laugh while she
hummed, a gorgeous laugh, pure music, pitch-
perfect. I picked C and tried to mentally rehearse
playing it. Adele looked at Savage and sang to him
that he wasn't nothing but a hound dog, and she and
I laughed loudly while out of the corner of my eye I
scanned the fretboard, hoping to figure out what on

earth to do with my fingers. Adele hummed, Karen covered her ears, then the cut-off point for changing chords arrived, like a train rolling towards me that I somehow had to jump aboard, and I tried to make my hands leap into place while maintaining the rhythm of my strumming –

There was a noise that sounded like someone turning off a burglar alarm by hitting it with a rock. Adele and Karen called out together: 'Woe!' and 'Aye!' – but my hands were still chugging and the plectrum ground into the strings once more, and this time the G came out true. I whooped; I couldn't help it; and I strummed.

Adele took Savage's ears in her gentle fingers and lifted them up, and sang about the hound dog not catching any rabbits or being a friend of hers. And I thought: O dear God above, it's miraculous but it is true: it has turned out that I, Neil Flack, am actually right for Adele, and she is truly right for me, and so this must be the day that I tell her it was me who sent her the card and wrote her a poem – and I knew in my heart that Adele would be glad it was me. Somewhere along the way I had managed to change chords again without even thinking, and everything was sounding just magnificent. Savage tilted his head and there was laughter, and then Karen shouted, 'Shut up!'

We all jumped, and my chord rang out, sounding suddenly buzzy and horrible.

Adele turned to Karen and glared. 'Why don't *you* shut up, Karen?'

'I think it's the door,' said Brendan in a small voice, but Adele wasn't listening.

'You're a moaning, miserable cow who just wants to spoil things,' Adele snapped. Karen was much bigger than Adele and normally looked as though she could squash her with her thumb, but Adele was fixing her with a look that came right out of voodoo myth. 'Someone's at the door,' Karen said quietly, and then she burst into tears.

Everything was suddenly silent apart from Karen's sobs. Then we heard a voice outside, calling, 'Let me in!' It was Harry.

'I'll get it,' said Brendan, scurrying out of the room. Over Karen's snotty plaint we heard Brendan hissing at Harry in the hallway. Harry laughed loudly and poked her head round the door, saw Karen sniffling, looked apologetic and went upstairs.

'Where's my bag?' Karen growled, at no one in particular. She scanned the floor and chairs, then jumped to her feet and stamped out of the living-room. I heard Brendan's voice coming from the hall, then Karen's brusque reply.

Adele and I were alone together, sitting in shock, staring at each other. 'God,' she said. 'What did I just do?'

'It was nothing,' I said. 'She *is* a moody cow.'

'Oh God,' whispered Adele. She stood up. For some reason I stood up too.

I whispered, 'I think she likes Brendan.'

'I think I really upset her.'

'I thought you did the right thing,' I said stupidly. '*Neil*.'

Brendan returned, followed by a suicidal-looking Karen, who slumped on the chair on which I'd been sitting, behind the amp. Adele sat down again. 'Sorry, Karen.'

Everyone sat staring straight ahead and saying nothing, except me: I was standing next to my school bag. Karen said, 'For God's sake, play some music.'

'Actually, I'd best go,' said Adele, her voice sounding incredibly posh compared to Karen's banshee-like emissions.

I began to panic. What had happened? Adele picked her peach scarf up from the sofa and I gazed at her. Everything was going wrong. Then I noticed something via peripheral vision. Karen had taken something out of her bag and was putting it in the back of my amp. She looked up and saw me observing her and fixed me with a freezing glare.

Adele had put on her scarf and was sitting on the very edge of the sofa, her shoulders hunched, her hands pressing palm-down on to the sofa at either side of her as though she were about to propel herself into the air and fly out of the room.

'What's in the back of the amp?' Karen asked. She pointed to the hollow space in the rear.

By now I was panicking. 'You put the lead in there when you're not using it,' I said. 'I mean the plug. The cable.' I moved swiftly towards her.

'No,' said Karen, pointing. '*That.*'

Before I could get to the amplifier she reached into the cavity and pulled something out. She yelped and looked up, and there was something in her eyes that filled me with terror.

'You filthy boy.'

She held up the mystery artefact so that Adele could see it. A single crumpled piece of paper. Karen cried, 'Well, look at this!'

Then Adele looked, we all looked, and suddenly Brendan and I were on our feet: Karen was holding a picture of a cartoon naked woman with giant breasts and a wild pubic forest.

'I don't know what it is!' I cried. I was unable to control the words coming out of me.

'Who put that there?' Brendan shouted.

'Agh! Fuck!' Karen screamed. 'It's sticky! Here, feel!' She flung it at Adele, who leapt back in horror.

'It's not what you think!' I cried. *It's not what you think*: the eternal, well-worn cry of the guilty. I felt an urge to add: *I can explain!*

'Sod this,' said Karen. 'I'm getting out of here. You people are dickheads.' Brendan looked at me imploringly. I looked imploringly at Adele.

She was squirming with embarrassment. 'I'd best go too,' she said quietly.

And suddenly Adele was on her feet, walking quickly to the door, following Karen. Then she stopped and walked back into the room, towards Savage, who was watching her from the middle of the carpet. Reaching down, she pulled her school bag from under his front paw, then turned and left the room. I heard the sound of shoes being put on, and then the front door opened and closed with polite urgency.

Frantic, I asked Brendan, 'Should I chase her?' – but Brendan was sitting with his jaw clenched, staring at the window.

He said, 'I don't fucking believe it.'

'It'll be okay!' I cried. 'Just tell me what to do!'

'How the *fuck* did that get in your amplifier?'

'She stole it from the bin!' I gasped. 'She planted it!'

Karen had stolen my rude pictures from Father Wigman's room and had kept one with her – why? Just in case the opportunity to demolish my life came along? But of course that was just the sort of thing bullies liked doing, wasn't it? I looked at the bit of paper. It was not the one with Adele's name on it, which was a blessing, I suppose, but not much of one.

After too much hesitation I ran out of the house with the picture in my hand, towards the shops – Budgens and the chemist and grocers and newsagent – and first I looked in the newsagent, then ran back past the butcher's and chemist back to Budgens, and I ran inside into the hallway of tinned food and I snaked wildly up and down the aisles, three trips down each aisle, loping, hurtling like a bird hurtles when it flies through an open window into your bedroom, but Adele was not there –

I had lost her.

movie flakes

That evening after a quiet dinner – quiet because there was perhaps too much that needed saying, and also because we wanted to show appreciation for the meal (chicken chasseur) – we watched television as a family, our last night as a family because Mum was going back to her flat later on.

I was aching to phone Brendan in the hope that he'd formulated a plan to reverse our hideous misfortunes, but I was too scared, and anyway I knew that plans could not rescue us now. We sat, and Craig and I waited to be informed of any noteworthy developments in our parents' marriage.

Eventually Mum said, 'Craig? Neil?' We both stopped slouching. 'Your dad and I have been talking things over, and I think I should talk things over with you two as well.' I noticed that Dad had started fidgeting. Mum continued. 'I'd like to see the both of you more often.'

Craig and I looked at each other. We both said, 'Great.'

'I was thinking perhaps you could stay at the flat some weekends, or I could come here, or maybe we can go out during the week.'

Craig said, 'And leave Dad alone with the drinks cabinet?'

'No, your dad can come too!'

'No more films about women crying all over each other, though,' said Dad with mock forcefulness.

This was a happy moment for us Flacks, but because I was a Judas and a pornographer who had lost his one chance at love, I could not feel in the slightest bit happy.

Mum noticed that something was wrong. 'Is that okay with you, Neil?' she said softly.

'Great,' I said again.

Now everyone was looking at me as though expecting me to pass the final verdict on whether we could be a happy semi-reunited family. I tried to smile but succeeded only in showing everyone my teeth.

Dad said, 'All settled, then! Neil, it's your turn to make a pot of tea.'

I went into the kitchen, still looking miserable, giving no thought to how Mum must have been feeling thanks to my sullen response to her good news.

In the kitchen, her things were still lying around: some books, her spare glasses, notepads, her white ballpoint pen. She left practicalities like packing bags until the last minute.

Dad came into the kitchen as I stood stirring the tea in the teapot. He said, 'Okay?'

I said, 'Eh?'

'Everything okay?'

I said, 'It's just brewing,' meaning the tea. My voice sounded far away.

'What's this that Mum tells me about you sending a card to a girl at school?' he asked. He was trying to sound interested but it came out as saucy, as though he should be winking at me while he said it.

'Oh, that,' I mumbled. 'I thought I'd might as well.'

Dad nodded. 'Nice?'

I squinted. 'Pretty stupid.'

'But it's the looks that count.'

'No, I meant the card.'

'But is she –'

'Oh,' I said, which wasn't really an answer to the question he was trying to ask, but it had been a long and disastrous day and I felt I might break into embarrassing sobs if I didn't minimize the amount of noise I was letting out of my mouth. I turned around and poured the tea.

'How come you never said anything about it?'

He meant, said anything to *him* rather than to Mum. Well, what did he expect? I hadn't sent Adele a card for his entertainment; I hadn't even sent it for *her* entertainment. I said, 'I don't know.'

Dad got some Digestive biscuits and put them on

a plate. He sighed. 'You would have liked Mum to move back in, wouldn't you?'

'I suppose.'

'It's been a really nice few days. Your mum and I will always be very good friends, but we see things very differently, which is a good thing in some ways, I suppose, but it makes living under the same roof a bit of a tricky affair. We decided it wasn't fair to you or Craig to carry on the way things were. But she really does want to see a lot more of you two. As much as possible. Of course, that might be a problem with all the hot dates you'll be having, eh, Valentine Man?'

'Yes,' I said.

Dad opened his mouth then closed it and shook his head, then took the teapot and biscuits, and I took four cups, and we went back to the lounge, which was full of the *Doctor Who* music: the credits were rolling, and there was a reminder that this month's copy of *Doctor Who* magazine came with a free sticker.

That was the closest Dad had ever come to explaining to me how he felt about Mum. I'd wasted the moment.

Later that evening, when Mum left, wearing the scarf she'd worn on arrival, we saw her to her car and ran in and out of the house bringing things she had forgotten to pack. There was light rain and darkness, the gloom of Odell Close on a February evening, the glowing of living-room lights and kitchen lights filtered through curtains; and house number twenty-one was expelling a mother into the night after a posh supper. Quiet suburban drama. Then you could see that the rain was in fact snow, or was at least mingled with it; small drops of snow terminating on the puddly pavement and road. We stood at the door to wave at Mum, me trying hard to smile, all hugging ourselves and bouncing up and down as Mum searched under the steering-wheel to locate the keyhole. She gestured at us to go indoors and when we didn't she opened the door and climbed out of the car and ordered us inside, saying we'd freeze, which was true. She looked so desperately sad, she couldn't hide it. We waved and Dad shut the door softly. We stood listening to Mum trying to start the car, usually a lengthy process. Craig ran to the toilet and Dad sat down on the sofa, and I thought about snow and about how if we were in a film, this would be the moment when the hero runs after the heroine – *now*, with it snowing outside (though the snow was pretty paltry if truth be told). Then I looked at Dad, who was looking at the gap between the curtains, a gap in which you could see only a reflection of a slice of living-room, but still you *knew* there was snow going on outside, and I entertained a possibility. I allowed myself to accept that Dad himself might be thinking the same

247

thought: *now is the time to go after her, now would be the time for action in any romantic motion picture worth its salt: now! With the snow coming down, damn you! What further sign do you need?* Dad looked towards the kitchen, forlornly, then at the coffee table; I felt suddenly embarrassed to be there. Because it was possible – wasn't it? – that I'd guessed what he was thinking. And later, days later, when I'd had time to fill out my hypothesis, other things occurred to me, such as: maybe my dad was actually a romantic like me, or like I was before God smote me with a rude picture and an amplifier and a bully; or like Craig once was, before that watershed incident with the love letter that got pinned to his bedroom door. Maybe Dad had started out as a romantic, but something had turned him. And maybe he did love Mum desperately, and *could* live happily with her, if only he'd stop acting so macho and just *speak* with her, which is all she ever wanted from us, and is what all three of us dumb Flack males should have learned to do years and years ago, instead of making Mum feel like a useless and invisible appendix in our house and driving her away.

And now Mum was leaving, and I thought about how she'd given us her news about seeing us every week, and I'd sat there feeling glum about disasters of my own making. Was anybody more selfish than me?

Outside, the car started and Mum kept the revs high, waiting until it was safe to drive off without fear of stalling. I went into the kitchen and softly lifted the bin lid, and looked at the baked bean cans, the variety pack cereal boxes, the food scraps that in Brendan's household would have ended up in the dog's bowl, and I lifted things carefully, peered about, and found what I had been almost certain was in there: a Valentine's card. I took it and went to the kitchen door and looked into the living-room. Dad was gazing at the television. I walked behind the sofa and opened the front door and mumbled to Dad, then walked outside and closed the front door and looked at Mum's rumbling car through the snowflakes, now becoming rain again.

I tapped on Mum's window and she wound it down. 'Dad didn't give you this,' I told her.

She didn't take the card from me. The envelope was covered in tomato sauce and the ink had run. Instead, she read the blue smudge. ' "To my randy woman"?'

'*Handy*woman,' I said. 'Like a handyman–'

'But female. I see.'

I realized that I was acting out the scene that my dad should have acted out. I was acting out my dad's romantic scene, with my own mother. It was an embarrassing thought, almost as embarrassing as handing my Mum a card covered in beans. I took it out of its envelope, and glanced briefly at the picture as I handed it to her. Flowers. I was dying of sadness.

Mum said, 'Thanks.'

I didn't ask her if she was going to read it. Instead, I said, 'When are you coming over next?'

Mum started crying. I put my hand through the window and she held my little finger. I looked up to see if Dad was watching our scene. He wasn't, but I did notice Craig in an upstairs window.

'This coming weekend, we'll all do something incredibly exciting,' Mum said. 'I don't know what, but it will be incredibly exciting.'

I said, 'I'm sorry I never told you I wrote poetry.'

Mum laughed and grabbed another finger to squeeze. Then, yielding to an urge to be honest, I said, 'It's mainly because I only started writing last week.'

Mum laughed more. 'I've been looking at some of the old photos of you and Craig,' she said, 'and you were definitely always a poet.'

She said she wondered why she'd never noticed it before. She squeezed my fingers and I grinned with pride, and then she let my fingers go and I waved as she drove away, and some cosmic director said that's a wrap, and Mum put her hand out of the window to wave, Hollywood snowflakes dropping one by one down her sleeve.

hand grenade

By Wednesday the 16th there was a more or less official story circulating, in which Brendan and I had lured Karen, Gillian and Adele back to Brendan's house, left the room and then returned with a shoebox or shopping bag full of pornography. It was also mentioned that I had some porn in my amplifier, adding an element of truth to this tale of mine and Brendan's endeavours to disturb the girls' gentle minds with X-rated grot. Basically, according to the story, Brendan's entire home was heaving with filth, which Brendan and I saw fit to dangle in Adele and Gillian and Karen's faces, leering, croaking *You like?* and laughing crazily. Actually, our mostly fictional exploits constituted precisely the kind of behaviour that would have been lauded if enacted by a bully (flinging porn at the prettiest girls in the school! Ha ha!) But when wimps did that sort of thing, it was a different matter.

Who'd spread the story? Karen was of course the chief suspect, but I wondered why there was no mention of the fact that the pornography in question was a picture I'd drawn myself and eaten one English lesson. I didn't think for one moment that Adele had spread the story, although she might have mentioned something to Gillian and Dean, who would have added the embellishments themselves.

Brendan, of course, wasn't talking to me. I had ruined his life. The task of apologizing to him, of enduring days or weeks of penance, intimidated me too much, so I didn't do it. I decided I wasn't going to grovel or beg for forgiveness. When Brendan was angry, he stayed angry until his system detoxified, and any admission of guilt or remorse on my part would just make him feel powerful, would go to his head, would make him want to draw out his rage.

So I resolved to lie low. Lying, apparently, was something I did well, sexily even, especially on floors. I tried to be invisible. Now that the idea that I had ever been a romantic made me feel embarrassed, now that I had flushed that image of myself out of my blood and bones, I felt clean and cold like scrubbed tin, and possessed of a new clarity. I decided that whenever I felt overly conspicuous sitting on my own, say at breaktimes, and could not find a neutral group to attach myself to, I would hide in the toilets, or go to the shops nearby and choose sweets.

I wondered whether Mum had felt this when

she'd first moved to her flat: the dark pleasure of finally giving up your hopes that someone will love you just the way you'd like them to; the liberation of resignation.

On Wednesday something astonishing happened. The girls of the second year at Denesgrove Secondary School started passing around a note:

WHO SENT ADELE COLLIER A VALENTINE
CARD
(IN A BLUE ENVELOPE)?
WRITE HERE NAMES IF YOU THINK YOU
KNOW.

There was also a question scribbled on the black-boards in two of the form-rooms:

WHO SENT VALENTINE TO ADELE C.?

I didn't see these scribblings. Apparently, under-neath one of these questions were written a few names, some of them comic suggestions like

MR LUND!

Also – I did not know it at the time, but girls had started gossiping in corridors. I later discovered that this gossiping had in fact started on Valentine's Day.

News of my mystery Valentine card soon spread to the boys of the second year, who didn't know how to respond to it. It was not the kind of thing that boys usually gossiped about. But this was not just a case of a mystery Valentine; it was a case of a mystery Valentine received by the most widely adored girl in the year. Boys wanted to know who their rival was. Some may have considered claiming it was them who sent it. All of them were wondering, *what's so interesting about the card Adele received?* This led to the next phase: the spreading of rumours concerning the specific qualities my card possessed. Depending on who you asked, my Valentine was:

- The most romantic card ever sent
- Really mysterious
- Brilliant

Nobody had actually mentioned poetry. Later, when I finally discovered that my card was famous, I chose to think that the terms 'romantic' and 'brilliant' etc. referred to my poem, rather than to the picture of strawberries on the front. Adele had apparently not divulged the precise nature of the card's content, which suggested to me that she was not sharing it with people, but was treasuring it in her heart.

(Of course it crossed my mind later that the card to which they were referring wasn't actually mine, that it was in fact someone else's. But I didn't take this possibility seriously. The note mentioned that the card was sent in a blue envelope. My card had been in a blue envelope. If anyone else had sent Adele a card in a blue envelope, surely the note that the girls passed around would have mentioned a different distinguishing characteristic? One thing I knew for sure from *Sweet Dreams* books was that when girls set their minds on reaching the bottom of a love mystery, they don't make a shoddy job of it.)

Earlier that morning I'd managed to encounter Adele in Drama. After the register was called, before being sent off with our Group Piece groups, we had a whole-class warm-up session, where we had to get into small groups and do humiliating physical things. I tried to stand near Brendan so I could wait till everyone had finished forming groups and then get put into his group by default: he looked pathetic and dejected and I wanted desperately to make up with him. But Brendan went with Martin and a boy called Chris, and soon everyone was in a group except me.

Somehow I knew that I was going to end up in the same group as Adele. It was all too easy: Miss Liptrot was walking towards me from the other side of the studio, and I was shuffling towards Adele, and the point where Miss Liptrot and I would meet was the point where Adele and the girl she was standing with, a girl of intellect called Teresa Shingler, would be the people nearest to me.

'Neil, get in a group,' called Miss Liptrot.

I looked at Adele, hoping she would invite me to join her group. She was standing on one hip, coughing into her hand. She appeared pained from the coughing. '*This* group?' I asked Miss Liptrot, pointing at Adele, who lowered her coughing-hand and regarded me with a sort of horror, as though she were a lobster I'd selected for my dinner in a seafood restaurant.

'Fine,' said Miss Liptrot. 'Chop chop!' She climbed the first amphitheatre step and issued the class instructions to form a machine with our bodies, making moving parts out of our limbs.

'Brendan's not in our group any more,' Adele told me in her clipped voice, slightly rough from a sore throat. She sniffed; I think she had a cold.

'Why?'

'I don't think him and Karen get on.'

I said, 'Those pictures were planted there.' Adele frowned at me. 'It was Karen who put them in the amplifier. She hates me.'

Teresa Shingler said, 'So what are we doing, then?'

Adele ignored her.

256

'Karen doesn't hate you,' Adele said. 'She definitely doesn't hate you.'

'Once, she attacked me.'

'Attacked you?'

Teresa Shingler was trying to win our attention: Miss Liptrot was talking, giving us more instructions.

'I didn't see Karen drawing the picture,' said Adele.

'She didn't draw it at Brendan's house,' I explained. 'She had it in her bag.'

Adele coughed, a tidy cough into her clenched hand. She looked at me, tired-eyed. 'Karen really likes you. Gillian says she's told people.'

I felt like I'd been stabbed. Karen liked me? 'She pushed me over once, and laughed at me!'

'It's because she likes you.'

It was too much to bear. But then I contemplated something even more unbearable: the Valentine, the one with the strawberries kissing, *was from Karen*. And when did she see me lying sexily on the floor? *When she pushed me over, last year, and laughed at me*. That wasn't Karen being a bully; that was Karen *flirting*. And why had she taken my rude picture from Father Wigman's bin and kept it with her? It was a *keepsake*. Did she have all of the pictures, including the one with Adele's name on it? Yes, presumably. Was she going to use them to avenge herself on me further?

'So if she likes me, why did she put that picture in my amplifier?' I asked Adele miserably, but I knew why: *Karen had realized, during the rendition of* 'Hound Dog'*, that I loved Adele, not her, and she'd wanted to make Adele hate me.*

Adele, beautiful Adele, narrowed her eyes at me. A month ago, a week ago – two days ago – I would never have imagined being this close to her, of being a person in her life; it was still thrilling, even if everything had gone dreadfully wrong. She looked at me and said, 'Did she really put the picture there?'

'I swear to God.' I held up my hand. 'I don't know why she did it, but she did.'

'Look, you two, we have to make a machine!' snapped Teresa.

'Some people do that sort of thing to people they really like,' Adele said. 'Try to hurt them on purpose.'

This struck me as slightly implausible, but then I thought of how Dad had accused Mum of staying away for a month just to make us miss her.

'Maybe to get their attention . . .' Adele mused, as though reading my thoughts.

The idea of being an object of unrequited love made my brain fizz. One would think I'd have felt a certain sympathy towards Karen, being an un-requited lover myself, but in fact I felt violated. I felt she had no right to be interested in me; our

258

incompatibility was so blatant, given our respective statuses as bully and wimp, that she must have been almost pathologically deluded not to have noticed it. It occurred to me that Adele might feel equally, or perhaps more, flabbergasted if she found out that she was *my* object of unrequited love. But no — Adele would at least understand why I loved her. But if Karen did love me, her love was clearly a kind of madness. I looked for her in the throng, and saw her standing silently, looking with great sadness at her dramatic partners as they struggled to find a way to resemble a motor.

'A *machine*!' Teresa said, chugging her arms. 'We have to make a machine!'

Too late; Miss Liptrot made us all sit down, then looked around the studio. She told one boy off for chewing, and then she told me off for sprawling. I wasn't used to being told off in Drama. I sat up. Then Miss Liptrot picked a group to perform their machine piece. They got up and made shapes, moving clumsily.

'She's going to pick us,' hissed Teresa. 'I know it.'

'She won't,' I said as the first group was told to sit down. Had I just cleared my name with Adele? Did she really believe I didn't draw that rude picture?

'Neil!'

It was Miss Liptrot. Teresa and Adele were on their feet, looking down at me. We had been picked to demonstrate our impression of a machine. I became animate and stood up. Adele, Teresa and I stared at each other, waiting for someone to do something. Tentatively, Teresa started to make her arms chug again. Adele and I looked at her like she'd gone insane. Then, swallowing any reserves of pride and dignity, Adele put a hand on Teresa's shoulder and started swinging her leg. I gazed in horror. Where should I put my hands? I couldn't think what to do, so I knelt on the floor by Adele's feet. Adele and Teresa were both moving rhythmically. I was just crouching there, motionless. I heard someone say something about me. I prayed for death.

'Do something,' whispered Adele.

I put my arm in the air, pulled an imaginary cord and made a noise that I hoped and imagined would sound like a train whistle, but which actually sounded like a violent fart. The entire room erupted with laughter. Sitting up, I let out a strangled laugh of my own, and accidentally spat on my own knee.

After the machinery warm-up was over, we got into our Group Piece groups. Brendan came over and joined ours: he didn't want to be with Gillian and Karen any more.

'So you're an item now,' Brendan said mockingly. 'Looks like your card paid off.' He laughed horridly. 'Looks like she doesn't mind people doing filthy pictures of her.'

I said, 'I cleared things with Adele.' I looked over

in the direction of her group, but instead caught the eye of Dean Millard, who was talking to Gillian. He pointed at me and mimed languorous self-abuse.

'You cleared things?' said Brendan snidely. 'My arse you did.'

But I *did* feel that I had cleared things, or had at least made real progress, and my recent misery was starting to feel a bit unfounded. Small hopes were beginning to stir in me, like sea monkeys. It occurred to me that Karen wouldn't tell Adele about stealing my rude picture, because then she'd have to admit that she planted it in my amplifier. Also, just because Karen loved me (a thought I could still not really process), there was no reason why Adele should not love me too. Perhaps Karen's ghastly affection for me would stimulate Adele's more refined affections. Maybe Adele would become jealous of Karen and they'd fight, and I would rescue Adele by flinging Karen from an open window! Hope was springing up; I felt a gentle wave of alteration pass through me.

Brendan didn't talk to me for the rest of the lesson, except in character: our Group Piece was going to be about the IRA, with Martin as an older brother who joins up. I didn't even know what the letters IRA stood for.

Martin had the good sense to wait until break, when Brendan was elsewhere, to notify me of the splash my Valentine had made. He walked over to

me with an amused expression as I sat on my own
on a workbench in CDT 1 reading *Sinclair User*.

'I just made a bit of a discovery,' he said, standing
over me. 'Something you might be interested in.'

father wigman

When confronted for the first time with the real possibility that somebody to whom you are intensely attracted has, or might develop, a real interest in you, it is like being created anew. So when Martin told me that my card, my poetic card, had affected Adele, had affected her so much that she wanted, perhaps needed, to know who sent it, it hit me very hard. My intuition at Brendan's — that I was right for Adele, and she for me — seemed woolly and ephemeral compared to this hard evidence. Now it really did seem as though my life was being manipulated by a mischievous but sympathetic deity; the Lord, having first decided to giveth to me and then to taketh away, had decided on a whim to giveth back again. I felt drugged, transformed, despite everything that had happened with Adele and the picture. Within minutes I was feeling so wildly euphoric that I wanted to run somewhere, or shout, or to phone Mum and talk about Adele, or just find

Adele and embrace her. Brendan was for the time being forgotten.

I went to the toilets, sat on a toilet seat in a cubicle and waved my hands around with happiness.

Initially, though, when Martin told me about the effect my card was having on a whole year-full of twelve- and thirteen-year-olds, part of me didn't believe him, even though most of me lurched straight away into chronic excitement. Martin was known for his deadpan humour, so it was hard to take him seriously; you were always expecting a joke. And because 2E4, our tutor group, was not exactly close to the throbbing heart of school life, was, rather, something of an appendix, or a patch of rough skin, there was no one readily available who could confirm his story.

Nevertheless, he explained that Adele was impressed by the card, and that her friends were wandering around trying to track down its sender. And there was a bit of paper floating around school, on which people were writing the names of boys who they thought might have sent the card. So, if I wanted Adele to know it was me, I would have to do something *now*, before the fuss blew over or someone else took the credit for my masterwork. In fact, Martin said, my name might already be on the bit of paper. But he didn't know who had it right now.

'You could ask someone,' he suggested.

'Who can I ask?' I looked eagerly around our tutor room.

'Liz and Abigail?'

'Will they know about the list?' I demanded.

Martin picked his nose. 'Probably.'

I couldn't think, I couldn't think. If I admitted to someone that I had sent the card, what would happen? Would they even believe me? Would Adele believe it was me? And if she did, would she just fall in love with me there and then? Or what?

Martin slapped my arm. 'Neil, I'm off. Well done. Speak to Liz and get yourself written down on that list of names.'

'Where? Where are you going?'

'I have to go to homework catch-up club.'

'What should I say to Liz and Abigail?'

'I don't know, do I? Just ask them if they've seen the list. Just do *something*.'

I let him go. Some worries bubbled up and then vanished. Brendan mattered briefly, then ceased mattering. I also worried briefly about Karen – not about her well-being, but about her coming over and punching my face in for trying to get Adele to think that she had drawn those rude pictures. Should I have mentioned Karen to Martin? I considered running after him and soliciting his advice on how to handle her. But before I could, my mind had returned to the more pressing matter of Adele, and my worries vanished, were drowned out. In fact I could not feel anything but wildly happy, because when I looked around everything was new. The future had changed. My young hormones knew that a portal had opened to a previously foreign, adult world, one that contained kisses and hand-holding and, yes, of course, in the distance, sex. A thin rope-bridge now connected the two sides of the chasm across which I'd spent so long staring.

I left the form-room in search of Liz and Abigail, the only girls I knew well enough to consider talking to about such sensitive issues as the contents of a list of would-be poets.

Problem.

Father Wigman nabbed me in the corridor. Worse, he nabbed me after shouting my name as I walked past the Graphics class-areas (cordoned off by large portable hinged carpeted screens) into which I was peering furtively, trying to spot Liz and Abigail while not being spotted by anyone myself. Worse still, Father Wigman shouted my name from afar, and in a tone that suggested that we were not teacher and pupil but were in fact golfing buddies. I noticed people staring.

Father Wigman loped towards me. He ran the way people run when they are too tired to run: without actually lifting his knees, all the motion taking place in his lower legs, which flicked backwards. When he stopped he looked concerned and exhausted.

'Do you have a minute, Neil?'

As a matter of fact I did not. 'Yes, sir.'

'Let's find somewhere.'

Let's find somewhere private, was what he meant.

We followed the corridor round a corner and then Father Wigman commandeered the office of the head of fourth year, Mr Bryant. It was minuscule. Mr Bryant was not in it.

Father Wigman sat on the desk, on some papers. This time he didn't invite me to sit down. There was no room; I would have had to pull out a drawer from the filing cabinet and get into it.

'Neil, I know you've got a lesson in a minute, so I won't see you now. But I'd like to book you to see me this week. I'll withdraw you for a half lesson. I'll put a note in the register that your tutor can give you in the morning. Or maybe at dinnertime. Okay? Right. It's just that I'm concerned. Since our talk – was it last week? – I've heard reports. Some people are worried. Or rather, I've heard complaints. From pupils. Actually, just the one in particular–'

My brain was having a hard time keeping up. *Who* exactly had been talking? Adele? Martin? Brendan? Karen? What was he talking about? The trouble with liberal teachers is they never just come right out and tell you that they think you're bad and need whipping into shape. They think they need to confront you with your own sins in as gentle a manner as possible, for fear that you might be engulfed by your own guilt and leap from an open window, which in my present case would have been pointless, as Mr Bryant's window was three feet above ground level.

Emboldened by recent events, I interrupted him. 'Sir, what have I done?'

He took a breath. 'Apparently you have been in possession of some objectionable material.'

I didn't even think to deny it. 'Who said that, sir?'

'Neil, I don't like to get into the issue of disclosing the names of those who've passed on a report to me until I have had the chance to ask you if you know anything about the issue and, if so, to hear your side of the story. You understand?'

'Well, no, sir.'

'You don't understand or you don't know anything about any objectionable material?'

'Um, understand.'

But of course I did understand: this was Karen's doing.

The bell went, and Father Wigman and I stared at each other. He didn't know whether to keep me from my lesson or defer the discussion until a later date. He was a by-the-books kind of person in many ways.

He sighed. 'I'll catch up with you tomorrow, Neil.'

'Sir, I've got you for English.'

'We'll arrange something. Probably at lunch. Okay? But until then I want you to think about this situation. Because it's serious.'

I wanted to go. Abigail was in my next lesson. 'Yes, sir.'

He got up off the table and all the papers that had stuck to his bum slid on to the floor with a shhhh! noise.

So that was that: I was officially in counselling.

En route to my next lesson I was busy planning what I would say to Abigail when I saw Gillian walking along with Karen and Crystelle Keane, and I had a panic attack.

Was I ready to come out of the closet right now and proclaim that I was Adele's poet? Someone like Dean Millard would have been ready – already handsome, popular, probably experienced with women. I was not prepared, not even close. I wasn't even sure how I should go about getting prepared. It struck me that I really needed Mum's advice. Or I needed to just sit in a room for three days and nights figuring out what first steps I should take into my new life with Adele. I wanted everything to be perfect. I also had to make absolutely sure she did not think I was a pervert.

There was of course the possibility that Adele would actually take her own life if she knew it was me who sent the card. She had, after all, been eager to tell me of Karen's interest in me, which suggested that she considered me the worthy consort of a she-bully. But now I knew for certain that the greatest things I had to offer – true romance and poetry – were, as I'd suspected and desperately hoped, precisely the things Adele was looking for. And although our meetings had been awkward and at moments horrific, I could not stop thinking back to Adele singing Elvis Presley in her sweet posh voice. The connection had been a romantic one. This much I knew instinctively.

One as inexperienced as I does not tumble head-long into one's destiny without first straightening one's collar, checking oneself in the mirror, taking a breath, steadying one's nerves and resolve, and getting one's plan firmly in focus. Adele and I, I reasoned, could bear to remain teetering on the edge of our romantic destiny for a day or two longer. Until after the weekend at the very latest.

This was Wednesday 16th February, two days before I told Adele, to her face, that I was her poet.

jigsaw theory

Thursday 17th February. Harry actually came up to me in school, something she had never done before, while I was on my way to my first counselling session with Father Wigman. It was bad timing, as Father Wigman deplored tardiness, but it was a nice surprise.

'Hey,' she said, approaching me in the Humanities block corridor. She did that stupid thing where you tap someone on one shoulder when you're actually at the other, except she wasn't at my other shoulder either, she had crouched down. She was agile, and thus well-suited to this brand of foolery. I turned around and looked down and saw her peering up at me.

'Oh, hi.'

'That dick brother of yours has asked Suzie out.'

'No.'

Harry said, 'I think so. I'm pretty sure. I've been watching him up in the sixth-form room.' Some sixth-formers walked past us, but none of them said hello to Harry. I wondered how many friends she had. I got the sad impression that Harry wasn't amazingly popular. I felt bad for her, but I also found myself thinking guiltily: I hope my brother doesn't humiliate himself in front of Suzie.

She leaned her head against the wall. I stood nervously next to her.

'People are looking,' I said.

'So?'

'Harry, please get your head off that wall.'

'God, he's obviously besotted with her. Fuck, I feel so stupid. I thought he was just using her.'

I waited a while, but she didn't move her head, so I said softly, 'Harry, sorry, but I have to go. I have to see a teacher and I'm late.'

She just leaned. Then she stood up straight and took a big breath, then stared woefully at the floor. 'Well, thanks for listening.'

On a whim, I asked, 'Shall I meet you after school?'

'What for?'

'To walk home. To talk. Forget it.'

'That would be nice.' I was about to walk away but she said, 'So, anyway, how are you? Did your parents sort things out?'

I told Harry about giving Mum a Valentine's card from my dad, in the snow. Harry frowned. 'And?'

'Well, nothing.'

'Did she open it?'

'Well, yes.'

'And was it for her?'

'For who?'

'For your mum?'

It hadn't occurred to me that it might have been for anyone other than my mum. I stared at Harry. 'Of course it was for her.'

'Ah, good. And she liked it?'

'I think so,' I said, starting to suspect that I had made a hideous error of judgement.

'Have you spoken to her since?'

'Yes,' I lied, awash with panic. 'She's coming over again soon.' How could I have been so brainless? Harry put her head in her hands. 'At least someone's happy. I'm fucking everything up.'

'No you're not,' I said, trying to reactivate my sympathy.

'Craig saw me looking at him and Suzie, and now he knows what a complete fucking drip I am.'

I said, 'Me too.'

'I act like I'm cynical, but I'm a complete eleven-year-old girl. Sometimes all I really want is to get married and wear dresses.'

I said, 'You don't have to get married to wear dresses.'

'Sometimes I sit down and read the same stupid girl books I read when I was ten.'

'I know,' I confessed. 'I'm the one who keeps borrowing them.'

She looked up at me with a confused frown. Then she half-smiled. Then the frown came back, much sterner this time. 'Fuck, you're serious.'

I realized that in my eagerness to provide her with a feeling of not being alone in her sappiness, I had just admitted to invading her privacy and raiding her pine cabinet.

'You little snot,' she said.

Ordinarily, in the face of being condemned by someone, I'd have launched into protestations of innocence, mainly because I genuinely did believe that most of the time I was innocent of anything bad. I never really considered myself substantial enough to be bad. Now I knew I was bad. I just stood there.

'This is a humiliating moment,' said Harry. 'I feel I should end it by leaving.'

She pushed past me, leaving me to marvel grimly at the way fortunes and situations change so quickly, just like that, sometimes several times in the space of a school breaktime.

I would have stood there fretting and biting my nails, but there was no time. Elsewhere in the school, a monk was waiting for me.

This week on *Oprah*: Pervert Teen Poets In Counselling. Meet Neil – tardy boy poet, sexual deviant, thief of girls' literature.

I ran to Father Wigman's counselling room with six minutes until the bell.

Was this an auspicious preamble to my career as Adele's boyfriend – having two secret personas, poetic Scarlet Pimpernel and porn fiend getting professional help? Was there a precedent in the world of literature? Was I setting it?

I was still dizzy with guilt from the episode with Harry.

Father Wigman's counselling room was like a cupboard with a window. Underneath the window, two soft chairs were squashed shoulder-to-shoulder. On the right-hand side of the room was a desk, on which sat a sloping row of ring binders detailing various professional codes of practice. Then there was another chair. The walls were covered with posters advertising telephone helplines, coded with symbols to show whether they were free, local rate or expensive. Behind the door was a giant poster of Shaun, A Homeless Boy, looking suitably bereft of abode as he hovered next to his lengthy life story. It was impossible to move around the room for all the furnishings, let alone hurl things in juvenile rage. I also noticed an upbeat poster advertising emergency contraception, with four small pictures of women of different races laughing, or talking excitedly with friends, beside the blurb. I didn't know what emergency contraception was, but it looked like it encouraged happiness and sociability.

Luckily Father Wigman took my apology well. I told him that I had bumped into my brother, who was upset because of a family crisis. I was quite a good liar.

'Well, we haven't much time, so we'll get started,' said Father Wigman in his gentle monotone. He was sitting on the desk. His eyes looked tired to the point of lifelessness. He gestured for me to sit on one of the spongy chairs under the window. I had a daffodil behind my head, on the windowsill.

'When I last spoke to you,' he said, referring to that day I ate the poem, 'I gave you something to think about.'

'Yes, sir.'

'Do you remember what that was?'

Something about lust? 'Lust, sir?'

Father Wigman was in his element. 'Well, I didn't ask you to think about lust, not in the sense of, you know, thinking about lust. I asked you to think, rather, about the girl in the drawing. I mean, to consider her as a person.'

There was so much I could have said in my defence that I found it hard to say anything at all. 'Sir, that time in your lesson, I wasn't drawing anyone.'

'I don't understand you, Neil.'

'Sir, I know that I wrote a name on the paper, but it wasn't anything to do with the picture.'

'It seems a bit of a coincidence, Neil. You have to admit that it all seems iffy.'

276

Iffy? 'Sir, I wasn't drawing anyone in particular. It didn't even look like her, sir.'

'Well, accuracy isn't really the issue, is it?'

'I don't know what I was thinking, sir.'

He picked up his notepad, a tiny thing with a small biro stuck in the spiral wire binding. 'You didn't know what you were doing? When you drew the picture?'

'Sir, I don't get why I'm here. Is it because of the picture?'

He put the pad down again. As long as he wasn't actively using it, I felt I hadn't yet raised any major psychotherapeutic red flags. 'Neil, is everything all right at home?'

'Fine,' I said, not wanting to go into details.

Father Wigman picked up his pad and manipulated the pages. He made a chewing motion that I assumed was supposed to mean something. Then he looked at me, leaning forward as he did so, leaning into his look, getting his weight behind it. 'Let me ask you straight out. Have you been using rude pictures to upset any girls?'

'What? Who said that?'

'Please, Neil, just say yes or no and we can take it from there.'

'No, sir, nothing like that. Sir, who said that I had done anything?' If it was Adele I would die. But – it wasn't Adele, was it? It was bloody Karen, and this was part of her ongoing project of getting revenge on

277

me for ignoring her. Saints akimbo, I was a plank. God knows what she had told Father Wigman. Using pictures to upset girls? Oh, Lord.

'Until I've established how much truth is in the claim – because, Neil, there usually is some truth in every claim, isn't there? – until then, I don't feel it would be entirely right to name the person who made the complaint, who is quite possibly very upset and scared–'

Karen scared? 'Sir, this is all a lie. Someone is trying to get back at me for something.'

'You're saying that these claims have absolutely no ground in reality?'

'No, they don't. I mean, yes, that's what I'm saying.'

He sort of chuckled. 'But, Neil, you see, from my point of view, I have no choice but to be of the mind that there are, in a way, already grounds for believing these claims, you see? Because it wouldn't be the first time that you behaved this way, you see where I'm coming from? So you see the position I'm in? It's simply not proper for me to give you the benefit of the doubt, right off the bat, and to send you on your way. It's a very delicate situation, Neil, and you have to consider how this looks from the outside.'

I protested, possibly too much, and Father Wigman sat watching me as though any second now I was about to slip up and give myself away, or break down and confess, like they do in *Columbo*, although they usually also pull a gun.

The bell went.

'We haven't made headway, have we?' Father Wigman asked. I opened my mouth and shut it and shook my head in a disbelieving way. 'Neil, we need to get to the bottom of this. I want you to understand that this isn't a disciplinary action. I feel there is something going on, and I'm concerned. Okay? That's all. You aren't being punished. But I'd like you to come back and see me, perhaps on a weekly basis, until we've sorted out whatever is going on, okay? Because that's what I'm here for. I know I'm also your English teacher, but people have to wear different hats, don't they?'

'Yes, sir. But I have to go. We've got a test.'

As I left, Father Wigman opened his pad and removed the pen from the spirals. I lingered outside the door, looking through the crack, to see if he was going to write something, but he didn't.

But as soon as I left the room I wanted to be back in it. Suddenly I wanted to argue my case. I poked my head round the door. Father Wigman looked at me.

'Sir,' I said, 'are you in here at lunch?'

He thought about it, wondering, perhaps, why I was asking.

'Yes,' he decided.

'Can I come here at lunch break?' I inquired. 'I have to ask you something.'

* * *

At lunch break Father Wigman sat at the desk eating a ham salad baguette and I sat in one of the soft chairs nibbling a blueberry muffin I'd bought from the canteen. I wanted to drink my orange-flavoured Calypso, as my mouth was dry, but every time you took a slurp of Calypso through your straw the resultant vacuum caused the plastic cup-shaped container to collapse on itself, and then when you stopped drinking it re-inflated, making a sound like the last of the bathwater going down the drain, or a very small toilet flushing, which wasn't something I wanted to inflict on Father Wigman. I tried to settle into the chair. 'Sir, I have to ask you a question.'

'Go ahead,' Father Wigman said.

'But, sir, I need you to sort of pretend to believe me about something.'

'Pretend to believe you?'

'Sir, I wrote Adele's name on the bit of paper in your lesson because I wanted to write her a poem.'

'A poem?'

'Those rude drawings, that you said weren't accurate, well, I don't usually do drawings like that. And also, I got a Valentine's card. From a girl. But I accidentally upset her, and I think she's the one who told on me. For revenge.'

Father Wigman was looking confused.

'And,' I continued, 'the stuff she said probably was based on something that really happened, but it wasn't anything to do with me, not really, and if you want you can ask Adele. She'll tell you.'

'Ask Adele? To vouch for you?' He sounded surprised.

'Well, whatever, sir, it's really complicated, but it's okay if you don't believe me, because what I wanted to ask was – well, if you *did* believe all this was true, then, well – actually, I need to say something else first.'

'First?'

'Right, I sent Adele a Valentine's card, with a poem, sort of based on that one by e.e. cummings.' I looked up at Father Wigman to see if he was thrilled and impressed. 'Anyway, now Adele wants to know who sent it. But I think my friends will be angry if I tell her it was me.'

'Of course they won't,' said Father Wigman.

'Because they think I'd be deserting them,' I explained. 'Because I'm doing everything without them.' I wanted to mention Harry, and my theft of her books, but I stopped myself. I couldn't even remember what it was that I came here to ask him. Perhaps there hadn't been anything. I just wanted to explain to someone everything that was going on, and also to try to shed this stupid image that Father Wigman had of me as some kind of pervert, and also to put everything into words to clarify it in my mind, and maybe get some feedback on—

Who was I kidding? I had become one of those

people who is desperate to just sit and talk to anyone, even their English teacher.

'So, Neil, let's say I believe you. Okay? What do you want to ask me?'

I slumped. 'I don't know, sir. I just don't want to have counselling.'

'But you can't run away from issues.'

'*Sir*, what I mean is . . . okay, here's what I want to ask. There's a list going around where – no, forget it, that's not it. It's just, I don't know–' What on earth was I doing here? Even the dining-hall, with its boisterous queues and lonely tables, was better than this.

Father Wigman leaned forward. 'Neil,' he said. 'Neil, stop panicking. Listen, I believe you. Okay? Does that help?'

I slumped back in my chair, surprisingly relieved. 'Really? Yes, thanks, sir.'

He leaned forward and peered at me. I held my breath. He said, 'In the very moment after you tell someone you believe him, you can usually see whether he told you the truth.' He sat back in his seat and folded his hands around his notebook.

'So did I?' I asked.

He laughed. 'Hopefully you already know the answer to that one.'

'Then, yes, sir, definitely. I am telling the truth.'

He laughed more, then grew solemn again. 'Something is obviously weighing on you, though.'

'But it's not, you know, lust, sir.'

'Okay, fine. Let me ask you some things.'

'Right.'

'You're in love with someone?'

Before I could help myself, I said: 'Yes, sir, Adele.'

I blushed. Father Wigman was trying to keep everything impersonal and I was ruining it. He waved his hand, welcoming into the forum my apparent eagerness to share detail. 'Okay, you're in love with Adele. And you keep getting into trouble.'

'Yes, sir.'

'And you wrote her a poem?'

'Based on e.e. cummings, sir. I've been reading poetry.'

'Excellent!'

'So—'

'So you want advice about love.'

I blushed again, violently. Was that why I had come here? To ask a monk about love? That was too disgusting for words. I cleared my throat loudly. 'Sir, I just don't want to be in counselling.' He looked at me with a kind of benevolent but amused look that made me feel foolish, like a foolish person who is asking his English teacher to explain love. 'I don't want to be treated like that kind of person, someone who needs help, because of a problem with lust, when I'm not that kind of person.'

He nodded and sighed. 'Neil, I'll tell you what I

283

think I know about romantic love, but bear in mind it will be coming from a different angle to your own.'

I put my head in my hands with horror. But I said, 'Okay.'

He waited for me to look up at him. Then he sighed and held up one hand and looked at it. 'When somebody meets someone who is truly right for them, it is always a miracle. And you cannot make miracles happen just through your own efforts. They are always a divine gift.'

'Okay,' I said. So far, so vague.

'And I think real love always involves divine grace. I don't think that God's grace is something that can only manifest in Christians. But I do believe that the only kind of romantic love that ever survives and blossoms is that which is infused with grace. Grace only exists where something is given for free, without charge. Grace is not like seduction, not like the kind of giving that you do when you want something in return, or when you feel attracted to someone and find yourself giddy and generous, just because you feel the pleasure of their company, and you suddenly become a giving person because you want to purchase more of the person's time and attention. Do you see? If you are in love with someone you must bear in mind that if you and she are truly meant for each other, it will not happen by force, because it is a miracle, and only God does miracles. So you must be gracious and have faith and not be afraid to give the other person every chance to reject you. You must not try to cover her eyes, as it were, and blind her to what you see as reasons not to love you. You must not be afraid to get things wrong, or say the wrong thing, or appear silly. Do you see?'

Yes, I saw. It smacked of romantic suicide. Father Wigman bent down and opened the desk cupboard and pulled something out and plonked it on the desk. It was a board with jigsaw pieces on it.

'My old spiritual director gave me this. It's just an ordinary jigsaw, nothing special. See?'

I looked at it.

'Now, Neil. Your situation is quite a mess. Yes?'

'Um, yes sir.'

He held up a jigsaw piece. 'Look at that. What do you see?'

It was just colours. 'Just colours?' I said.

'It's also a bit of a mess, isn't it?'

I nodded.

'Certainly not a recognizable picture. And look at these curvy bits sticking out of the side of the piece.' I looked. 'Untidy edges. They stop it from fitting with any piece other than those it was made to fit with. See?'

'Yes, sir.'

'Now, if I really wanted to make it fit with, say, this piece–' he picked up another jigsaw piece and

tried to make them fit together, which they didn't
'– then what would I have to do?'

'Um, you could squash it in really hard.'

Father Wigman laughed. 'True, I could just squish
them together, ruining them both in the process. Or
I could cut off these knobbly bits, make the edges
nice and straight and uniform. Then I could paint
over both pieces with the same colour.'

'Yes, sir.'

'Now. Do you know how sometimes you speak to
someone and you just don't get on? It's a real effort,
and everything you say sounds silly?'

'Yes, sir.'

'And you try your hardest to come up with interesting things to say?'

'Yes, sir.'

'It's because you're trying to fit with someone you
don't really fit with. And sometimes when people
don't get on, they start to *hate* each other, because
when they try to speak to each other they feel boring
and misunderstood, and all their jokes fall flat.
Really they're just hating who they are when they
are with that person. But jigsaw pieces don't hate
each other, do they? Of course not! When they
don't fit, they accept it, they are polite about it, but
they also accept that they all belong in the same
picture, and one day – this is of course where faith
comes in – one day the picture will be whole, complete, and you won't be able to see the joins between

the pieces. We'll *all* belong to the same picture, indivisible, all at peace with one another yet each retaining our uniqueness, just as the pieces in a puzzle remain individual.'

What did this have to do with Adele?

He continued. 'You don't have to force yourself to be liked, or to like people. Do you have any friends whose company you really enjoy?'

'One,' I said. I meant Brendan. 'Maybe two.' I meant Harry. 'But they both hate me at the moment.'

'But at times when you've been able to get along, Neil, do you ever need to plan what you are going to say to them? Do you have to put on an act? Is it an effort to laugh with them?'

'Not really. No.'

'So that means you fit together. Right now your place is next to them. The jigsaw analogy isn't exact; in real life the jigsaw evolves . . . But how about Adele? Is it easy to get on with Adele?'

'Sir, I think we fit.'

'Time will tell, Neil. But if you try to force yourself to fit next to her, but in fact you *don't* belong together, then eventually you will hurt her, because not only will you have to cut yourself into shape, you'll also have to turn the scissors on her, if you see what I mean. And if you keep trying to fit in different places on the jigsaw, you will always provoke anger and resentment in the pieces you were *meant* to fit with. Yes?'

'Yes.' When I heard the words anger and resentment I thought suddenly of how my dad would feel when he discovered I had tried to squash him and Mum together by giving her his Valentine.

'Accept it, Neil: we are all a mess! Some of us try to paint over our jigsaw pieces, don't we? *Most* of us do, in fact. We paint complete, miniature pictures on them, so that they will look *whole* and *complete* and *well-rounded* and we won't need anyone else. But we will continue to be messy until the jigsaw puzzle gets finished. You have to submit to the hand that moves the pieces. Do you know what I mean?'

'The hand of God, sir?'

He patted his thighs and stood up. 'Well said.'

It was finished. 'I think me and Adele fit, sir,' I said again.

'Maybe you do,' said Father Wigman, and I almost vocalized my happiness with some sort of cry.

'Thanks, sir,' I said, suddenly embarrassed.

Father Wigman didn't answer, he just waved his hand as though to waft me, odour-like, out of the office. The session was over and he had more important matters to turn to. But I could see that he was struggling to suppress the outward appearance of a deep professional satisfaction. It was the first time I'd ever seen Father Wigman look as though he believed he'd managed to say precisely the right thing.

dregs of anonymity

After school on Thursday I lay on my bed and fretted about having ruined my parents' marriage.

Mainly I was worried about what Dad would say and do to me when he found out that I had given Mum his card, a card probably written for some floozy at the fleet hire company. I tried to convince myself that the card was for Mum, but there are some things a boy just knows. Craig would not be happy with me either. Why hadn't Mum phoned? Perhaps she was too upset to call. I wondered if I should phone her. And say what? That I'd written the card myself? That it was a joke?

Downstairs, the phone rang. I went to the top of the stairs. The call was taken by my dad, who shouted up to me that a girl was on the line.

I went down and took the receiver. 'Keep the bastard books,' a miserable voice said. 'Just help me with this Suzie and Craig thing.'

'Harry?'

'Yes. Hello. Wait. That *is* Neil, isn't it?'

'Yes.' There was a pause. 'I'm really sorry about the books.'

'Thieving shit,' she said. 'I'm too depressed to be as angry as the situation demands. Help me slander Suzie and turn your brother against her.'

'I'll try,' I said.

'I was going to hang up if Craig answered.'

'He never answers the phone. It would mean moving.'

She asked me whether I'd got into trouble for turning up late to see Father Wigman.

'No, he was okay,' I said. 'I told him about Adele.'

'Did he give you advice?'

'Sort of.'

'What did he say?'

'It was religious advice.'

'Religious seduction advice? That sounds suspicious.'

'Some of what he said was good. Like you shouldn't push things.'

'Hmm. Neil, my advice is: spend the whole weekend reading those stupid books you stole off me, you little shit, then get yourself fired up and roar into school on Monday and tell your girl that you hoped she liked her poem, then – just smile and walk away! If someone did that for me, I'd definitely react.'

'You mean if *Craig* did it.'

'Oh, sure. Like Craig would actually write a poem.'

'What if my teacher was right, and you shouldn't push these things?'

Harry went quiet for a moment. 'Are you talking about you and this girl, or me and Craig?'

'Neither,' I said. 'Or both, or whatever.' I told her about the jigsaw pieces not fitting, and how you shouldn't just paint them and cut bits off them. It was a hard theory to explain, and Harry didn't let me finish.

'Neil, that's a completely *stupid* theory,' she said. 'I mean, fine, yes, it sounds all well and good, and yes, it's obvious that we should only fall for people who we know fancy us already, and blah, and blah, but who in the name of shit is supposed to actually live like that? You can't control how you act with someone you're crazy about!'

'But maybe we should,' I said.

'So you're telling me that if you were to realize that you and this girl, Adele, don't just *fit together naturally*, you'd be ready to give up and shrug your shoulders and walk away?'

'Well, maybe. I don't know.'

'Fucking bollocks, Neil! Even if you knew there was a dirty great ninety-nine-point-nine per cent chance that she thought you were sheer *snot*, you'd still have some sort of hope that one day she'll come to her senses. Bloody hell! I thought you were romantic! That jigsaw stuff isn't romantic! It's like science!'

291

'But my teacher thinks that there's one person for everyone,' I said. 'But most people don't find their person because they've, you know, done things to their jigsaw pieces.'

'Oh, fine,' snapped Harry. 'Go into school on Monday and stand near Adele for a few seconds, and see if your jigsaw pieces suddenly fit together, and if they don't, then go ahead and abandon her for ever and go through the whole female population of earth until you slot into place. Okay? How fucking poetic! Avoid heartbreak by becoming a jigsaw piece. Oh, and while you're at it, give Craig my blessing, and wish him happiness with that horse-faced rump-fed hag, because she's obviously closer to him on the love jigsaw than I am, even though I've known him for eight bloody years. God, Neil!'

'Harry, forget it, you're right.'

'You're completely bloody right I'm right! Don't tell me I'm right! Just be a friend.'

This struck me as a weird thing to say.

'Okay,' I said.

'Romantics should stick together,' she said.

That evening, in an attempt to do something nice for Harry, I decided to tell Craig that I thought he should ditch Suzie and go out with Harry instead.

'Why would I do that?' Craig asked. We were in the lounge, watching a cowboy film while Dad rustled up steaks for dinner. Craig was still excited because Suzie Winstanley had agreed to go out with him next week sometime, to the pictures and the pub, and had virtually guaranteed him some sort of opportunity for groping.

'Well,' I said, 'because Harry's not a hooker.'

'Exactly! She's a friend.'

'But it's obvious that, you know—'

'No, what?'

'That you should go out with each other. She obviously likes you. You obviously still like her.'

'Still? What do you mean, still?'

'From when you went out with her before.'

The hero on television leapt behind a rock. Craig said, 'I was ten. We were ten. *Ten*. We were, you know, playing at boyfriends and girlfriends. Just like when you were eight and you and that albino girl with the blue NHS spectacles told Mum you were going to get married.'

'Shut up.'

Craig looked at me. 'I don't want to go out with Harry.'

'Why not?' I demanded.

'Well, for a start, um, I just *don't*. You don't need a reason not to want to go out with someone.'

'But you're virtually the same person.'

'Who wants to go out with themselves? Just carry a mirror. Me and Harry just get off.'

'Get off?'

'Neil, do I have to explain everything to you?'

'Get off?'

He waved his hand at me. 'Oh, *sod* off.'

Dad walked into the lounge with an apron on. 'What's happened?' he asked.

'Neil wants me to go out with Harry.'

Dad gave me a murderous look, then I think he realized I was talking about Ariadne, not some boy. He laughed loudly. 'Good idea. But, anyway, I meant in the film.'

'The guy has been taken prisoner.'

We had dinner in the lounge, as a treat. Craig was in love, I could tell. He laughed at the bit in the film where the hero's friend was rolled to death by a crocodile. Dad and I exchanged looks over our steaks, and I considered confessing to Dad that I'd potentially wrecked his relationship with Mum by fishing his card out of the bin, but I was not sufficiently daring; as long as there remained a possibility that I might not get found out, my general policy was to admit nothing. Dad gave me a concerned look and I realized there was terror all over my face.

After dinner someone knocked on the door and Dad answered. It was Harry, with whom Craig apparently got off. All of a sudden I wasn't sure what to think of her. Why had she been pretending to me she was fawning after him, when all along she and him had been in a sort of relationship?

Or didn't getting off count as a relationship?

Harry asked Dad if Craig was in. Craig came downstairs and Harry came in and they sat in the lounge. I sat at the top of the stairs, listening, because I was terrified that Craig would confront Harry with what I'd told him earlier. They were talking quietly; I could only pick out odd words. Then Harry said, 'Oh, Craig, get Neil for me.'

'Neil?' Craig seemed suspicious. Perhaps he thought that I was going to come downstairs with a vicar and some witnesses and we were all going to force Craig into marriage. He came to the bottom of the stairs and looked up. By now I was hiding round the corner but I think he saw my foot. 'He's lurking up here,' he told Harry.

I came down. Harry said, 'I need to talk to you about Brendan.'

Craig looked sceptical.

Harry and I went into the kitchen. 'Is he okay?' I asked.

'Well, I'm sorry to say it, but no. Brendan is dead.'

'You're kidding!'

'Of course I am, you retard,' she said. She appeared to have reverted to her normal self after yesterday's emotionalism. 'Have you two fallen out?'

I said, 'Kind of.'

'He doesn't look happy.'

'I know.'

'Are you going to get it sorted out?'

'Yes,' I said.

'Okay, that's all I wanted to know. I won't pry. Anyway, we're going out, me and Craig.'

'You *are*?' I was astonished.

'No, I mean, we're going to the shops, then to the library. Listen, did you say anything to Craig about Suzie Winstanley?'

'I said she's a dirty hooker.'

'Good, good.'

'But, trouble is, I think that's what he's looking for in a girl.'

Harry looked thoughtful.

I said, 'No! Don't become a dirty hooker.' But I thought: if she was getting off with Craig (whatever that was supposed to entail), but not going out with him, then were she and Craig not dirty hookers both?

'I may have to,' she said. 'Next week I might buy a tight T-shirt and a PVC miniskirt. It's worth a try.'

This made me blush. Harry noticed and laughed horribly. 'Would I suit crotchless leggings?' she asked. She laughed harder when she saw me try to hide my face.

'What are you two cackling about?' Craig shouted.

Harry sang back, 'Coming.' She said to me, 'Wait till we're gone. Then look in the bushes next to the fence.' She looked out of the window. 'Shit. Do it quickly. It's starting to rain.'

After Craig and Harry left, I went into the front garden and stood in the drizzle and looked in the bushes. There I found a slightly damp white cardboard box bound with masking tape. I took it inside and opened it and found the remainder of Harry's collection of romantic novels.

Night-time. Mum still hadn't rung. I wondered if Dad had noticed that the card was missing from the bin, but had not yet connected its absence with his sneaky thieving youngest son. At eleven in the evening I decided that Mum was not going to phone tonight, and what with it being school the next day, with its attendant horrors, my worry mechanism short-circuited and I filled with an unsettling kind of calm.

Lying in bed I found myself thinking about Harry and my brother. It really had never occurred to me that intelligent and sensitive people embarked on sexual relationships in the hope that they would evolve into love affairs. The logic seemed skewed. Sex seemed to me such a potentially humiliating thing that I could not imagine engaging in it with anyone who had not previously made an adamantine commitment not to dump me if I proved clueless and uncoordinated on my first few hundred attempts at it. A person, that is, who already loved me.

But if Harry and Craig were close friends, and also

got off, why was she so unhappy? The way I saw it, Harry had pretty much what she wanted: a *de facto* boyfriend – girlfriend relationship. It strained my mental powers to see exactly what Harry was so miserable about; I would have given a kidney to be Adele's virtual boyfriend.

Wide awake, with nothing else to do, I picked a good book from Harry's collection and started to read it, in her honour.

I didn't know it just then, but I had reached the end of my last day as Adele's secret admirer.

mystery poet revealed

Friday the 18th.

Brendan and I hadn't hidden behind our tree for a while now, and I missed it. I considered calling for Brendan early in the morning and asking if he wanted to spy on girls, but I decided against it. Acting like a pervert is okay so long as you have not in fact achieved infamy throughout school by being a pervert, but this was no longer the case with Brendan and me.

But I was ready for school early on Friday because, having guessed correctly that Craig would spend all morning in the bathroom making himself look dapper for Suzie, I got up at some stupidly small hour and ended up with time on my hands. Also, my leg was feeling better, enabling me to get ready for school with more speed and less stumbling. So I called for Brendan and let him set the agenda. Since I'd told Adele that Karen had planted that picture in my amplifier, the stories of Brendan's perversion were beginning to die down, at least enough to allow him to speak to me a bit.

It became sunny and damp, a nice morning. Brendan and I walked along the cycle path, then crossed a field to the bench beside the lake that the second cycle path passes, and sat waiting for the day to begin properly. We were invisible to passers-by, except for people walking their dogs, because the bench was round the side of the lake that you only got to if you walked through about a mile of mud, which we were more than happy to do. We were beneath the droopy branches of a willow, right next to the lakeside. This little grotto was another of our discoveries. In a year or so, it would be taken over by sixth-formers, who would use it for smoking and littering.

Going to the grotto on Friday morning was Brendan's idea. I think he had started to meet Martin there before school. Martin turned up after about ten minutes, and seemed surprised to see me.

None of us talked about girls. Instead, we talked with great animation about what it would be like to be tree dwellers who cannibalize passers-by. There were, of course, certain people we would not eat, on grounds of ethics and culinary preference. Then we talked about our Drama piece, and how it would be funny if Paul Thorpe somehow managed to get his goolies squashed during the staging of the play, despite his best efforts to keep away from all potential danger. We discussed ways in which we could theoretically make this happen.

A swarm of gnats came over to me and started flitting around my head. One wandered over to Brendan and flew in his mouth. Brendan started hacking and we all laughed like fools. Then I moved to the other end of the bench, but the gnats followed me, bypassing Brendan and Martin.

'That's freaky shit,' said Brendan. 'They like you.'

'Don't flies hang around dead people and turd?' asked Martin.

I said, 'No, but I do.'

'Good one,' said Martin, which made me feel mature.

Brendan said, 'Imagine if you were sitting somewhere trying to be smooth, and people were going past, and you were in this cloud of flies, and you kept moving, but they kept following you, like you were a moving bit of crap.'

'They just want some manly company, these flies,' I said.

'It's not their lucky day, then,' said Martin.

'Those flies are *gay*, Neil,' warned Brendan.

'Fruit flies,' I said. The flies went over to Brendan. Martin and I laughed at him without mercy.

'They heard you mention gayness,' said Martin. 'They seek their own, those gay flies.'

We were totally happy.

* * *

Karen came up to me before registration, as we milled around the CDT block waiting for Mr Lund to open the doors to the workshops. He was never on time. I saw Karen approaching and turned away and tried to occupy myself with my school bag.

'Neil.'

Terrified, I attempted to maintain the pretence of being interested in the zip. I ventured a glance at her, mostly out of politeness; she may have been the person who got me put in therapy, but I was her Valentine, and she was standing right in front of me, and I wasn't daring enough to pretend she wasn't there. It occurred to me that she might get rough. But she smiled at me, a pleasant enough smile. She was surprisingly nice-looking when she smiled. The smile broke down all of my fears and I said the first pleasant thing I could think of, which happened to be, 'The card was really nice.'

'What card?' She was grinning now.

'Oh, sorry, forget it,' I said.

'You fancy Adele, don't you?' I frowned at her and tried to think. 'You'd might as well admit it,' she said casually, inspecting her fingernails. 'And you sent her that card. It's really obvious. I figured it out at your friend's house. It's fine.'

I didn't know what to say. I suspected a trap of some sort, but I couldn't figure out what that might entail.

'Sorry about Father Wigman,' she said. Then she

302

laughed, implying she wasn't sorry at all. 'He caught me with one of those other pictures. He caught me throwing them into the skip at the back of the Science block at break. I told him you'd planted them in my bag and I was trying to get rid of them. Ha!'

I said, 'That's okay.' I didn't know what else to say.

'Those pictures were hilarious. But I thought when you did one of Adele with massive tits and crossed eyes you were taking the piss out of her.'

'It wasn't meant to be a picture of Adele.'

'I thought they were funny, because the picture had massive tits, but Adele's like a twig ... I thought you didn't like her because you thought your friend Brendan had joined our Drama group because of her. God, I am a fucking idiot!'

'No you're not.' I felt really bad.

'You know that Dean fancies her as well, don't you?' Karen asked, her voice getting spiteful. 'You realize if I'd shown anyone the picture with Adele's name on it, he'd have kicked the shit out of you.'

I wanted to know why she'd stolen the pictures in the first place. But she'd only done exactly what I'd have done in her situation. If Adele had left pictures in a school bin, I would not have rested until they were in my possession. I said, 'I thought Dean fancied Gillian?'

'Ooh! Look who's all interested in who fancies

who!' She laughed and wiped her nose unself-consciously on her hand.

I said, 'Does Adele know?'

'That Dean fancies her? Probably. I think she likes him. I bet she does.'

This hurt horribly. 'I meant, does she know about the Valentine?'

'The one you sent? You mean, does she know you sent it?'

I didn't answer; I was pretty certain she was just trying to get me to admit to sending the card. She was probably Adele's agent, sent to extract a confession. I blushed, which virtually equalled an admission of guilt. Karen said that Adele didn't know who the card was from, and said that she hadn't shown it to anyone. 'She *wants* to know, though,' she added.

I asked, 'Are you going to tell her?'

'Look, what I wanted to tell you is that Dean said something about how if no one admits to sending the card to Adele by breaktime today, he's going to say it was from him, to see what happens, you know? Because he thinks it would be a waste if no one owns up. So I thought you should know what he's up to.'

'He can't do that! That's really unfair!'

'So just tell her it was you.'

I fretted. 'Can't you tell her?'

'Fuck off, Neil. Don't use me to set you up with Adele.'

304

Just then Karen saw Dean standing outside his tutor room, and she shouted over to him. He stopped and looked round comically, then spied her and broke into a big grin. Then he saw me and grinned even more. He came over.

'Marshall Man,' he said to me, an obscure phrase which I later realized was a reference to the brand name of my amplifier.

'Wotcha,' I said.

'Neil sent that Valentine to Adele,' Karen told him.

Dean didn't look surprised. He nodded slowly. 'Ah. Thought so. You stare at her too much.'

'I never said it was me!' I objected.

Dean leaned against the wall and laughed softly. 'Oh, right,' he said. 'So it could've been anyone. Could've been me.'

Karen said to Dean, 'I told him you were going to say it was you.'

'It would be *well* funny. I bet you anything I could make her believe me.' He turned to me. 'What was in the card? If you're not going to admit it was you, you'd might as well tell me what was in it.'

I said, 'You can't say it was you if it wasn't. That's lying.'

'He's sharp,' Dean said to Karen. 'Actually, it *was* me who sent the card, so I'm not lying. I can't wait to tell her.'

'But you don't know what's in it!'

305

'Neither do you. Do you? Doesn't look like it. I'm going to tell her at break.' He looked at Karen. 'What do you reckon? I'm going to tell her I sent it. See what she says.'

Karen shrugged, then turned to me. 'I'd tell her if I were you.'

'I can't!'

Dean hoisted his bag on to his shoulder, getting ready to move away. He looked over his shoulder and saw Mr Lund creeping through the crowd of kids, heading towards Dean's tutor room, keys in hand. Dean patted me on the shoulder. 'Let me have a bit of fun, yeah? If you're not going to tell her it was you, you can hardly get all worked up about me saying it was me, can you? You can't just, you know, let the card go to waste. That would be stupid.'

I looked at Karen, who shrugged again, and gave me a scaled-down version of the smile I got earlier. 'See you then,' she said, and she and Dean walked away.

During registration I organized an emergency meeting with Brendan and Martin.

We lingered outside the room where the circular saw was kept, off CDT 1. Dean's tutor room was next door; you could see it through the glass door. But right now we couldn't be seen through the door, as the entrance to the circular-saw room was round a corner. I didn't want Dean to see me in urgent conference.

306

Martin and Brendan didn't seem thrilled about being asked to help me now with my Valentine plan, at the eleventh hour, but they listened as I told them about Dean's decision.

Martin said, 'I already heard about it. I thought he was kidding.'

'He told you?' I asked.

Martin shrugged.

Brendan said, 'He's got a point, though, hasn't he?'

'What point would that be?' Martin asked.

'Well, if you're not going to own up to it, then it's just a big waste, isn't it? Because Neil isn't going to do anything, so, you know . . .'

'Anyway,' said Martin. 'I smell a rat.'

Brendan sniffed. I said, 'What do you mean?'

'I'll try and talk to Dean, but slyly,' Martin said.

'If you don't admit to sending it, can I?' asked Brendan. Then he saw my face. 'No, I'm just kidding.'

'Dean says he's telling her at break, if no one else admits they sent it,' I said. 'I don't know where he'll be doing it.'

'We're going thieving at break,' said Brendan. 'You should come. Forget about Dean Millard.'

'I should speak to Adele,' I said. 'God. Where is Adele at break?'

'Her tutor room,' said Brendan. 'You know that.'

We were told to come in and sit down and then

we answered the register. Then everyone started packing up to go to first lesson.

'I'm going next door to speak to Dean,' said Martin. 'It's too weird that Karen told you about Dean.'

'You think it's a trap?' asked Brendan.

'I know it's a trap,' said Martin.

'He feels it in his giblets,' said Brendan.

By breaktime I was a wreck. Brendan and I stumbled out of Geography, into the corridor, then Brendan stopped suddenly. 'Did Martin say he was going thieving or not?'

'I don't know,' I said sharply. Martin hadn't come back to see me after dashing off to speak to Dean. 'I'm going to Adele's tutor room,' I said. 'Are you coming?'

'This is going to be really embarrassing for some-one,' foretold Brendan.

Maybe I should just let Dean take the credit, I thought. I didn't want to admit my love for Adele just because of some ultimatum. Why not just let Dean play his trick on Adele, and then own up at a later date? I put this suggestion to Brendan. I could tell that he didn't like the fact that I was suddenly involving him, having got myself into this situation without his assistance, but he said wisely, 'If Dean tells her it was his card, and she believes him, she'll probably go out with him.'

'But she'll ask him what was in the card.'

'You know Dean. He'll blag it.'

I didn't really know Dean, as it happened, but if anyone could blag it, I imagined it was him.

'We have to stop him!' Brendan declared. 'He must be stopped.'

We headed for Adele's tutor room, with no plan, no clue as to how to behave, no weapons or armour. I was the true poet, a poetic Elijah, godly and upright, and Dean was the false poet, the priest of Baal, and we were to undergo a trial by fire, and Adele was the one we were hoping would go up in flames of love, and there was a good chance that someone was going to be laughed at or beaten up, and there was an even better chance that I would be that person.

I had never been so terrified.

Please note that the following happened at great speed. In zen-time, with no space for leisurely thought, no intervals in which to insert reasoned calculation.

We went to CDT 3 (actually a Graphics room). For a few awful moments we hovered outside the room in which we would find Adele, me clutching Brendan and begging him to tell me what to do. He was as scared as me. Then I leaned against the door handle accidentally, in a spasm, and fell into Adele's form-room with Brendan bumbling behind me, and as soon as I saw her sitting at a desk eating a bun I felt as though I had found her at the centre of the labyrinth. She looked up at me as though she knew why I was here – knew that I had come to admit to her that I was her poet, the one who loved her. And there was Dean Millard, sitting slightly apart from her, laughing at something Gillian was saying, and sitting with Gillian was Karen – holy cowpats, *they were all here*, the whole gang, all witnesses to the perversions and failings of these two nobodies, these wimps, me and Brendan, who had just walked through the door and were standing wide-mouthed and petrified. *And there was Martin*, looking up at me with a weird pained expression that I couldn't decipher because my eyes were refusing to settle on any one individual, but were roaming, roaming – and the worst thing was that everyone seemed to know why I was here.

Then Gillian jumped to her feet and ran over. Karen stood up, looking agitated. Martin gesticulated – to whom was he gesticulating? My eyes wouldn't stop; they were like the eyes of a hangman who has arrived home and walked into the living-room, switched on the light, and there, sitting in his chairs and on his sofa, are the vengeance-seeking zombies of his many victims – and Karen was shouting something at me – she had set me up somehow, I didn't know how – and why was Adele just sitting there, looking forlorn and dumb? Focus, eyes! Stop this darting! Settle long enough on one person, any person, to see what the hell is going on! And now Dean is up and on his feet, and Martin is coming forward, and perhaps it's a surprise party. I can sense Brendan, tense and alive with excitement and foreboding, next to me, rigid like a cornered animal—

'Neil!' cried Gillian, laughing. 'All right, let's settle this now, was it you or Dean?'

'What?' I blurted.

'It wasn't Neil!' shouted Martin in an angry voice.

Gillian said, 'The *card*, Neil, the one Adele got on Valentine's Day. You or Dean. Who sent it? The one in the blue envelope?'

I couldn't look at Adele.

'It wasn't either of them,' said Martin. 'Neil, just forget about it.'

Was I walking into a trap? Was he trying to save me? Did he himself fancy Adele, and wanted to stop me from admitting my love? No, no – it was a trap: Dean and Karen and Gillian had planned all this because they suspected me of loving out of my league, of loving the most beautiful girl in the school.

The fact was that they'd got me. I couldn't extricate myself from this now, I lacked the cunning, lacked the talent for improvisation. I had few options. I could deny outright that I had sent the card – and give up ownership of my poem, that beautiful poem, and give up my claim to being a

311

poet, and then listen to the cock crowing three times, like it did with St Peter – or I could claim that it was Dean who'd sent my beautiful card, which was even worse, as I would be handing him Adele on a platter, handing him my poet's mantle (or whatever poets wore). Then he'd trounce me, whap me in front of Adele, and Karen and Gillian would pin me down while he moved my nose around my face; or – and this is the option I was fast settling on, I *could just leave*. I could try to ignore them as they laughed behind me, and move schools, disappear.

Or I could just admit it. I could say: it was me. Three words.

Before I'd had a chance to consider this last, outrageous option, one based on a logic that was utterly alien to my thirteen-year-old psychological make-up, my mouth had made my mind up, and I had selected an option.

'It was me,' I said.

'He's *lying*!' shouted Martin. 'Neil, shut your mouth.'

'*You* shut *your* mouth,' I said.

Everyone was laughing, crowding round, except Martin, whose hands were fists, and Karen, who was shaking her head for no reason I could discern, and Adele, sitting looking up at me, looking queasy and appalled, obviously regretting it was me and not someone desirable who sent her the card –

But *fuck it*, I had written the poem, I had sent the

poem, and if there were consequences, good or bad, then they were my consequences and nobody else's. Screw them all – all I wanted, I now decided, was to possess for myself, as part of my own personal history, the wonderful thing I'd done in writing a poem for Adele and having the nerve to give it to her. And so it hardly mattered now that I knew from the way she was looking up at me (she looked sick) that she was incredibly disappointed that it was me and not Dean who'd sent the card. At that moment I felt untouchable, because I wasn't wasting time and energy defending myself any more. I had thrown myself on their spears, and it wasn't so bad. So sod them all; they had beheaded me (or beaten me to death with clubs, according to another tradition) and yet I had left behind me my legacy, my Valentine, and maybe, you never know, Adele would look at the words in it one day and read them with open eyes – one day in the future when she was cynical and sad – and be cured of the belief that there were no romantic people in the world; and it would be like getting her sight back.

'Nice card, Neil,' said Gillian. And she took the card in its blue envelope from behind her back and threw it at me, and I didn't catch it, so it fell to the floor and landed at my feet. Looking down at it, I saw that it was unopened.

Dean Millard clapped and shouted, 'We have a winner!'

At that moment Martin grabbed me and bundled me out of the room, and I didn't resist.

We stood outside and from the sound of things every single person in the tutor room was laughing outrageously. Martin said 'Stay here' to me and pushed open the door, and I saw him walk towards Adele, who was still sitting there forlorn, and he shouted 'You fucking evil bitch.' And then, as the door swung closed, I saw, through the gap, Dean Millard step towards Martin as though to calmly restrain him, then punch him to the ground.

I walked into the room. Martin shook his head and sat up. There was blood all over his face. I walked over to my card, which was face-down on the dirty green carpet, and picked it up. There was what looked like a pubic hair attached to the envelope, trapped underneath the Sellotape that I'd put on the back. This was why they'd wanted to find out who'd sent it. This was why the card was such a talking point. Because of the accidental attachment of a pubic hair. Because it looked like the least romantic Valentine's card in history. Because it was a card furtively written and packaged on the hirsute floor of the bathroom of a house populated by three hopeless males.

I was staring at the card when Martin came over to me and put his hand on my shoulder and urged me gently out of the room once more. Brendan came too.

'Your face,' I said to Martin. I felt suddenly nauseous.

'They're just evil people,' said Martin. 'All of them.'

'I think I'll go home,' I said, and I did.

avenge my death

Recently I asked my brother how to end this memoir, because it seems wrong to leave anything dangling. But things do dangle, we all know that. And that's what Craig said: let dangling things dangle. Relationships, above all, dangle, and can dangle indefinitely over the precipice of extinction, never quite falling into it. Dad and Mum dangled, Craig and Ariadne dangled, even me and Adele continued dangling for a short while, despite her unwanted acquaintance with one of the Flack family's pubic hairs. But I might say something about how we dangled, with the hope that if I describe the dangling in the right way, it will seem more positive, less like dangling.

So: I walked out of school. There was one week to go until the half-term holiday, but first there was the weekend.

As promised, Mum took Craig and Dad and me out, though she couldn't think of anywhere exciting to go, so she opted for something that she thought us boys would like: bowling. Dad humiliated us by dancing whenever he got a strike. Craig started badly but won the last game spectacularly, picking up a seven–ten split at some point, which meant nothing whatsoever to Mum and me, but was apparently an impressive thing to do. Mum distinguished herself by being the only person to throw her ball down someone else's lane. I was the only one who fell over. Afterwards we went out for hamburgers and I didn't mention my Valentine; what's more, nobody mentioned Dad's Valentine, which convinced me that I had not damaged relations for my parents. It was a big relief.

The following week I pretended to have a bad stomach-ache, and Dad let me stay home from Monday to Wednesday.

On Wednesday, Brendan got suspended from school for writing something rude in a lesson.

It was in CDT – the class had a supply teacher, who told them to design an advertisement for something, and Brendan, sitting with Martin, started to draw rude designs in his notebook, and just as he was drawing a picture to accompany the slogan

Need a smooth shave?

Try

DOG SPUNK

he realized the teacher was at his shoulder. He was sent to see the deputy head, who was apoplectic, and then Brendan got the giggles and the deputy decided to send Brendan home for the rest of Wednesday and all of Thursday.

I would have visited him, but he wasn't allowed visitors; neither was he allowed out. I did get a phone call from him, though, on Thursday. Cruelly, the suspension was too short by a day – one day longer and it would have taken him up to the holiday. But a two-day suspension meant that he had to be back in school, with his work up-to-date and an essay on the importance of good manners written in neat, on Friday.

It was a good job the supply teacher didn't see any of Brendan's other adverts. Brendan told me about them. They were disgusting beyond belief.

I wanted to apologize to Brendan for the whole business of sending Adele a card behind his back, as it were. But I had watched enough television to know that true friends, especially male friends, don't just apologize to each other. They make some sort of symbolic gesture, something subtle and unsentimental, and the other guy understands the implications, and confers forgiveness through some equally cryptic medium. Manly men are unvocal, preferring to give and receive forgiveness by means of exchanges like:

LANCE: Hey, Buck, about that thing–
BUCK: Forget it, man. I know. I know.

Or:

RANDY: Jake—
JAKE: *Yeah*.
RANDY: Huh.

Never:

STEVE: Bud, do you have a minute? I'm really sorry about
         what happened. Really sorry. Do you think you
         can forgive me? Could you find that in your
         heart?
BUD: Oh, come here, you big silly lug.

So I phoned Brendan, having heard from Craig, via
Harry, that he'd been suspended. Brendan's dad
permitted him five minutes on the phone.

'It's rubbish that you were suspended just for
writing something rude,' I said.

'It's criminal,' said Brendan. 'But Mr Snell said it
was also because of disturbance in class, and
because of laughing at him, and he didn't show my
mum the bit of paper, which was good, but I knew
she'd ask what I'd got done for, so I tore out all the
rude things from my notebook and made up something that was rude, but not *too* rude, so I could

320

show it to her. But it was hard to know how rude I should be. I couldn't put anything about fanny, or bush, or dick, or nob, or cock or baps. But I couldn't make it, you know, *not* rude, or Mum and Dad would have said, this isn't rude! and probably complained to the school.'

'So what did you write?'

'I wrote *Dog Willies – The Dangly Snack*. And I drew a picture of someone with a big grin and a bulge in his cheek, to show he was eating. But I didn't draw an actual dog willy.'

'Did your mum and dad mind you using the word "willy"?'

'Willy is okay,' said Brendan. 'I can't believe they suspended me. It's an injustice.'

I had been trying to think of a suitably manly way to apologize for all that had happened concerning the Valentine and my rude picture, but I couldn't, and I sensed that the five minutes were almost up, so I said, 'I'm sorry about the Valentine and the rude picture.'

And Brendan said, 'Don't worry about it.' He put on the voice of one who was dying from a gunshot wound. 'Just go back and avenge my death.'

Which struck me as a strange thing to say, but was, I suppose, a pretty manly way to bestow forgiveness.

People forgot about the hairy Valentine incident after a while, of course, just like they forgot about the rude pictures. A stray hair stuck to an envelope is no big deal if you think about it. I decided to tell Dad about how the girl to whom I'd sent a Valentine hadn't even opened her card, hadn't read the poem, and Dad, incensed by Adele's rudeness, said I should go into school when I felt better and confront her, tell her off for being a snob, and I decided that I'd take his advice. It struck me that this was perhaps what Brendan had meant by avenging his death: it was time to reject the active pursuit of Adele and Gillian and get back to business as usual. Pick some new girls. Place ourselves firmly at the outskirts of their lives. Adele may have been the most beautiful girl I'd known, but she didn't have any right to crush my heart in her fist. And neither did Gillian or Dean. But it was Adele I was most angry with.

Mum phoned on Wednesday night and I told her about Adele not reading my card. She said that one day when I became a famous poet she'd look back at her crime and weep.

I took a breath and asked Mum if Dad's Valentine had been for her. She was silent for many moments. She said, 'Who else would it be for?'

'I don't know,' I stammered. 'It could have been a joke card for his friend Terry.'

'Terry is your dad's Handywoman?' Mum asked.

Embarrassed, I asked, 'Was it a nice card?'

'Just lovely,' she said.

One day Mum would show me Dad's card. It had a very long, silly poem in it. There was nothing pragmatic about it at all, no references to how they might reach an amicable cohabitation arrangement. It was a kind of verse story about them growing old together and bickering, throwing things, becoming increasingly cranky. And then there was a bit that described how they would be after a big row:

> But never mind.
> I'll have you on good terms again tonight
> and lie quietly nose to nose, or thereabout,
> and when our lights and
> teeth are out, I'll thank my stars that you're
> the one I smile my gummy smile about.

They got divorced about ten years ago, and they still live apart, but I see no reason why the poem should not prove true, since neither has found anyone else they like quite as much, and they seem to like each other more and more as years pass. Harry (these days it's only me who calls her Harry) says they are 'dating', but I disagree; nobody wants to think of their parents as dating, even if they are.

I walked to school early on Thursday, ten days after Valentine's Day, and waited outside the school grounds, near Budgens, hiding round the side near the big steel bins, and when Adele and Gillian walked past me I came out of hiding and strolled right up to them.

She was still the most beautiful person I had ever seen, looking shy and a little afraid – with her dark vertical hair like a waterfall and her sad tired eyes underscored with those endearing shadows.

'Can I talk to you?' I asked, and to my surprise, she turned to Gillian and said in her clipped posh voice, 'I'll meet you in school.'

Gillian went, and we were alone.

I told Adele several things I'd been yearning to tell her, things about how she wasn't any better than me, not really, and about how I'd tried really hard to write a nice poem, and she didn't even bother to read it. And how it was only a bloody hair, probably my brother's, and I wrote the card in the bathroom because being romantic was banned in my house, as was poetry, on pain of death.

Adele said, 'Honestly, I thought it was from Dean.'

'Well, it wasn't.'

She said, 'I thought the hair was a nasty joke, because it was, you know, stuck down with Sellotape. I told Gillian I'd got a card, and she said, "We'll find out who sent it" – meaning her and Dean Millard and Karen. But Karen thought it was you who sent it, I don't know why, and I didn't believe her, because you didn't seem like a nasty person at all.'

She didn't love me, I could tell. But she *was* feeling guilty, I could tell that too. She said, 'It didn't even enter my head that it was a proper Valentine, because I just looked at the envelope and got upset. Honestly. And after you went that day, I read it, and it was brilliant.'

Not beautiful, not romantic, just brilliant.

'You read the poem?'

'Honestly! I think I can remember some of it.' And she started to recite a few lines, though not amazingly accurately.

When I heard them it struck me that the poem was not really brilliant; it sounded as weird and over-wrought as some of the less artful poems in Mum's books; but that wasn't the point.

Adele stopped reciting. 'Did you know? – after Dean punched your friend, Karen called me a bitch! She does like you. And later on she had a fight with Gillian, because of what happened with the card and everything.'

I laughed with shock. 'Who won?'

'Hard to tell. Gillian definitely lost the most hair.'

I thought: I will have to find Karen, and thank her for being so very much nicer a bully than I would ever have suspected her of being had she not assaulted someone on my behalf.

I had a smirk on my face. Adele said, 'It was a really nice card.'

* * *

So much for avenging Brendan's social and academic death by confronting Adele.

The real death, of course, was of Brendan's pursuit of Gillian and my pursuit of Adele. At least, it was the death of our first attempt to seriously pursue romantic love, as opposed to just ogling girls from afar. We were clearly not capable of relating to girls as lovers yet. Like all thirteen-year-old wimps, even romantic thirteen-year-old wimps, we were created for the joy of viewing the world of sex and love from behind a fallen tree, from which standpoint love and sex may not have been accessible, but at least they were *funny*. At least they made us *bond*, and made us giggle till we ached and snotted. Love and sex were our greatest pleasures at thirteen, not because we were anywhere near to experiencing them, but because we could concoct speculative dreams about them. Love seemed unthinkable and sex ridiculous, yet they were at the same time the most tantalizing things on earth, the two things we could never tire of talking about. This was true of Brendan and it was true of me and I believe it is true of all hormonal teenagers who giggle together, irrespective of whether they consider themselves perverts or romantics or poets.

And would love and sex ever be this enjoyable after we stopped giggling and marvelling at them, and started experiencing them? In time we would become mature about relationships and mature about our sexuality, and by the time we became adults, we would be – what? Like Brendan's parents – sane and serious and comfortable? Or like my parents, miserable and on their own? Love and sex would one day become realities, but would they become humourless realities?

The official code of sexual conduct was established for us by Hollywood: soft-focus, grimaces, saxophone music, arched lower backs. It all seemed so earnest, and bore little relation to the things we found so funny as teenagers. It seemed that taking it seriously (at least while actually performing the act) was the price you paid for actually experiencing it. Ditto romance. Consequently, the (*serious*) relationships we would have with our future partners were doomed never to be as giddy and vital as those we'd had with our school-friends.

I had what you might call a premonition, or perhaps just a hope or wish. It was this: that I would somehow manage to recapture and then retain the peculiarly childish irreverence that constitutes the only real respect for love; the ability to see love as something profoundly foolish and worthy of tender derision. Thus I would of course require a certain kind of partner, one of similar outlook, one not given to taking things too seriously. Such people exist, and I'm one of them. Brendan is too. Adele, wherever she is now, might be one. Harry Keetley is.

Such people do exist, scattered around the globe. We locate each other eventually.

Adele

I can't imagine your
        elsewheres
But told a friend of you
        Saying
Like the poem of ee
        cummings
About the little tree
        is every
Moment with she
And though
I steal through the deaths of each
        glimpse
of a too-beautiful
        beauty
now I perceive
The heart of your tiny
        witcheries
And I am faint with loves
And imagine always your everywheres
You are even here
        there
Where like a meadow
        reclining
Between twin horizons
        is Spring,
The horses racing to
        and fro

Imagine one and two
      are
I and you, and one
      horizon
Dips to its lover,
      holds us

(There where I fell
one day, if I could
again, would stay)

acknowledgements

I would like to say a special thank you to the following who have all been such a great help to me during the writing of this book: the incomparable Antony Topping at Greene & Heaton, Selina Walker and all the lovely folk at Transworld Publishers. The Hannons, especially Margaret, Debbie Megnauth, Hilda Tidball, Magga Dog, Kay Hixon, Toby Vaughn and to James Hall and Peter Camichel – may crops always grow in your beards.

THIS IS YOUR LIFE
John O'Farrell

'A SPLENDID SATIRE ON OUR CELEBRITY-HUNGRY AGE'
Daily Mail

Jimmy Conway always wanted to be famous. As a teenager
he even stashed away a series of letters advising his future
self on how to handle the fame and fortune coming his
way. And so when he's reunited with these rather
embarrassing predictions in his mid-thirties he can't help
feeling he must be a bit of a disappointment to himself.

Thus begins an extraordinary journey into the world of
celebrity. Jimmy bluffs and stumbles all the way to the very
top until he finds himself about to perform stand-up
comedy in front of a packed theatre and a live television
audience of millions. There's only one problem he's never
preformed anything before – ever . . .

With his second novel, John O'Farrell has written a
compelling, funny and acutely observed satire on our
shallow celebrity-obsessed culture in the vain hope that he
might get to go on telly occasionally.

'EXCELLENTLY DONE . . . O'FARRELL GIVES AN EXTRA
SQUIRM TO THE TRADITIONAL ENGLISH COMEDY OF
EMBARRASSMENT'
Sunday Times

'VERY FUNNY'
The Times

0 552 99849 4

BLACK SWAN

BLESSED ARE THE CHEESEMAKERS
Sarah-Kate Lynch

'GENUINELY ORIGINAL . . . THE PLOT UNFOLDS WITH
HUMOUR AND EMOTION AS ALL SORTS OF PECULIAR
THINGS HAPPEN IN THIS STRANGELY MAGIC PLACE'
Daily Mail

Blessed are Corrie and Fee, for theirs is the kingdom of the
world's tastiest farmhouse cheese. Tucked away in a corner
of Ireland, the lifelong friends turn out batch after batch of
perfect Coolarney Blues and Golds, thanks to co-operative
cows, non-meat-eating fecund milkmaids, songs from *The
Sound of Music* and the wind blowing just so in the right
direction across the green meadows of County Cork.

Add to this mixture Corrie's long-lost granddaughter
Abbey, fleeing from a remote but by no means backward
Pacific island and an unfaithful husband. And stir in New
Yorker Kit Stephens, heart-broken burned-out and looking
for a purpose to his wasted life.

The magic that Corrie and Fee weave in and out of the
cheese vats is legendary, but can they use their powers to
turn bitterness and betrayal into love – or will the secret
ingredient be lost to Coolarney cheese forever?

'A TRULY LOVELY READ . . . SEDUCTIVE AND FEELGOOD'
New Zealand Herald

'A MAGICAL DÉBUT NOVEL THAT CHARMS TO THE
LAST PAGE'
Good Housekeeping

'WARM, WITTY AND MOUTH-WATERING'
Hello!

0 552 77103 1

BLACK SWAN

EVERY GOOD WOMAN DESERVES A LOVER
Diana Appleyard

A warm and compelling novel about a woman who has to
break free.

Sasha feels that she is captive in a life which no longer
satisfies her. Her children are critical, her husband
unsupportive, and she is bored and unfulfilled. So, with
two good women friends, she escapes to darkest Peru. To
take on the challenge of a lifetime – to walk the Inca Trail.
Amongst the grandeur of the mountains, and the glorious
ancient civilisation of the Incas, she discovers that she can
grab hold of her life and wrench it back before it's too late.
She embarks upon a love affair which takes her completely
by surprise; she also finds disaster and the sound of her
own laughter once more.

0 552 99934 2

BLACK SWAN

BIG JESSIE
Zane Radcliffe

'She emerged from a flurry of windblown rose petals, her pale skin interrupted at regular intervals by bands of red – scarlet bob, scarlet lips, cropped scarlet top, scarlet mini, scarlet knee socks, scarlet boots. She looked like a barber's pole, or a lolly that *had* to be licked.'

Scarlet plucks her twelve-string guitar with nails the colour of glazed cherries and Belfast music hack, Jessie Black, is smitten.

He charms his way on to her tour bus as her band head for Dublin. But the second they cross the border Jessie feels the heat of a sniper's bullet. . .

Who wants him dead? Rather, who *doesn't* want 'Jay' Black dead? Any number of people might justifiably have pulled the trigger.

There's Scarlet's stalker, a gun-toting shoe fetishist. And the still-grieving widow of Northern Ireland's international goalkeeper, Miles Huggins, who Jay inadvertently killed. Not to mention the property magnate who was blackmailed into handing Jay Belfast's first-ever million-pound flat. Or the RUC Chief Constable who has given Jay an ultimatum. Or, now you come to mention it, Sinn Fein *numero uno* Martin O'Hanlon, who Jay has to expose.

It's when Scarlet goes missing that things start getting serious, and Jay has to go it alone.

A story of blackmail, corruption and exploding peacocks, *Big Jessie* is the new firecracker thriller from the author of the WHSmith Award-winning *London Irish*.

'FUNNY, ABSURD AND MEMORABLE. RECOMMEDED'
FHM

0 552 77096 5

BLACK SWAN

A SELECTED LIST OF FINE WRITING
AVAILABLE FROM BLACK SWAN

77084 1	COOL FOR CATS	Jessica Adams	£6.99
77115 5	BRICK LANE	Monica Ali	£7.99
99934 2	EVERY GOOD WOMAN DESERVES A LOVER	Diana Appleyard	£6.99
77105 8	NOT THE END OF THE WORLD	Kate Atkinson	£6.99
77131 7	MAKING LOVE: A CONSPIRACY OF THE HEART	Marius Brill	£6.99
99947 4	CROSS MY HEART AND HOPE TO DIE	Claire Calman	£6.99
99979 2	GATES OF EDEN	Ethan Coen	£7.99
99686 6	BEACH MUSIC	Pat Conroy	£8.99
99990 3	A CRYING SHAME	Renate Dorrestein	£6.99
99985 7	DANCING WITH MINNIE THE TWIG	Mogue Doyle	£6.99
99995 4	HIGH SOCIETY	Ben Elton	£6.99
99935 0	PEACE LIKE A RIVER	Leif Enger	£6.99
99966 0	WHILE THE SUN SHINES	John Harding	£6.99
77082 5	THE WISDOM OF CROCODILES	Paul Hoffman	£7.99
77109 0	THE FOURTH HAND	John Irving	£6.99
77153 8	THINGS TO DO INDOORS	'Sheena Joughin	£6.99
99859 1	EDDIE'S BASTARD	William Kowalski	£6.99
77103 1	BLESSED ARE THE CHEESEMAKERS	Sarah-Kate Lynch	£6.99
77200 3	NO WONDER I TAKE A DRINK	Laura Marney	£6.99
77090 6	HERDING CATS	John McCabe	£6.99
99901 6	WHITE MALE HEART	Ruaridh Nicoll	£6.99
99970 9	FALLING OUT OF CARS	Jeff Noon	£6.99
99849 4	THIS IS YOUR LIFE	John O'Farrell	£6.99
77096 5	BIG JESSIE	Zane Radcliffe	£6.99
99645 9	THE WRONG BOY	Willy Russell	£6.99
77000 0	A SCIENTIFIC ROMANCE	Ronald Wright	£6.99